Gate of Heaven

By the same author

Jolly Rogerson
A Narrow Time
The Priest

Gate

of

Heaven

Ralph McInerny

Harper & Row, Publishers

New York, Evanston, San Francisco,

London

Designed by Gwendolyn O. England

Library of Congress Cataloging in Publication Data

McInerny, Ralph M.
  Gate of heaven.
  I. Title.
PZ4.M1514Gat3   [PS3563.A31166]   813'.5'4   74–15877
ISBN 0–06–012941–7

75 76 77 78 79 10 9 8 7 6 5 4 3 2

For Richard Sullivan

Gate of Heaven

1

SEEKING RESPITE from the roar of television in the recreation room, Leo Phelan left the building and walked across the front lawn toward the lake. He wore a windbreaker and a baseball cap, and a huge pair of binoculars were slung from his neck like a penitent's affectation. How noisy the natural world was with its hums and songs and sighing leaves, yet people complained about the city. Phelan had always loved cities. Most of his active ministry had been spent in them and he had learned not to hear their noises. Now, after the better part of a year at Porta Coeli, the retirement home of the Society of Saint Brendan, he still felt assailed by the shrillness of bird song, the chattering of squirrels, the incessant not quite supersonic buzz of bugs. He imagined a plane coming in low across the lake, trailing swirling clouds of DDT. Peace through chemistry. Leo Phelan smiled joylessly.

He stopped at his favorite bench and sat. Plunging his hands into the pockets of his flimsy jacket, he was reminded of their new name for Stokes. The windbreaker. An old man's weakness,

1

the taunt funny but a little cruel. It was as though they were again in the grip of boyish meanness. Of course they meant no harm and Stokes took it well enough. And went on earning the name. Age. Great cloudy thoughts drifted across Phelan's mind. They were all old now as once they had been young together. He was not really tempted by such musing; he had grown wrathful rather than melancholic. He brought his binoculars to his eyes and sighted across the lake at the college campus. He saw a milky blur. He adjusted the lenses and what they all called Little Sem, the society's first building, came into focus. It still stood, looking much as it had when they were boys there. He moved the glasses slightly. The arm of a crane came into view. A wrecking ball hung from it. Phelan's smile was grim with satisfaction. The hand of destruction stayed. At least for now. But how long, O Lord, how long?

Though he might wish destruction on the annoying creatures of God, Phelan felt a visceral obligation to protect the works of man. That building must not be destroyed. Despite his arthritis, his grip on the binoculars tightened. Tumulty. Tumulty was the enemy within the walls, trying to persuade the occupants of Porta Coeli to give their assent to the destruction of Little Sem. How confident of success the enemy was, his wrecker already in place. Only a few strong wills restrained it.

At the sound of footsteps behind him, Phelan turned to see Michael Tumulty walking swiftly along the gravel path in front of the house, chin high, determination in the set of his jaw. Tumulty came to the door, opened it, paused and looked back. His eyes grazed Phelan, lifted, continued on across the lake. He turned and went inside, sped on his way perhaps by the binoculars Phelan trained on him.

Once inside the cool waxed vestibule, Tumulty stopped. He was out of sight of Phelan but not, he was sure, out of mind. The man had become his nemesis. Leo was intransigent about Little Sem. There were others, too, but their opposition had

2

some modicum of subtlety about it. Tumulty did not like the fact that he was handling the matter of Little Sem badly. It was a small assignment as assignments go—or at least as they had gone. Father Hoyt, the president of Saint Brendan's College, was relying on him to secure the agreement of these old priests to the taking down of Little Sem. That so small a thing had grown large was due to the most incredible fluke. At first Tumulty had welcomed the discovery of an old document in the society's archives which put the fate of the first building in the hands of the senior members. After all, if there had been no problem, Michael Tumulty would not have been asked to resolve it. But matters had taken an unexpected farcical turn. Tumulty was stymied by a willful band of cranks, men who in all other respects were content to waste their declining years in this house. They belonged here. Michael Tumulty did not. That was his conviction and his cross. The institutional smell of the vestibule filled his nostrils and he closed his eyes as if fighting off dizziness. He did not belong here. He would be reassigned. He had only to keep a cool head. The wrong reaction toward the opposition might seem to justify his having been assigned to Porta Coeli. But success in his assignment from Hoyt meant freedom.

The Founder had not come to the refectory for lunch. This was not unusual. Father Cullen, the Founder of the Society of Saint Brendan, was ninety-three years old. He had moved to Porta Coeli as soon as the retirement home had been completed two years before, had come here without murmur or complaint. Tumulty knew this because it had fallen to him to tell the old man that he was to live here. At the time it had never entered Tumulty's mind that a day would come when he would receive the same grim message. Did others think that he had taken the blow as well as the Founder himself? He could not believe that others saw him as finished, no longer active, retired. He was seventy-two. Of course there had to be rules about retirement, there could not be a society without rules, but reasonable rules were flexible and applied with an eye to excep-

3

tions. Tumulty was certain that he would still be active today if it were not for his enemies. Well, he would get out of this house. All he needed to do was clear the way for the tearing down of Little Sem.

The outside door opened and Phelan came in, tugging at the bill of his baseball cap, those absurd binoculars bouncing off his pouter-pigeon chest. His eyes glinted with knowing suspicion.

"Going to see the Founder?"

Tumulty gave the slightest nod and started down the hall, aiming himself toward the Founder's room; purposive action, a man with things to do. His movement had the effect of tugging Phelan along with him. He felt that he had been surprised in a moment of indecision and doubt, and had to make an effort not to stop and tell Leo to go away. That was the worst thing about people like Leo: they dragged others down to their childish level.

"Isn't it time for your nap, Leo?"

"Any time is nap time here, Tumulty. You should know that by now."

They approached an intersection of hallways where the glass-enclosed nurses' station faced the infirmary wing. Miss Bishop sat at a desk, smoking a cigarette, lost in thought. At their approach she leaped to her feet. The girl was underemployed here, bored to death. Did she sit there dreaming of the day when they would all fall ill and be transferred to her domain? The Founder was her only patient and he refused to be fussed over. Tumulty asked if the old man was awake.

"He was a minute ago." Miss Bishop checked her watch as if taking the pulse of the house. "Dr. Dowling is due in half an hour."

"How is he feeling?"

She was momentarily puzzled. Had she thought he meant the doctor? No doubt Dowling was the object of her daydreaming. Poor girl. She had told Tumulty of her mother and not without

4

embarrassment he remembered now his promise to visit Mrs. Bishop. Phelan was shuffling off toward the Founder's room. Tumulty decided against giving chase.

"How is your mother, Alma?"

Reticence and long suffering settled like cosmetics on the nurse's pudgy face. They explained why she had marched crepe-soled into her thirties still single. Alma represented a way to be useful, a way for Tumulty to prove to himself that he was not yet filed away, finished, worse than dead. If only he had more time.

"I shall go see her, Alma."

The nurse smiled. "It won't do any good."

"These things have a way of working themselves out."

"You don't know my mother."

Father Tumulty's expression indicated that handling Mrs. Bishop posed no problem to him. He was a priest with decades of service behind him. He would get Alma out from under that maternal thumb and free to marry Dr. Dowling. Dowling was a widower in his late forties who might well consider himself fortunate to win so exemplary a young lady as Alma Bishop. Tumulty imagined himself saying the nuptial Mass, perhaps right here at Porta Coeli. No. The chapel would be cluttered with aged priests, their eyes brimming with memories of marriage rites performed, baptisms, too, and funerals, endless parish Masses, the church crowded to the doors. The past hung in the atmosphere of the house, stifling the present. There were times when Tumulty felt physically incapable of breathing and had to burst out of doors to assure himself that the world was still there, life going on, the future over the horizon.

Miss Bishop was studying the Founder's chart. There seemed little written on it.

"Is he running a temperature?"

"Nothing serious."

She had hesitated. Tumulty was sure the Founder had

5

shooed her from the room. If anyone took his temperature, it would be old Sister Diotima, and she would forget to write it on the chart.

"He says he has a touch of grippe."

The phrase echoed with the old world, an Irish ailment.

"I'll stop in and see how he is."

Phelan stood beside the Founder's bed, listening to the old man. The bed had been cranked up so that the Founder's head seemed displayed on his pillow, a prehistoric egg.

"It is only a building, Leo," the old man said.

"Only a building!" Phelan glanced angrily over his shoulder at Tumulty as if *he* had used that diminishing phrase. "It is where you began, Father Founder. Where the society began. It is a symbol."

The old man's eyes became admonitory and bright. He breathed deeply as if respiration had become a conscious task. He had not noticed Tumulty in the doorway.

"Life is a symbol," he whispered. "A trinket. A toy. Let go of it, Leo. Let go of everything that binds you to this world."

"No." Phelan remembered the cap on his head and snatched it off. He was agitated that Tumulty should be hearing this. He moved closer to the bed, putting himself between the Founder and Tumulty.

"Little Sem must be preserved, Father. They want to tear down everything. They want to destroy what you have built. They will destroy the society itself."

Tumulty entered the room. This was a decisive moment. Phelan could scarcely refuse the Founder's request that he stop his silly blocking of the college building plans. The Founder had closed his eyes. He made a gesture with his hand and Tumulty noticed the liver spots; the old man's skin had the basted look of a holiday fowl's. His gesture clearly dismissed the idea of preserving that old building across the lake in which Phelan and Tumulty and all the others had spent their first years in the religious society founded by this old man.

6

"Is your life's work to go down in ruins?" Phelan's voice rose.

"Perhaps, perhaps."

Phelan was shocked. His mouth gaped in disbelief. The Founder opened his eyes and saw Tumulty at the foot of the bed. He took Phelan's hand in his. His breathing had become a labored rasping.

"Let go, Leo. Let go."

His gripping hand contradicted the plea. The Founder's breathing became more audible. Suddenly his eyes rolled upward and his body went rigid, bending like a bow. Alarmed, Phelan freed his hand and stepped back from the bed. Tumulty quickly took his place, stared down at the Founder, then hurried from the room. He was calling for Miss Bishop before he got into the hallway.

The nurse came, on the run, followed by Sister Diotima. Phelan lingered in the hall, his cap back on his head, looking confused and frightened. Tumulty wanted to be of help, but the two women pushed him aside. He did not like that. He was not a bewildered old man like Phelan.

"It was delirium," Phelan said when Tumulty came outside.

"It's a stroke, Leo."

"I mean what he said. He didn't know what he was saying."

"Don't be foolish, Leo. He knew perfectly well what he was saying. More important, you know. I advise you to heed his words."

"I do not need your advice."

"It is not my advice. It is the Founder's."

"He was out of his head!"

Phelan turned and went off down the hall, his shoulders rounded in his jacket, his head hung low, though that might have been due to the binoculars. Tumulty felt a fleeting pity for him. Until now the Founder had resisted Tumulty's request that he lend his authority to the effort to stop the opposition to taking down Little Sem. The Founder had not wanted to make

7

it a matter of obedience. Now, at last, he had spoken, and none too soon.

Dr. Dowling arrived, a gaunt, lanky man who looked as if he had never relaxed in his life. He was immediately drawn into the activity in the Founder's room. Tumulty withdrew to the nurses' station, where he sat at Miss Bishop's desk. He pulled the phone toward him. Others must be informed of the Founder's attack. Phelan would spread the word in the house. It seemed only fitting that it should fall to Michael Tumulty to inform the current leaders of the society. The moment was historic. A giant of a man was sliding from the shelf of life. Even as he formed the phrase, Tumulty realized for the first time that the Founder could be dying. He might already be dead. The impact of the thought wiped the rhetoric from his mind. He got up and went back to the sickroom and looked in. The two nurses were on either side of the bed, pitching a plastic oxygen tent over the fallen Founder. Dowling had a syringe in his hand. Tumulty succeeded in getting Alma Bishop's attention and beckoned her into the hall. She told him somewhat impatiently that the Founder had suffered a stroke and was now comatose. The prognosis was uncertain. Tumulty nodded gravely and returned to the desk and phone to convey the sad news to Father Hoyt, the president of the college, and Father Faiblesse, superior of the Society of Saint Brendan.

In the recreation room the television was aroar with more worldly news when Phelan made the announcement.

"They go in threes," Butch Henley sighed, his eyes not leaving the screen.

"What?" Phelan asked.

"Threes. They go in threes. Usedom. Now the Founder."

Henley's voice trailed off as if in search of a third. It had been only a week since they had buried Usedom.

"The Founder isn't dead," Phelan said sharply. "He has had some kind of stroke."

8

"He is dying," Henley said lugubriously.

Leo stared at him. Henley had taken on the mannerisms of his enemies, the television commentators. He sat before the set for hours, talking back to them.

"Hey," Henley protested when Leo turned down the volume of the television.

"The Founder has had an attack." Phelan removed his baseball cap and brought it to his chest, covering his binoculars.

"I heard you the first time." Henley got up but his body retained the angle of the chair. He was trying to reach around Leo in order to turn up the sound. A digital clock, an insert in Walter Cronkite's chest, ran counterclockwise. Over the newsman's shoulder another digit pointed toward the sky. Fifteen minutes and counting.

"That should be turned off," Phelan said. He wished some of the others were here. Must he carry the news to each room separately?

"Don't you see what's on?"

"Out of respect."

Leo's eyes closed and he pressed his cap more tightly against his binoculars.

"They go in threes," Henley said again.

Phelan glanced at the screen and the encapsulated astronauts. "I know they do."

"I mean deaths."

Henley had got hold of the volume knob and Walter Cronkite's voice, laden with arcane lore, became deafeningly audible again. Phelan clamped his cap back on his head.

"The Founder is not dead," he said angrily. "We should go see him. We should say a prayer for him."

"After lift-off."

Having made his telephone calls, Tumulty came out of the enclosure of the nurses' station. His eyes were drawn down the length of the western corridor to the doors of the chapel. Of

9

course. He set off down the corridor, which was empty save for Harrington, who was adjusting the rear-view mirror mounted on the arm of his wheelchair. Tumulty nodded but did not stop. Harrington had Parkinson's disease and a conversation with him tended to become an exchange of shouts and whispers. To bellow the news that the Founder had fallen into a coma would have destroyed the solemnity of the moment.

Inside the chapel, Tumulty saw Goudge puttering with the candles at the altar, his biretta pushed to the back of his head. Goudge was still a sacristan at heart, molding new candles from the stumps of old. Tumulty let the door hiss shut behind him and knelt in a pew. Lowering his face into his hands, he murmured a Nunc Dimittis for the Founder.

How easy it was in the warm pink dark of his hands to exchange the image of a stricken old man for memories of the vigorous blue-eyed mentor of his youth, ramrod straight, lantern jawed, sternly loving, totally immersed in his priestly vocation. Father Cullen had never doubted his vocation and he intended that those who joined the society should be men of discipline and devotion.

My yoke is sweet and my burden light. Those words, uttered in a thick Hibernian burr, were the text of the annual conference the Founder delivered to his assembled seminarians. Tumulty remembered the first time he had heard it, Father Founder standing on the stage of the auditorium in Little Sem, the whole school arrayed before him. Little Michael Tumulty, a first-year man in the front row, looked up at the priest, at the piercing eyes, the chin thrust over the high Roman collar, at the descending row of buttons on his cassock. The sun which that day slanted across the stage had never set for Michael Tumulty. He had listened, not to words, but to a man, a man of God, a priest such as he hoped to become himself. His youthful enthusiasm was enlisted for life. Remember how our hearts burned within us when we walked with him on the way. Tumulty was in his late sixties before he had even so much as

10

wondered about the wisdom of joining the Society of Saint Brendan.

Father Cullen had come as a young priest from Maynooth to the vineyard of America. It was early in the century and he saw the land with an apostle's eye. He acquired this site in northwestern Ohio and raised first one building—the now threatened Little Sem—and then another and another, gathering young men about him to help in the various tasks which fell to the infant Society of Saint Brendan. The Founder was the only religious superior Tumulty had ever had; Faiblesse did not really count. No bishop could compete with the Founder for Tumulty's loyalty, and several had tried. Members of the society, which was independent of the nation's dioceses and enjoyed virtual autonomy, had always been attractive targets for ambitious bishops eager to increase their clergy on the cheap. How convenient to pick up a man already trained, already ordained priest, ready to go to work, luring him with a plush parish. One more man incardinated into a diocese, as such transfers were called, one less member of the society. Rome had always been too quick to certify such transfers and the Founder had tolerated defections with equanimity. Of course in those days vocations had been plentiful and Little Sem teemed with students. Michael Tumulty would as soon apostatize as leave the Founder. He had been true to the dreams of his youth. How bitter that those dreams were tarnished and mocked by the easy way in which he had been shunted aside to Porta Coeli.

Through the interstices of his fingers, Tumulty watched Goudge step back from the altar and make a bobbing curtsy in lieu of a genuflection. Goudge up there now, an aging priest, but also in all those mornings of the past, five-thirty in chapel, cold and sleepy, the student sacristan putting out the cruets, marking the places in the altar missal with ribbons, lighting the candles. Noonan had said he preferred High Mass with its six candles since then the chapel was almost warm. In January the leaden dividers in the stained-glass windows went white with

11

frost. Boys wore sweaters under their suit coats, knelt shivering through morning prayers and Mass, sustained by the promise of breakfast. So many memories. Tumulty shook them away. One of the annoyances of this house was the constant reminiscing, the hunt in the past for the image or event that justified a lifetime. How easy it would be to share their delight in recollection. Dear God, did that explain his presence here? Had he taken to telling endless stories of the way it used to be? It seemed to him that he might have done that. If so, no wonder they had thought his day was over.

Tumulty stirred on his knees, his posture erect again, eyes straight ahead on the tabernacle. Goudge had left the chapel. Goudge liked it here; most of them did. They accepted the verdict that their lives were all but over. But, dear God, look at the Founder. Ninety-three years old. Tumulty saw no reason why he himself would not live as long and the prospect of spending the next twenty years in Porta Coeli was intolerable. He had to show them all that he was the same man who for nearly fifty years had held positions of high responsibility in the society. He had to get out of this house. Tumulty squeezed his eyes shut and said another prayer for the Founder. Sadness welled up within him and he felt tears press against his lids. He let them come. In part, at least, it was the Founder for whom he wept.

When, late in the afternoon, they were allowed in to see the Founder, the old man lay flat on his bed under the oxygen tent. There was a stainless steel stand beside the bed and from the bottle it held fluid flowed through tube and needle into Father Cullen's arm. Oxygen was tapped from a fixture in the wall. It was the staff's first opportunity to show how well equipped for illness Porta Coeli was. Usedom had died without fanfare in his sleep. The old priests gathered about the Founder's bed and did not seem impressed by the marvels of medical technology. They might have been making an act of faith that the Founder

12

was still alive. His pillow had been taken away and the mattress cranked level so that his sharp nose pointed upward as if to sustain the tent. Light played off the planes of plastic and Tumulty could not get a clear look at the Founder. No one spoke.

Tumulty was oppressed by thoughts of the indignity of age, of illness, of death. The Founder's toothless mouth was open and in his throat his Adam's apple bulged grotesquely. He lay stiff and unrelaxed as if supported on his shoulder blades. The thin, high rib cage pressed against the flimsy garment he wore. Tumulty shut his eyes, seeking a more worthy image of the Founder. The gleaming efficiency of the room served only to remind him of the inevitability that made it necessary. He wished that someone would make a move so they could leave the room. He did not like being here. Did the others? Surely they could not. He remembered the words the Founder had addressed to Leo Phelan.

Let go, let go. Loosen your grip on life, let your fingers open, slip into a coma or worse. No wonder Leo had connected the words with the attack that had followed their utterance. It was advice to die. Tumulty opened his eyes but did not look again at the inert figure beneath the plastic tent.

When finally they were outside, Leo said, "Noonan should be in charge. While the Founder's ill."

Others nodded assent. It seemed settled. Tumulty turned away. Noonan had been the head prefect of the school when they were boys. Leo's suggestion seemed somehow right though Noonan had done nothing in subsequent years to fulfill the promise of student days. Tumulty had not anticipated this. With Leo, Noonan opposed him on the matter of Little Sem.

"The name of Little Sem should be changed to Founder's Hall," Phelan piped. "As a memorial."

Tumulty felt that he was being taunted. "If that is the best we can offer as a memorial, I suggest we forget it."

"He loved that building, Tumulty."

13

"Of course he did. We all did."

"You do not tear down what you love."

Tumulty would have liked to remind Leo of what the Founder had said to him before the attack but he sensed that it would be both wrong and ineffectual to try to use those words against Leo now. It would degenerate into an irrational brawl. Besides, Garrity had put a hand on Tumulty's arm.

"Let us go for a stroll, Michael."

Tumulty agreed. Garrity, too, was opposed to the destruction of Little Sem but Garrity was wise and kind. Moreover, he was the key to Tumulty's plan for fulfilling his task of overcoming opposition in the house.

Garrity said. "He is ninety-three years old, yet I am surprised to see him at death's door."

"I know."

"The man was a giant." Garrity spoke softly, as if trying out the past tense. "A saint."

The remark did not seem hyperbole. How odd to think that one had lived with a saint.

"Yes," Tumulty said. "Yes, he was."

2

SOME SIXTY YEARS AGO and more, little Michael Tumulty had first imagined himself a priest. It would have been difficult not to, serving Mass in the parish church in Minneapolis. Holy Rosary was a Dominican parish from whose pulpit members of the Order of Preachers thundered and imprecated by the half hour at all the Sunday Masses while the altar boys, seated in cassock and surplice beside the celebrant, understandably came to feel themselves on the safe side of the fulminating preacher, in some way allied with him, half clerical already. By the age of eleven, Michael was something of a connoisseur of the homiletic art as well as an aspiring practitioner of it. If his attention wavered during the long sermons this was because, in imagination, he was delivering one of his own.

He saw himself standing silent in the pulpit, brooding over the congregation until not a single cough or clearing of the throat was audible. Like the pastor, he would be tall and thin, his wavy hair brushed out from his skull in such a way that, with the sun behind him, a moted polychrome light arriving through the stained-glass windows of the sanctuary, it seemed an aureole. One long-fingered and consecrated hand lay lightly upon the red-bound book from which he had just read the gospel in a rich and sonorous voice. Now every soul before him was in an agony of longing for him to break this intolerable silence. Finally the hand that had been hanging loosely at his side would begin to rise slowly and as it did Michael's head would tilt back, his chin would thrust up and out. His eyes closed as his arm rose upward. When it had described an arc of 180 degrees, three fingers sought the thumb and the index finger pointed at the great vaulted ceiling as if to hold off destruction.

"My friends in Jesus Christ," he would whisper, allowing his eyes to open. His arm dropped and he was pointing at the pews. "There are those among you who will spend an eternity in the unquenchable fires of hell. Your lives make a mockery of the suffering and death of Our Lord Jesus Christ. You have been offered the kingdom of heaven and you have sold it for a mess of pottage. You have left your father's table to wallow in filth with swine."

And little Michael Tumulty, wallowing in imagined oratorical power, scarcely understanding the words the preacher spoke, would, for the space of the Mass, imagine himself a priest, a Dominican, a preacher as effective as the pastor himself.

That vision faded in the afternoon and was gone entirely during the week, when Michael's fancied self was modeled on his father, a motorman in a streetcar. To the son, Mr. Tumulty's solitude in the swaying car—sealed off as he was in a glass compartment from the passengers on their wicker seats—seemed regal. His father worked with levers to start and stop the car, he opened and shut the doors with other switches, he was not so much commanded as released by the conductor's all-clear clang. But the following Sunday Michael became again an imaginary priest.

It was on a Sunday in his eleventh year that thoughts of the priesthood passed from fantasy to resolution. The change was occasioned by a visiting priest who was not even a Dominican. He was young and of middle size and his cassock and surplice seemed no more impressive than an altar boy's when he mounted the pulpit. Taking his cue from the Dominican celebrant of the Mass, Michael settled back with a smile of benign condescension on his lips. And then the priest began to speak—to speak, not preach, to talk directly and without rhetoric to the people before him, his voice soft and musical and Irish but only an instrument for what he had to say, the words clearly coming from his heart and soul.

His name was Cullen and he belonged to the Society of Saint Brendan and of course he didn't for a moment imagine that any of them had heard of it or of him before but he wondered if they could believe, members as they were of this lovely and prosperous parish, that they lived in what was still a mission country. Their lot was not the usual one—oh, no—however familiar it must be to them. Why, there were areas of the land with scarcely a priest for miles and miles, no father to say the Mass and hear confessions, to baptize the children and anoint the dying, whole dioceses without a parish so grand as Holy Rosary. Would they put their minds to thinking of the souls in need of Christ's grace and mercy this very moment who could not be waiting for some distant day when things would be for them as they were now in this fortunate place in south Minneapolis? The priests of the Society of Saint Brendan were doing the little they could here and there about the country, mainly in Ohio but in other places, too, and he was here today, as they would all have guessed by now, to ask their help and support. Their money, of course, but their prayers as well, and he wondered, too, if there were any young people listening who might feel stirring in their breast a call to join in the work of the Society of Saint Brendan. They must nurture these thoughts if they came and parents should encourage their children to ask if God was calling them to a special life, one to be lived entirely for souls. Fathers and mothers might wish to imagine

17

him as their own son returned to ask their prayers and financial support of the work of the society. For that they would have his own thanks, of course, but more importantly they would know they had responded to the Lord's desire that the gospel be preached to all nations, even our own. Yes, ours. Father Cullen smiled. He wagered that he was newer to this land than any of those to whom he spoke but perhaps for that very reason he had the newcomer's first fervor of love for it. Their pastor had generously authorized a second collection, for the work of the Society of Saint Brendan, and Father Cullen thanked them in advance for whatever they might be able to give. God bless you.

Michael got through the rest of the Mass in a kind of daze and when he swept ahead of the celebrant into the sacristy afterward he looked around for Father Cullen but the priest was not there. He wanted to hang around for the next Mass and talk to the visitor before he went out to preach again but they would be waiting for him at home. Michael had to settle for one of the envelopes that gave the address of the headquarters of the Society of Saint Brendan in Fort Elbow, Ohio.

The nun who taught the eighth grade at Holy Rosary made a special effort to interest the boys and girls in religious vocations. To aid her in her task she had collected catalogs and literature from various religious orders and, in the case of some of the seminaries, the student magazine as well. Thus it was that Michael Tumulty had come to read a smudged hectographed publication from the seminary on the shores of Saint Brendan's Lake in northwest Ohio. He was captivated. The printed official brochures and catalogs had intimidated him, though he liked to read the *horaria*. Rise at 6:00, Mass at 6:30, breakfast at 7:30, first class at 8:10, and so on through the day. The catalog from Saint Brendan's took on life when read in conjunction with the student magazine and Michael would turn from his efforts to decode a humor column entitled "Quid Nunc" to the photographs of dorms and study hall and chapel, peopling them

18

with boys whose names he had read in the magazine. It was in the latter that he first encountered the name of Frederick Noonan.

Michael wavered once in the direction of the Dominicans when the young priest who was in charge of the altar boys took them by train to Minnehaha Falls for a picnic. There under giant cottonwoods along the creek the priest had told anecdotes of his own days in the seminary and Michael was visited anew by the image of himself in a Dominican habit mounting the pulpit at Holy Rosary. The difficulty was that joining the Dominicans would have seemed too much like moving into the parish rectory, going to live with men impossibly older than himself. It helped that his parents were impressed by the society because of its Irish origin. Mrs. Tumulty had already made up her mind to accompany Michael on the long train ride to Ohio and it would have been cruel to deny her the trip now by switching to the Dominicans and the paltry journey to Dubuque.

For years afterward, certainly throughout his years in Little Sem, Michael winced in embarrassment whenever he remembered his arrival at the school. His mother was what he would learn to call a *mulier fortis*. She descended on the seminary with her eldest son determined to get him off on the right foot. There had been a long session in the Founder's office, where she managed to whittle down the ordinary board and tuition to a payment of two dollars a month. "Mr. Tumulty is a motorman on the streetcar" was a recurring line and for the first time in his life Michael felt ashamed of his father's occupation. The Founder nodded in feigned comprehension. He had only the vaguest notion what compensation workmen received for their labors in this allegedly wealthy country. The tuition had been set somewhat arbitrarily at ten dollars a month; he did not really know if that sufficed to keep a boy in school but it did seem to him a princely sum. Mrs. Tumulty balked at the laundry costs as well, wondering if Michael couldn't package his dirty clothes and send them home to be washed. The Founder waived

19

the laundry fee. After that Mrs. Tumulty took Michael off to bargain for his books. He got everything he needed, second-hand, for two and a half dollars, though toward the end the outhaggled brother in the bookstore seemed about to make a gift of the lot. But the dormitory was the worst. There his mother made his bed for him, accompanying her actions with a loud didactic commentary. This was the way he must do it every morning. Her deft handling of the problem of the corners almost but not quite put out the glint of amusement in the eyes of the witnessing student prefect of the dormitory. When the school carriage took his mother off to her train, Michael could have shouted with relief. That terrible experience saved him from the bouts of homesickness which during the first weeks filled the freshman dormitory with imperfectly muffled whimpering when the late autumn winds keened round the corners of the building and the mournful trees sent shadows leaping about the darkened room. Michael remembered his mother right there in the dormitory, making his bed for him as if he were a kid, and it was easy to snuggle under the covers and sleep a contented lonely sleep.

Perhaps he would have seemed a baby to the upperclassmen even without the anecdotes they traded of the redoubtable Mrs. Tumulty. Little Michael, they called him, and he was little indeed, physically small and just turned thirteen, with thick black curls and wide Irish eyes. He became an object of pity, too, since his mother had skimped on the suggested clothing list in the school catalog. She thought it was nonsense to demand that so young a boy have two suits of clothes. Little Michael wore his one suit seven days a week throughout his first year. He had only one pair of boots as well—he had never had more at home—and in these he went to class and onto the playground, which was dusty or muddy or deep in snow. And he loved the school. It was even better than he had imagined. At thirteen he belonged to a student body which ranged through six years, the four of high school and the first two of college, so that his heroes were chosen from among boys who were quite literally young men. He became almost a mascot of the college men, of Tracy and Goudge and Huff. Noonan was the head prefect of the school and thus beyond the range of intimacy, but little Michael worshiped him from afar. Indeed he felt some affinity with those upperclass luminaries since in his first year he was selected to serve the benediction, which was given each afternoon at three in the convent chapel.

He would leave his last class with Father Casey, the teacher, and they would go down the hall and through the refectory and into the kitchen, where a door gave onto the cloistered convent wing. Beyond that door was a dimly lit corridor that seemed always freshly scrubbed and waxed and Father Casey's shoes made an odd kissing sound as they walked the length of the corridor and into a miniature sacristy. Michael had to take his cassock into the corridor to have room to slip it on and give Father Casey an opportunity to vest. Sister Diotima, the superior, had everything in readiness on the altar: the charcoal glowed in the censer, the candles were lit, the monstrance stood beside the tabernacle. The voices of the nuns singing the Little Office had been audible from the moment they entered the cloister. Father Casey waited until the hour they were reciting was done and then, pressing back against the vestment case, he would nod to Michael, who preceded him into the Lilliputian sanctuary. In prayer and song the brogue of the nuns thickened to unintelligibility and, kneeling beside the priest, Michael felt asea in a tide of Hibernian piety. At first he would steal a glance at the nuns upon entering the sanctuary but there was nothing to see but a field of black tents; at prayer the nuns unpinned their veils and covered their faces and Michael had had the disconcerting thought that they were facing away from the altar.

By three-twenty he was free and on the way to the dormitory for his sheepskin jacket. It was a distinction to be so delayed. At Christmas the nuns gave him a holy card and Father Casey presented him with a rosary; that card had gone through life

21

with him and even now was a marker in his breviary, the Verna volume, a reminder of innocence and beginnings and thirteen years of age, a palpable link with his first days in the seminary. The rosary had gone the way of rosaries: an undone link, missing beads, a misnamed decade and then into a drawer to be forgotten, replaced by another.

If it was a distinction to serve benediction in the convent chapel, the job Goudge gave him was more prestigious still. On Sunday mornings, between the low and high Masses, he set off with a pitcher of holy water to fill the fonts of the faculty and, better, those in the rooms on the college corridor.

Thus one bright Sunday morning in April, 1912, little Michael Tumulty, wearing his only suit, his curly hair beginning to free itself from the slicking down he had given it at dawn, a glass pitcher of holy water in his hand, came along the college corridor. The linoleum floor of the hallway stretched ahead of him, ending in a blaze of double windows that looked out over the playing field. The smell of roasting chicken lifted from the kitchen two floors below. Michael stopped at each door, knocked, waited a moment and then, with or without an answer from within, opened the door and reached inside with his pitcher. The holy water fonts were nailed to the wall just inside the door, above the light switch. In the course of the week they ran dry and the little sponge in each had shriveled and lightened in color. *"Ecce aqua benedicta,"* he sang when he opened the door and, if the occupant was in, he would reply, *"Sit nobis salus et vita."* Michael quite literally sang the announcement, the exuberance and delight he felt at being on the college corridor and of being welcomed like a little brother by its denizens making song a necessity. His choice of the tune of "Clementine" had been as spontaneous as the need to sing. It had just burbled forth that way, much to the delight of Huff, who had been unable to match the response to the tune. Huff had accompanied him along the corridor that first Sunday, making certain that the others appreciated the musical innovation.

Recognizing that he was on the thin edge between being amusing and a clown, Michael had retreated to *recto tono,* but Huff had insisted on "Clementine" and "Clementine" it had remained.

On this April morning the college corridor seemed deserted. His knocks received no answer, his announcement no response. He tipped his pitcher, watching the little sponge absorb water, grow dark, swell and lift with the rising liquid, then sink. Now when the college men entered or left their rooms they could dip a finger into the water, make the sign of the cross and receive the standard indulgence for performing this gesture reverently. Down the corridor Michael went, toward the blazing windows. He no longer sang his announcement, he hardly said it aloud. He found himself eager to finish and get outside with everyone else before the High Mass began. At the end of the corridor, on the left, was the room of the head prefect. Noonan's room. Michael approached it with appropriate reverence. Noonan was the top man in the school, almost as exalted a personage as the priests on the faculty.

Michael tapped on the door and opened it. A startled Noonan stared up at him. He was kneeling on the floor and the top of his footstool, oddly, was opened, lifted like the lid of a trunk. There were headphones on Noonan's head; their wires led into the footstool. As if that were not enough, a cigarette dangled from Noonan's lips. The supposed embodiment of the seminary rules was thus caught *in flagrante delicto* by a freshman bearing holy water. Both the radio and smoking were prohibited in the most emphatic way. Michael was so profoundly surprised and shocked that, without filling Noonan's holy water font, he closed the door and fled down the corridor. Before he reached the stairway he heard Noonan calling after him but he flew down the steps and ran all the way to chapel, the holy water sloshing out of the pitcher and getting his shirt wet. In the sacristy he stood very still and felt that he had not breathed since closing the door of Noonan's room.

23

"You should knock before entering a room," Noonan said to him that evening. He had come to the door of the high school recreation room and sent a boy in search of Michael. They now stood in the hallway outside, in an island of shadow between two feeble overhead lights.

"I did knock."

"And what are you supposed to announce when you knock?"

Michael looked up at Noonan; he was talking to an adult but one to whom he now felt strangely superior.

"*Ecce aqua benedicta,*" he said, and his voice was thin.

"*Sit nobis salus et vita,*" Noonan replied.

"Amen."

Noonan smiled, a smile of complicity, what seemed to Michael in his innocence a Judas smile. "I guess my ears were occupied."

Michael said nothing. Noonan put a hand on his shoulder, lightly, but it had the feel of menace. They began to walk down the hall, away from the recreation room. The receding happy voices might have been those of a lost Eden.

"The radio comes with the room, Tumulty. My predecessor bequeathed it to me."

"I don't believe you."

And he didn't. Noonan was asking him to believe that the school's code of honor was a fraud, that head prefects systematically and as a matter of tradition flaunted its rules. The thought was vertiginous. Noonan's hand seemed heavier on his shoulder; its fingers now gripped him slightly.

"Well, it's true."

"You were smoking."

They had come under one of the feeble lights. Noonan stopped them by gripping Michael painfully by the shoulder. The light was behind his head and Michael looked into shadowed features. The prince of darkness. Noonan had become the embodiment of evil.

"Not so loud," he hissed.

"Are you afraid I'll tell?"

Noonan's face in shadow seemed to be considering that. "No. Of course not."

"I won't."

"Good boy."

"You don't understand."

"I don't understand?" They were walking again. Noonan wore a rueful smile. It was bitter to Michael that once he would have been bursting with pride to be walking with the head prefect.

"It's not you I'm thinking of."

"I see."

But did he? Michael saw the point only imperfectly himself. He had to protect the others from the dreadful knowledge that was his. The head prefect is a hypocrite. He assumed that every younger boy idolized the upperclassmen as he had. The past tense was appropriate. He no longer had any desire to see the college men except from a distance. He tried to give up his holy water job but Goudge would not let him. He seemed to know the reason for Michael's desire to resign.

"Phelan would like the job," Michael said.

"Phelan won't do. The college men wouldn't hear of it. They like you, Tumulty."

Michael said nothing.

"Before you know it, you'll be a college man yourself."

Michael nodded.

"You might even become head prefect."

Michael looked at Goudge and tears started up in his un- blinking eyes. "I wouldn't want to be. I'd turn it down."

How easily at thirteen he had hung the millstone around Noonan's neck, and around Goudge's, too. Woe to those through whom scandal comes. And little Michael Tumulty had been profoundly scandalized. The wonder was that he did not go to Father Cullen with the story. Saint Brendan's was never quite the same for him again. At midyear Noonan resigned as head prefect, pleading that his studies suffered from the extra work. Garrity was appointed to fill out the term but of course everyone continued to think of Noonan as head prefect. Michael Tumulty became in his second year a sarcastic boy, masking his love of the school behind a stream of tart remarks. In his final year he did not have to turn down the job of head prefect. It was not offered to him; Father Cullen wanted Michael's help in an untitled capacity in his office. As other college men had before him, Michael smoked in his room, though he did not have a radio. Sunday mornings after Low Mass he gave his room a thorough airing and, if he happened to be in when the first-year boy came along the corridor with the holy water, he contrived to be busy at his desk. "Behold the blessed water," the tiny voice would say, and Michael Tumulty, turning to the opened door, addressing his own lost innocence, would respond, "May it be for us both salvation and life."

3

Noonan's room was blue with smoke and Garrity, come there reluctantly at Phelan's insistence, was reminded of meetings in the head prefect's room so many years ago. Had Phelan been present then? Garrity could not remember. He accepted a water glass into which Phelan had poured a dollop of Jameson's.

"The Founder," Noonan said, and tossed off his whiskey.

Garrity drank his; it would ensure that his nap was sound. He had been on his way to his room and forty winks when Phelan had caught him. Phelan, having sipped to the Founder, now lifted the remainder of his drink to Noonan.

"The new superior of the house."

"The man is not yet dead," Noonan chided.

"To the new acting superior, then," Phelan amended.

Garrity disliked the lilt of triumph in Phelan's voice. What earthly difference did it make who was superior at Porta Coeli? He expressed the thought aloud.

"You'd know the difference if Tumulty had taken over," Phelan said. "And don't think he wouldn't have if we hadn't spoken up. You've seen how he haunts the Founder. Tumulty spends more time in the office than the Founder ever did." Phelan turned to Noonan. "You have to take over the office."

"And do what?"

"Just sit there. Assert your right to it. It's a matter of principle."

"I doubt that it will be contested," Garrity said, putting down his glass. He felt drowsy. The thought of a nap was inviting.

"You don't understand Tumulty," Phelan said. "Good Lord, you've seen how he proceeded on Little Sem. He was collecting agreements before we even knew what was going on."

"Without our agreement nothing can be done."

"No one would have agreed if they had understood, if it had been put to them in the proper light. There should have been unanimous opposition. That would have shown them."

"Hoyt must be furious," Noonan said, holding out his glass for a refill. "Imagine being stopped by the likes of us."

Phelan's laughter turned into a fit of coughing. Slapping his back, Garrity felt that he was administering punishment. Surely the Founder had not imagined this kind of division when he set down the somewhat Byzantine regulations of the Society of Saint Brendan.

Father Cullen, smitten by the political ideals of his adopted country, had sought to introduce into his society a complicated machinery of checks and balances. A more worldly, less inexperienced man would have foreseen that an excess of democracy is a guarantee of inertia. All positions in the society were elective but it was forbidden to campaign for them. A ward heeler from Chicago, a generous donor, the source of his largesse mercifully obscure, had spoken glowingly of the caucus system and the Founder had seized upon the idea, moved by the thought that the election of men to the highest posts would repose on a pyramid of previous elections. Each member of the society was likely to vote several times in various capacities in each election but the final choice came to seem terribly remote. They elected electors who elected electors who elected electors so that the ultimate result burst upon the society with as much surprise as an autocratic appointment would have. Garrity sometimes suspected that it had been the illusion rather than the reality of democracy that the Founder had been after all along. The suspicion was enforced by the fact that the Founder and/or the father superior—until a few years ago Father Cullen had been both—could veto the result of any election.

The case of Little Sem did not exactly fit this pattern since here the veto was invested in all members of the society who had celebrated the golden anniversary of their profession of vows. Oscar Shively, a convert to Catholicism who had donated the first tract of land to the society, drove a hard bargain. The land was a gift but in return for it Oscar wanted the assurance that Masses would be said for the repose of his soul so long as there should be a society. The Founder gladly agreed but Oscar required more. He asked to be buried in the chapel, in the middle aisle, his bones resting beneath a slab which extolled his generosity in Latin words that came to be shuffled indistinct by generations of student soles. Assured of Masses and of a resting place in chapel, Oscar, one might think, should have been content, but he had one more anxiety that had to be allayed. His mind now being turned to thoughts of eternity, he was nagged by an awareness of the transitoriness of the things of earth. Recently his barn had burned. He brought his concern to the Founder. That zealous priest fairly itched to tell Oscar that he could not guarantee that moth and rust and theft, not to mention fire, would no longer wreak havoc in northwestern Ohio after Oscar passed on. But the Founder needed and wanted the gift of land. It must have seemed attractively quixotic, all those years ago, to tie the future use of Oscar's gift, in perpetuity, to the will of a group of senior members of the society whose far-off existence required the stoutest act of faith. At the time, the society had consisted of the Founder, one other priest, three lay brothers and half a dozen seminarians. That any of them, including the visionary Founder, should survive to celebrate his golden anniversary, that there should even be a society of which one could be a member fifty years hence, was not a proposition on which the normally shrewd Shively would have placed a bet in ordinary circumstances. Needless to say, Oscar could not have bargained in this way with any established religious community.

Had the Founder himself been certain that his society would flourish? What had his thoughts been when he wrote out his promise that Oscar's gift of land and his tomb in the chapel to be raised on it could never be put to a different use without the unanimous consent of a hypothetical group fifty years hence? The same question might have been asked of the country's founding fathers. What is it that prompts men to sit around a table and draft guidelines for generations yet unborn? Among a host of noble motives and apart from the necessity to placate Oscar Shively, the Founder was gripped by that fierce passion for possession which visits men who have taken the vow of poverty. Forgoing the joy an individual feels in claiming a corner of the earth as *his,* as if the possessive somehow defines the very composition of the soil, the religious feels a compensatory need to employ the additive "ours."

But whatever his thoughts had been some sixty years earlier, the Founder's solemn promise to Oscar sifted to the bottom of a drawer in the remotest corner of what had come to be called the archives of the society. The building erected on that first gift of land housed every facet of the society's work: the Founder lived there, the brothers lived there, appeals to Irish bishops were penned there. The seminarians were taught there. As the society grew, other buildings went up, more land was purchased until, within ten years of its erection, the original building became the preparatory seminary, Little Sem, the house in which the first six years of preparation for the priesthood were passed. It was only after the First World War that Saint Brendan's College became a separate entity which was opened to laymen—a select group, not many, and of those a significant portion discovered in themselves a vocation to the priesthood. The college had flourished, it continued to flourish, plans for expansion and building stretched into the next decade. So it had come about that the land on which Little Sem stood was now required for another purpose. It had seemed a simple matter to knock it down, clear the site and build anew—until that old promise of the Founder's had come to light. Father Corcoran, a cagey canonist, still filled with the frenetic energy that made retirement at Porta Coeli distasteful to him, had been given the task of putting some semblance of order into the jumble of documents which were the society's archives. By some it was regarded as an unpropitious day when he had discovered the document in which Father Cullen had placed such fanciful restraints on the use of the site of Little Sem.

With one exception—and he, poor devil, was mad, *hors de combat* in a state institution—the class of priests envisaged by the promise were residents of Porta Coeli, the home for retired members of the society recently constructed across Saint Brendan's Lake from the college, itself a gift of a septuagenarian benefactor in Fort Elbow, a not far distant city. At first it had seemed only an annoying technicality, that document, a matter of gathering signatures from the occupants of Porta Coeli, then on with the work of destruction. Father Hoyt, when he placed the matter in Tumulty's hands, had even imagined that the old priests would be flattered to be consulted on the matter. Not that he was so maladroit, when at Tumulty's behest he addressed them in the recreation room, as to suggest that they had veto power over his wishes. No man in whom administrative work had rounded the rough edges of frankness and honesty would have committed such a faux pas, least of all Father Hoyt.

"I have come to seek your counsel," he told them. "As you know . . ."

What they were presumed to know was that the fortunes of the college had brightened considerably under his own and his predecessor's guiding hands; the enrollment was up, new buildings had been built, the quality of the faculty had improved dramatically. It did not occur to him that this final point might be ungracious to the emeriti among his listeners. Nor did he take into account that other and, as they thought of them, saner times haunted the souls and memories of these priests.

"Coeducation," growled Phelan. "The campus is crawling with half-clothed females, Father. I suppose that is progress, too."

"Their presence is progress, Father, whatever we may think of their attire."

"Think of it? What have you said about it? What have you done about it?"

The president's smile might have been painted on his lips with holy oils. "I have avoided the role of fashion expert, Father."

The sentence did not quite end. Hoyt had clearly wished to address Father Phelan by name and equally clearly he did not remember it. That as much as anything had altered the tenor of the meeting. Phelan had been a teacher at the college when Hoyt was a babe in arms. A sense of their expendability, of their pastness, came over the old priests. The president plunged on.

Garrity interrupted to ask what other sites had been considered for the new girls' dormitory.

"The site I have mentioned is so obviously ideal that others have not been considered."

"Then why have you come to us? You said you sought our counsel."

32

"I would not want to go ahead without the approval of the senior members of the society."

"We've never been consulted before."

"Ah, but before you were scattered. Now that you have all come together in this beautiful house, it is easier to ask your advice."

"He needs our agreement," Corcoran said.

"Needs it?"

Corcoran explained the nature of the document he had found. It was a bad moment for the president. He had been made to look devious. The negative feeling spread to Tumulty, who had been himself less than a model of candor on this matter although he had been, it appeared, more forthcoming than Hoyt. Phelan announced that he for one was adamantly opposed to the destruction of Little Sem.

"Then it cannot be done," Corcoran said. He took no apparent relish in this announcement; it was merely a fact. Documents do not lie.

The president had had to retreat, if not in disarray, nonetheless without the agreement for which he had come. He was not amused. A self-liquidating government loan had already been approved, a wrecker had been engaged, there was no obstacle to his plans for the new girls' dormitory except these crotchety old priests. He would have thought they presented no difficulty even if his approach had been more transparent. He had not wanted to trouble these old heads with the details of current campus activities. They were in their way alumni and, as with alumni generally, the less said the better.

What the Founder had put together the Founder could put asunder. Thus reasoned Father Hoyt and, before leaving Porta Coeli, he went with Tumulty to the old man's room. His slight pique at Father Cullen's failure to attend the meeting was gone. All the better that the Founder had not witnessed that absurd reversal. Hoyt had had little experience of being thwarted; indeed he had been seldom bothered by delays. The talk with the

33

Founder was not brief. When Father Hoyt emerged from the room he wore a frown upon his face and he tugged his necktie tighter about his throat. Phelan, who had been loitering in the hallway to see the outcome of the meeting and report to the others, noticed the activity with the necktie. He would have liked to give that gaudy garment a tug or two himself. The president had let it be known that his duties—lunching with politicians, local, state and national, pilgrimages to the Mecca on the Potomac to wrest public moneys from bureaucratic hands—were best performed in other than clerical clothes. In the atmosphere of Porta Coeli, both in the rec room and with the Founder, he would have been well advised to wear a black suit and Roman collar. How odd that Father Tumulty had not told him as much.

Garrity had been an almost disinterested observer that evening. He shared without intensity the oldsters' delight in the defeat of the young. That, he sensed, was what the opposition largely was, age versus youth, a false nostalgia for the past against a thoughtless hurtling into the future. Garrity had tried without success to be an admirer of Hoyt. The young man—Father Hoyt was in his mid-forties—was the first member of the society to have been noticed by the world outside the Church. The column and a half devoted to him in an issue of a weekly newsmagazine had sent a tremor of vicarious pride through the society, but Garrity had experienced it as a shiver. There had been a photograph of the president, too, wearing clericals and standing at his desk, behind which was an easel heavy with his plans for the college's future. He had been described as of a new breed, and so he was, almost parthenogenic. Hoyt hungered for excellence, spoke of relevance and priorities, he hated war and was learning from the kids. The novel adjectives used to describe his person and efforts seemed wholly appropriate: in the annals of the society the president was himself a neologism.

"What goes up must come down," Noonan had said at the time.

But Garrity was more interested in the missile than in its trajectory. What did Hoyt stand for? Garrity was prepared to believe that the society must change, adapt, grow, but he could not see Hoyt as an instrument of organic development. The president seemed to regard the society as shapeless clay to be molded without consideration for its past. And what spirit would he breathe into it when he was done? Garrity doubted that it would be a spirit akin to the Founder's, though Tumulty disagreed with him on this and Tumulty was no fool.

In any case, the president had belatedly discovered that his vaulting ambitions were misplaced in the mediocre society to which he belonged. The somewhat cruel wording was Noonan's; he predicted that the president would resign and let the society and college sink without a trace. It was difficult to know if Noonan was even half serious in making these remarks. If he did indeed expect Hoyt to resign, he simply did not understand the man. The president had immediately made Michael Tumulty his agent in order to overcome the opposition to him in Porta Coeli.

"Surely you don't think that old building is a shrine," Tumulty had said to Garrity.

"Of course not."

"Then what is the problem?"

"Hoyt."

Tumulty was silent for a moment, then he nodded. "Don't overestimate his importance."

Faiblesse? Irony was an unaccustomed attitude for Garrity but he could not imagine Faiblesse diverting Hoyt from whatever plans the younger man had for the society. It was a melancholy thought that Hoyt represented the only leadership left in the society and he was a leader Garrity could not follow. Thank God he had no religious obligation to; thank God as well for the discovery of the Founder's half-forgotten promise to Oscar Shively. That the feeble occupants of Porta Coeli should be able to stop the vigorous young president had an almost biblical fittingness to it. But Garrity did not regard his own opposition as petty. He was not enamored of the past as such, but neither could he deny the vision that had guided him, and the society, throughout his life. Tumulty, to his credit, had not tried to persuade him otherwise, at least not yet. Garrity could not believe that Tumulty, Hoyt's man at Porta Coeli, would long leave him unproselytized.

Not that he stood alone. Noonan and Phelan, Corcoran and Stokes had also withheld consent. And Goudge. Garrity did not really relish these cohorts. If need be, he could stand alone between Hoyt and his destructive plans. Stokes, of course, was a special case.

Phelan had not made clear to Stokes that his decision would be lost in a collective opposition. He had made the mistake of suggesting to Stokes that he held the fate of the society and the college in his hand. Stokes had panicked at the thought of possessing such power and Phelan pressed him until Stokes seemed on the verge of one of the nervous breakdowns that had blighted his career. Stokes had ended his active life as a chaplain to nuns in a convent in Fort Elbow. Many things had converged to bring him safely into Porta Coeli: his advanced age, his inability to adjust to the new liturgy bringing on as counterpoint to this antinomian age a classic bout of scrupulosity. This had waxed as the convent waned: young nuns went with regularity over the walls while the old ones faded into senility, almost tugging Stokes with them. The convent closed its doors just when Porta Coeli opened its and Stokes had been absorbed into the most congenial atmosphere he had known since seminary days. Now Phelan threatened the idyll by demanding a decision whose importance he had painted in exaggerated colors. Stokes fled in panic to Tumulty, the mentor of his youth.

"Tumulty made the same mistake I did," Phelan said defensively to the others gathered in Noonan's room. "He made Stokes feel it all depends on him."

36

"Tumulty knows that eventually Stokes will run with the herd."

"What is Tumulty up to anyway?" Goudge asked, his eyes narrowing with sedulous wisdom. Perhaps only Garrity recognized that crinkled expression as an imitation of Noonan in a thoughtful mood.

"Tumulty is a devious lad," Noonan said. "He always was."

Phelan and Goudge agreed. It occurred to Noonan that they had little curiosity about their own motives. Perhaps it was just as well. He had not told them that he had been summoned by Hoyt to a presidential audience. His own recent past, indeed the preceding fifty years, made that occasion stand out like the steeple of the German church in a small town. A better man than Noonan would have been forgiven for taking pleasure in the fact that Hoyt had called on him in his hour of need, though Noonan had suspected the fine hand of Tumulty behind the invitation. Noonan's breath had caught at the functional opulence of the presidential suite of offices. He had not visited them since before Hoyt became president of the college. The air of teleological efficiency, so alien to the society as Noonan had known it all his life, intimidated. Noonan arrived with a soul inflated by righteous resistance, which almost immediately dissolved at the graciousness shown him by Hoyt's receptionist, the concern with which he was asked if he could wait, the care that went into the selection of the chair to which he was directed. Not that he had had to occupy it for long. The president came out to greet him, to shake his hand and explain to the secretary just who Father Noonan was. Not even Hoyt had been able to make Noonan's career sound distinguished. In the president's office, Noonan was flattered out of his shoes by Hoyt's monologue. He was given a personal account of where Hoyt was trying to take the college. For reasons Noonan did not understand, Hoyt had not pressed him to consent to the destruction of Little Sem then and there. Almost certainly he would have given his

37

consent. Sitting in that office, Noonan felt that he had been brought back from the dead, from a pagan, Virgilian nether world from which he emerged wraithlike into the flesh-and-blood reality of Hoyt's busy day. How dare he oppose his ghostly self to these vital plans? No wonder he had not cared to tell the others of that visit. His was an untested virtue, his strength merely an unprobed weakness. Had Hoyt seen him as an adamant opponent? But there were further reasons for Noonan's silence.

Phelan and Goudge looked up to him now as they had in the old days, he the head prefect, they the underclassman and sacristan. Garrity was different. Before succeeding Noonan as head prefect, Garrity had had the task of assigning the weekly seating in the refectory. Each week he had posted the new seating chart in the bookstore window. By frequent changing of table mates, particular friendships, a taboo the Founder had brought from Maynooth, were avoided. Garrity's power had been as naught compared to the head prefect's, of course, and even after his resignation Noonan had retained the panache of the top job in the school. Porta Coeli had reestablished old relationships and Noonan, returned to his room from the visit to Hoyt, was ashamed of the delight he had felt at Hoyt's attention. The president had not been born when Noonan was head prefect of Little Sem, already a promising young member of the society.

Noonan had tried to be a good head prefect and by and large he had succeeded. Doubtless the responsibility of the job had helped keep him in the seminary. The thought that others looked up to him helped to resolve doubts when doubts came. He had been at the age when the prospect of a celibate life seems grimmer than it turns out to be. There had been no lapses along those lines, thank God, but he had not been an exemplar of the school rule. Goudge and others had accompanied him on those afternoon walks when they had stopped for a hasty beer at a roadhouse not a mile from where Porta

Coeli now stood. To have been discovered would have meant instant expulsion. Noonan smiled with remembered dread. How serious those old prohibitions had been; boys were indeed sent home for violating them. No liquor, no tobacco, no newspapers or radios. For the rest of their lives indulgence in any of these would carry the faintest aura of the illicit. Recalling the Sunday morning when he had been surprised by little Michael Tumulty, Noonan recognized it as a turning point in his life. For a week he had waited in apprehension for the Founder to call him in. Surely Tumulty would take his tale to Father Cullen. Finally, unable to bear the suspense, Noonan had gone to the Founder and resigned as head prefect. His excuse had been that he had insufficient time for his studies. It was accepted without question. He would have preferred some reluctance in Father Cullen but ten minutes after entering the Founder's room he had emerged, reduced to the ranks. Ever since, his life had been a long declension from eminence. How odd that now, at Porta Coeli, Phelan and Goudge, and Garrity, too, in a way, seemed intent on returning him to a position of authority. It was a late but welcome turn in his fortunes.

Goudge had wondered what Tumulty was up to. Noonan thought he knew. His old nemesis still haunted him. Feet of clay. How relentless a punisher Tumulty was.

39

4

SEEN FROM THE AIR, Porta Coeli had the look of a somewhat stylized pontifical key cast among the trees on the north shore of Saint Brendan's Lake: its circular western end was the chapel, its tapering body ran uninterrupted until, tooth-like, two northern projections, the kitchen and the infirmary, completed the effect of a key. Porta Coeli: Gate of Heaven. Odd that a gate should be shaped like a key, but then the image was likely to suggest itself only to errant aviators and the more imaginative who studied the floor plan posted just inside the main door. The main door, however, faced the lake and was seldom used by visitors. They entered the building from the parking lot behind, came through a single door near the kitchen, down a brief hall, and found themselves in the central corridor. To the left were four rooms equipped with all the paraphernalia of hospital rooms, in one of which the Founder now lay in a coma; to the right, the corridor stretched toward the doors of the chapel; ten doors on the left, on the lake side, were resident rooms; on the right side of the corridor were five more resident rooms, a guest suite and the refectory. At two-thirty in the afternoon the corridor was empty, the building silent. Nap time.

Ambrose Huff was not in bed. His room, like all the others, was reminiscent of a motel. A single piece of furniture along one wall was dresser and desk and diminutive bookshelf in one. Huff sat at his desk and was repeated in the mirror before him. The mirror should be moved to hang over the dresser. Better still, it should simply be removed. He had no need of mirrors. The one in the bathroom sufficed for his shaving and he had no other reason to see himself. On the paper before him he had written a single line.

> The leaving leaves have left

He was trying to write a poem. He had been trying to write a poem for the past three months. Once he had written a couplet that seemed perfect to him, as well it might have.

> It is the fate man was born for,
> It is Margaret you mourn for.

So Ambrose wept when his too faithful glass reflected to his eyes the ruin of his face. Written dry-eyed, the lines had not been dictated by the old man's face that peered from the mirror as from another room. How could he know if his poetry was his own? It did not matter. If memory was jogged by mimicking the act of creation, so much the better. When he sat in his easy chair and read, he quickly dozed off or found his mind drifting away, set in motion by a few syllables. He had no settled tastes in poetry. Newman, John Banister Tabb, Belloc, Lanier, Van Doren's anthology . . .

He had put poetry behind him when he left Saint Brendan's, off for Maynooth to study theology, left it behind him with the other things of the child. Sometimes in the interval he had glanced at Pound and Eliot. A glance had sufficed. They were

41

mad. They were not poets. Huff could hear no music in their lines. Poetry took him back to school days, to his days as editor of the magazine. How easily verse had come then, imitative, of course, yet in some way his own, far more his own than what he managed to write now at his desk in Porta Coeli. That conversation with Corcoran . . .

"What sorts of things are in the archives?" Huff had asked.

"Records. Papers. An enormous pile of things."

"Do you have a list?"

"I am cataloging it now."

Corcoran retained the frightening efficiency of a fifty-year-old. His face unlined, his eyes clear. Each morning he walked off along the path toward campus as if restraining himself from breaking into a run. Everyone ages differently, but Corcoran seemed not to age at all. It was not canon law that had done that for Corcoran, but his interest in history. He had learned to think in terms of centuries, epochs. Had Huff suspected this earlier, he might have indulged a vagrant interest in archaeology. Look at that maniac Toynbee.

"Do you suppose the school magazine was saved?"

Corcoran said he would see. A week later he was able to report that a complete set had been found in the attic of Little Sem.

"I went up there to look at it. They are not in good condition but it is a complete set. I made a note of it."

"You left them there?"

"For now."

During several days Huff had entertained himself with the thought that he would go over to Little Sem and take a look at the issues of the magazine he had edited during his final year at Saint Brendan's. He felt no urgency about it. The prospect of walking to the opposite side of the lake and the campus was unwelcome. He would have to see about getting a ride over, perhaps with Flamingo. And there were no elevators in Little Sem. He would have to mount the four flights to the top floor, and where was the attic? He tried to remember and the effort set his mind drifting. Sitting in his room with his eyes closed, it was easy to visualize Little Sem. When he saw it across the lake, the physical reality, it seemed foreign and strange. He realized that he really did not want to see those old issues of the magazine, his hectographed poems. He had no idea what they had been about. It would not displease him at all if those old issues were brought down in the rubble and dust when Little Sem was razed.

In the mirror the old man he had become yawned. His eyes squinted and his teeth slipped. He did not stop them. His upper denture hung over his lower lip. He kept his eyes squinted. He laughed. When he was a boy they had called him Chink.

Father O'Leary lay on his bed, staring at the ceiling. He had taken off his cassock and put on his bathrobe. His hands were plunged in its pockets. His right eye was closed. The left, where the cataract had formed, gave him a fuzzy view. He was thinking of the real distinction between essence and existence. As a teacher he had stoutly defended it for years but now, in retirement, in the privacy of his room, he could admit to himself that he had never really understood it. The attacks on it seemed unanswerable. Strange how little of it made sense, the arguments for, the arguments against, when put into English. It was a disturbing thought that philosophical problems were classifiable by the language which generated them. Latin difficulties, Greek problems, and of course in German they positively pullulated. German begat philosophical issues like an Old Testament patriarch. Were there any specifically French philosophical problems? Not really. *Esprit de finesse.* Bridge. He shook away these subversive thoughts.

Thoughts of the Founder took their place. The distinction between essence and existence was far too recherché when one was confronted by the stark fact of mortality. How wasted the old man had seemed, lying there. Two days before, he had sat at table with them, erect, alert, a stern amusement in his eyes at seeing these ancients he had known as mere lads.

"Are Latin texts still in use?" he had asked O'Leary when he told him he was revising his *Cosmologia.*

"Not in the classroom, Father."

"It will be read by professors, then?"

"I hope so."

"And who will publish it?"

"That remains to be seen."

"I should like to read it when you are finished."

"It's very technical, of course."

"Of course."

"Perhaps it would be wiser to write it in English," Father O'Leary said gloomily.

"I myself was never overly successful in philosophy. Not that I regret having studied it. Even I profited from it in some way, I'm sure."

"Theology would be impossible without philosophy."

"So I was taught."

A conversation with the Founder made one a child again, though O'Leary did not feel that he was being humored. The Founder could rekindle the difficult hope that age contained a wisdom worth living for. The rest of them seemed children still. It was as though the roll had been called once more and only these few had survived to answer it, scattered representatives of different classes. The years had provided no dwelling, only Porta Coeli. Yet O'Leary liked it here. Thank God for this new building. Thank Flamingo, too. They might have been put in Little Sem. Why did Phelan pester everyone to save Little Sem? Let it fall, let it fall. No Troys were to be left for the future to find.

Stokes was not in his room. After the visit to the Founder's bedside he had put on his coat and walked away from Porta Coeli. He did not like to take a nap. He slept poorly enough

44

at night without coddling his body during the day. He walked around the lake and across campus, ignored by the young, ignoring them, to the bus stop. Downtown he transferred and took a number 36 to the airport. It was a favorite spot. He went up to the observation platform and looked out over the field. Orange-colored racks of landing lights marched to the east; turned on, they became an illusory avenue down which at night planes descended to the runway. No need for lights in the daytime, of course. He wished he could come here at night and see the place lit up. Not that many flights came into Fort Elbow, commercial flights. Smaller craft came and went constantly, the same plane making countless takeoffs and landings, up and away and then within minutes back again. Practicing, Stokes supposed, or just learning. Such planes seemed mere toys, like the thousands of boats moored along the Great Lakes, on the rivers of the nation, on either coast and in the Gulf as well; expensive toys. Putt, putt, putt, over the water or into the air. How wealthy the country had become. Automobiles everywhere, two chickens in every pot. It had not made people happier, this prosperity. That should not surprise me, Father Stokes thought; riches are not happiness. But he was surprised.

A commercial jet approached from the east, most likely from Cleveland. Stokes leaned on the railing and watched it come down, tons and tons of machinery gliding to earth as gracefully as a feathered bird. Tumulty had flown everywhere in his time. There were plaques on the wall of his room, gifts of grateful airlines. Stokes had preferred trains but there were no longer any trains. How dismal the Fort Elbow depot had become. He had gone there one day to find it locked, the windows boarded up. The New York Central and Grand Trunk trains did not stop there anymore. For years the railroads had systematically discouraged passengers, letting the cars become shabbier and shabbier, the service a parody of its former self. Stokes had been one of the last to ride the Twentieth Century from Chicago to New York, taking a compartment. A sentimental journey. It had been a great disappointment. The shoes he had left out to be shined were untouched in the morning but his copy of *The New York Times* had been put in the little cubbyhole provided for it. He had read it in the dining car as they came down the Hudson valley. Breakfast had cost four dollars. A crime. America had been ill served by the railroads; there had been something crooked about them from the start. All those government subsidies. And the full-page ads preaching free enterprise. Dishonest. Robber barons. Of course trains could not compete with the airlines, with their swift efficiency and free meals. They had not wanted to compete. They did not know how, they had never had to. They would settle for freight and some of the mail.

The jet had taxied to the terminal and now stood on the ramp below him. Passengers were disembarking. The luggage train drew up beside the plane. He turned and stepped to the pay phone behind him. He rang the number of an airline counter on the main floor below.

"Would you have Father Stokes paged, please? It's very important."

"Would you repeat that?"

He repeated it, spelled his name.

"Is he on our flight?"

"I'm sure he's in the terminal."

"I'll page him."

"Thank you."

He hung up the phone and started for the stairway. He came into the main waiting room with the sound of his name reverberating. There was a nice note of urgency in the pager's voice. Father Stokes assumed an expression of concern and hurried through the crowd. One or two faces connected his clerical figure with the announcement that had just been made. There were lines at the counter but he caught the eye of one of the clerks and raised his brows quizzically.

"Are you Father Stokes?"

"Yes, I am."

46

The man beckoned him forward. People stood aside. "There was a call for you, Father. Funny thing; they seem to have hung up." He presented the phone to Stokes. The old priest held it to his ear.

"Curious," he said. "No one's on the line. Did it seem important?"

The man shrugged. "I'm sorry, Father."

Stokes turned. Again people parted to let him through. He went to the waiting room and sat down. Everyone would know now that there was a priest in the terminal. Perhaps someone would have need of him. He could easily be found, sitting here. He opened his topcoat, to make sure that his Roman collar was visible.

He should have left the phone upstairs off the hook. A simulated conversation would have made an impact. Some poor devil on the verge of suicide, desperate for discussion. Of course he would telephone Father Stokes. Just an outside chance that he might be caught at the airport. A busy man, always on assignment by his society, please God, let him be between planes. Only his voice on the phone could restrain the hand of despair. *Sed tantum dic verbo* . . . A tiny plane dropped in for a landing and Father Stokes smiled at it, a proprietary smile, the smile of a man on the ready. Fear not. The plane landed safely. Stokes relaxed. He was not needed. Yet.

Henley, seated in front of the television, was startled by the hand laid on his shoulder. The nurse, Miss Bishop.

"You should be taking a nap, Father."

"Have you been following this charade, nurse?"

"The moonshot? Not really. I've heard a few bulletins on the radio."

"Radio." Henley snorted. "They might have gotten away with it on the radio."

"Got away with it?"

"It's a fake, woman. Look at those pictures."

"But that's a simulation." On the screen a maneuver being performed in space was being illustrated with models, an animated cartoon.

"The whole thing is a farce. I suppose it's a way of scaring the Russians but they have no right to make a mockery of the nation's trust."

"Father, it's all going on right now."

"How do you know that?"

"I've seen it. I saw the lift-off."

"You saw the same picture I did."

"I'm sure I did. It was perfect."

Henley looked at Miss Bishop. Oh, let her believe it if she wanted to. There were millions like her. Of course the newspapers must be in on it, and the politicians. Well, it was probably cheaper to stage this hoax than to try the real thing. Go to the moon! Henley snorted. The gullibility of man.

Miss Bishop sat on the arm of the chair next to his. "You really don't believe those men are on their way to the moon?"

"It doesn't matter what I believe."

"You don't, do you?"

Henley grew wary. No need to insist on it to Miss Bishop. She and Dowling had a way of acting like keepers. With old Sister Diotima he could have been frank; he doubted that she was misled by these shenanigans, if she was even aware of them. He asked the nurse where the old nun was.

"She is with Father Cullen. She insists on keeping vigil there. There is really nothing to do but wait."

Henley nodded, himself waiting for Miss Bishop to go away. She was a plump, kindly woman and seemed to have settled for a chat. Henley turned more decisively toward the television. Miss Bishop, too, watched the set. She said, "You were pulling my leg, weren't you?"

"Hardly that, Miss Bishop." He managed to wink. Her little mouth rounded in pretended shock. She slapped his arm.

"You're as bad as Father Phelan."

Watching her leave the room, Henley thought that pulling either of her legs would be a major operation. What had she meant about Phelan? He turned back to the television.

There were moments when he wavered and felt credulity cresting within himself. Would they really go to this much trouble to perpetrate a hoax? Of course they would. And they weren't going to fool him. Not again.

Father Henley could never forget the ass he had made of himself back in the thirties. He had been giving a mission in New Jersey and had been listening to the radio in the guest room when "War of the Worlds" came on, the Mercury Theater Production, Wells by Welles, but of course millions of Americans had not realized that. The Martians are landing, and in New Jersey! Henley was gripped by a panic he had never known before or since. He ran down to his car, leaving his bag in the guest room, jumped behind the wheel and began to drive westward. There had been no radio in the car. He drove recklessly since half the time he had his head out the window, searching the sky. He drove all night. When morning came he was in western Pennsylvania. He stopped for gas, for news. His wild questions were not understood at first and, when they were, were greeted by derisive laughter. The gas station attendant would not stop laughing. Obviously he had not heard. Henley drove away, furious, hoping that damned rube could still laugh when the Martians descended upon him. He entered a town and, more cautious, went into a diner and asked for coffee. The radio was on and he strained to hear it. The waitress put a newspaper before him. It was all over the front page. His relief became anger and then the head-spinning realization of the absurdity of his situation. He was hundreds of miles from where he was supposed to be. He had not preached a sermon last night. He should be saying Mass in New Jersey right now. It took him half an hour before he could steel himself to call

49

the New Jersey pastor long distance. He lied, shamelessly. He had been called away so suddenly he had been unable to leave a message. He would be back in time for the mission that night.

And he was. He drove all day, retracing his harrowing drive of the night before. He was so weary he could hardly keep his eyes open. He rolled down every window of the car so that the blasts of air would prevent him from falling asleep. He was in the parish house before five. He had hoped to slip inside and upstairs to wash and shave before confronting the pastor, but the man met him at the door. Henley was undone by the stubble on his face and his bloodshot eyes.

"You're back," the pastor said.

"I told you I would be."

"You look a mess." The pastor came closer, sniffing none too slyly. He clearly suspected that the preacher of his parish mission had gone off on a toot. Henley breathed open-mouthed in the man's face and that backed him away.

"There was an emergency. I've been driving all night and all day. I've been to the other end of Pennsylvania and back. I haven't slept."

"You look it."

"I explained on the phone. I'm sorry I could not leave a message."

There was a flicker in the pastor's eyes. "Oh, I know you left in a hurry. You left the radio on in your room. I turned it off when I went up to see why you hadn't come over to the church."

"I'm sorry."

"Too bad you had to go. But maybe you heard. We had Martians last night, little men from Mars, all over the state."

Henley tried unsuccessfully to laugh in disdain.

"Little men from Mars," the pastor repeated. "Too bad you couldn't stay."

Henley glared at the pastor, who was Polish and no doubt had a heavy sense of humor. Why didn't he just say it and get

50

it over with? If he had, Henley might very well have knocked him down. He preferred being thought a drinker.

Ever afterward the memory of that ludicrous all-night drive could fill him with shame and something worse than embarrassment. He dreaded that news of what he had done would reach the Founder. In a like situation, Father Cullen's impulse would doubtless have been to go out and meet the invaders, preach the good news to them, save their little Martian souls, if they had any, if they were in need of salvation. Walter Cronkite doubted that there was life on other planets, but what did he know? Henley had half expected one of these moon trips to end in disaster: a pretended trip, a pretended disaster; why not? But that would not have dissuaded the Russians from making a real try. Better to create the impression that if the Commies ever got there, they would be second.

Not that being first guaranteed anything. Columbus had not been unseated by the knowledge that the Vikings had discovered America and, before them, the Irish monks. All of them Catholics, too. Henley had written Walter Cronkite to suggest that a priest be included on the first trip to the moon, citing the case of Columbus so as not to seem controversial. Of course there had been no reply. They could hardly expect a priest to go along with a hoax.

Michael Tumulty lay supine on his bed in the ultimate pose; the hands crossed over his chest lacked only a rosary. Afternoon sunlight played upon his closed lids, stirring a whole spectrum of color. Nap time. The truth was that he needed the rest as much as anyone else in the house. Indeed, lying down for fifteen or twenty minutes in the early afternoon had been a habit of his for decades, a brief refueling which enabled him to keep up the pace long after others his age had dropped by the wayside. The wayside being now defined as Porta Coeli. And here he was at rest with the rest of them. The thought chased any possibility of sleep away, not that sleep was what he wanted;

the trick was to clear the mind, make it a blank slate, let the tensions go. It was marvelous how restful a quarter hour of mindlessness could be. And of course it was fatal to dwell upon his grievances and discontent. Retired.

He sat up and swung his legs off the bed. Refastening the cassock buttons he had loosened before lying down, Father Tumulty stared at the drapes drawn across the window. As his closed lids had earlier, the beige drape caught shifting shafts of sunlight, mottling spots which altered with the play of branches in the breeze from off the lake. Tumulty got up from the bed, crossed to the window and rang up the curtain. Fittingly, perhaps, Little Sem sprang into view on stage left.

There was little point in trying to rest when his head pulsed with thoughts of undone work. His father's business. He closed his eyes and shook his head, rejecting the biblical phrase. How humiliating that he should have become his protégé's protégé. But what other ticket out of Porta Coeli did he have? God knew that his desire to get the job done did not hasten progress. The ideal would be to find a perfect point of balance between Hoyt's vexation and the final gathering of agreements from the residents of the house. It did no harm for Hoyt to realize what a difficult task Tumulty had undertaken for him; at the same time, too long a delay would render success meaningless, the annoyance of being stymied overwhelming any relief Hoyt might feel at being able to proceed. Of course Hoyt had wanted to direct the campaign from afar. What could the president do? Tumulty had suggested that he talk to Noonan. Even if Hoyt succeeded there, which was unlikely, the winning of Noonan's consent would scarcely settle matters. Garrity remained the key and Tumulty intended to persuade him without interference from Hoyt. For that matter, if he could not develop an argument good enough to convince Garrity, Tumulty did not wish to succeed. It was imperative to have Garrity's respect. Second only to the Founder, Garrity represented for Tumulty the conscience of the society. That was odd, since they had never been close. For Garrity to agree to the destruction of Little Sem would be sanction for more than the removal of a building. It would mean that helping Hoyt was more than disguised self-serving. And if Garrity refused? Tumulty acknowledged the possibility with the chill sense that that would be the end. Inactivity, however righteous, would be a living death, the indefinite prolonging of days like this one.

When Tumulty stepped from his room Miss Bishop was coming from the recreation room. She came toward him wearing a quizzical smile.

"Is Father Henley some kind of joker?"

"How do you mean?"

"He was just telling me he doesn't believe those men are really on their way to the moon."

"He doesn't."

"But that's silly."

"Yes, it is. There are many silly things in this house. How is Father Cullen?"

"There's no change, Father."

"Poor man."

"Oh, there's no pain."

And how could she know that? Still, there was little point in questioning the statements of medical people. God knew that he himself had given assurances about the next world that had been, to say the least, speculative. People would ask if the dead know what goes on on earth. As a young man he had answered yes but, with experience, had learned to be more circumspect. They know what God permits them to know. Safe as a tautology, that.

"Father, you don't have to visit my mother if you don't want to."

"But I want to. I shall go tomorrow or the next day."

"Does she know?"

"I shall call her first."

"With the Founder ill, you won't want to be away from the house."

How had she known that he wished to be at Father Cullen's bedside at the last moment? Surely it was absurd to expect that, at the end, the old man would become conscious and address words of wisdom to his spiritual children. For better or worse, the Founder's last words had been addressed to Leo Phelan. Let go, let go. But the Founder's own unconscious hold on life was tenacious. Father Cullen's mode of life, not those enigmatic words to Phelan, was the old man's message to Michael Tumulty. Don't stop, go on, there is still much to do.

He had started in the direction of the infirmary wing, falling in with Alma Bishop. The medicinal smell grew more noticeable.

"Has Father Faiblesse been to see the Founder yet?"

"No, he hasn't."

Tumulty was sure that he would have seen the father superior if he had come, but it was always well to check. Hoyt had not come either. Tumulty tried to think of the two men as callous but of course the explanation was that they both had things to do, functions to fulfill. His own day had become an open calendar, hour after hour without appointment, meals looming as massive milestones on the journey toward sundown. A vegetable. Perhaps he should become a vegetarian. He parted from Miss Bishop at the Founder's office. He would telephone Faiblesse again.

Leo Phelan sat improbably behind the desk, turned away from the door, looking out the window through his binoculars. Tumulty cleared his throat and Phelan spun in the chair. It might have been a turret. Phelan let his glasses fall to his chest. There was a strange expression on his face.

"Yes, Father?" A small businessman greeting an infrequent customer.

"I wanted to use the phone."

Phelan pushed the instrument across the desk. "Feel free."

Tumulty removed the receiver and stared at the dial. He expected Phelan to get up and leave him alone. The sound of muted whistling drifted across the desk. Tumulty realized that he had forgotten Faiblesse's number.

"I'm sitting in for Noonan," Phelan said.

"Oh."

"No need for him to spend all his time here."

Why should Noonan spend any time here? Then Tumulty remembered that Phelan regarded Noonan as acting superior of the house. He put down the phone. Phelan's shaggy brows lifted in a question.

"I'll make the call in my room."

Phelan made an expansive gesture, as if conferring on Tumulty the freedom of the house, the city, the universe itself. In the hallway, Tumulty hesitated. He might pay a visit to the Founder. He decided to return to his room. Phelan ensconced behind that desk confirmed his feeling that he had fallen among fools. With exceptions, of course. But Noonan and Phelan, ye gods. Faiblesse should come quickly and see what Porta Coeli threatened to become.

5

CAVIL BOULEVARD in Fort Elbow, Ohio, runs roughly north and south, a wide, tree-lined avenue flanked by huge old houses set far back on what elsewhere in the city would be triple lots. The boulevard is a four-lane thoroughfare, a major artery and thus a perennial point of reference when the city's traffic flow comes under review. Like every other city, Fort Elbow is coping unsuccessfully with the mad multiplication of automobiles; its center has become a maze of one-way streets and there has been much tearing down of buildings and the subsequent layering of their sites with asphalt or the elevating on them of poured-concrete open-ramp inside parking structures.

The past fortunes of the city are strung out along Cavil Boulevard. Where it leaves the downtown area, called now of course the inner city, the houses along Cavil date from the nineties, are made of wood, have barnlike carriage houses and, where the driveway sweeps past the front of the house, porte-cocheres. These houses have of late been bought by flaky but affluent liberals and been repainted pink and Prussian blue and various phosphorescent pastels, their occupants deriving from these anachronistic dwellings a false sense of living shoulder to shoulder with the black and poor. Some blocks further south, the mansions of the twenties begin and it is in one of these, a four-story brick affair, a substantial rectangle whose slate roof blends with the surrounding elms and the gouache of the sky, that the father superior of the Society of Saint Brendan, the Very Reverend Philip Faiblesse, resides.

The neighboring houses have been converted to insurance and real estate offices, they have been subdivided into suites for orthodontists, urologists and obstetricians or, a new trend, have become headquarters for the various social agencies that dispense from federal coffers moneys meant to uplift the lowly of Fort Elbow. The house that is called the generalate of the society sits on a lot surrounded by a high wrought iron fence set in a base of brick and seems unaffected by the falling fortunes of Cavil Boulevard. Neither the Disneyland effect of its northern beginnings nor the increasingly commercial aspects of its southward descent detract from the sumptuous isolation of the house. When the iron gates close off its driveway from the boulevard, it seems protected from the sad disintegrating world outside. The occupants may be forgiven if they feel that the house's thick Harding-era walls preserve from time's corrosion an island of order and peace. Within one can sense the conviction that the world has been made safe for democracy, that the economy is on a rising curve, that the Society of Saint Brendan and its work go on much as they always have and will continue to do, forever and ever, amen.

Such, at any rate, was the mood the house induced in Philip Faiblesse. He was a portly man of sixty, his face too full and pink with a pinkness that extended to his scalp and, shining through the sparse white hair, conferred on it an almost albino look. Now in the beginning of his second six-year term as father superior of the society, Faiblesse still regarded himself as a reluctant occupant of the post. When his name had first been mentioned for it, put forward by a champion whose future power then seemed the flimsiest promise, Faiblesse had thought it would be immodest to withdraw since that might have conveyed the suggestion that he had the slightest hope of being elected. "You'll make it," Father Hoyt had said. "You're as good as in." Father Faiblesse had only smiled. Hoyt was Tumulty's protégé and the confident prediction seemed a move in some terribly complex diplomatic game meant to make Michael Tumulty the Founder's successor as father superior. It had long been the custom, as it was the rule, of the society that offices were neither desired nor campaigned for. Steeped in this tradition, Faiblesse felt protected by the unthinkableness of the thought that Father Cullen could ever be replaced.

"While the Founder is still alive he will always be our real superior."

"That's not the kind of thinking the society needs now, Father," Hoyt had replied. "Ask the Founder. He wants fresh minds in control."

Fresh minds? Faiblesse felt that his had not at any rate been put to the uses of such intrigue. More certain than ever that Tumulty was the object of Hoyt's machinations, he yet had difficulty seeing how Michael was meant to benefit from the nomination of Faiblesse.

"It's hard to believe that the Founder is stepping down."

"Well, he is and we have to step forward. We have become stagnant, Father. There has not been a truly new idea in the society for over twenty-five years."

At the time of this conversation, Faiblesse was treasurer of Saint Brendan's College, a post he had held since ordination, largely because in an unguarded moment he had mentioned to the Founder that, before entering the seminary, he had imagined that his life would be spent in business as his father's had before him. Faiblesse senior had made a comfortable living manufacturing grape jelly, apple butter and strawberry jam which, under a variety of labels, was sold in grocery stores from coast to coast. That little family business had long since been swallowed up by a national concern and, in the moments of his discontent, Faiblesse reflected that he might have been living off coupons on some Florida key or, more likely, become a minor executive in the cannibal company, waiting for the ax to fall. The Founder had confused his biographical remark with a claim to understand money and finance; he handed over the college ledgers to Father Faiblesse with the same sighing relief with which, years later, he was to bequeath to him the office of father superior of the society. The affairs of the former had been as snarled as those of the latter. Somewhat to his own surprise, Faiblesse had discovered in himself that streak of deviousness which is the *sine qua non* of keeping a good set of books. His spiritual life had been given an impetus by the faintly larcenous nature of his daily work and the disturbing pleasure he took in it. So, too, as father superior he had quickly acquired the knack of donning a meaningless receptive smile when controversy arose. He reacted to conflict among his subordinates much as the Italian reacts to war. It was never a question of winning; the trick was to lose as little as possible and, in losing, convey the impression that the winner has taken an excessively narrow view of things. Beware of answered prayers: that had become his favorite bit of gnomic advice to suppliants. It might have been his own motto. Eight years ago, in a moment of weakness, he had actually prayed that Hoyt could deliver and he would be elected to succeed the Founder as father superior of the society. Provided, of course, that it was the will of God. That *pro forma* proviso had never seemed less sincere. The truth was that Faiblesse still had difficulty taking himself seriously as father superior. Nor had he ever understood the campaign that had put him into office. Tumulty had still been president of the college in those days, Hoyt a mere vice-president, and it had seemed logical that Hoyt was really working for Tumulty. Tumulty had not treated the outcome of the election as a disguised triumph. Indeed it was clear to Faiblesse that Tumulty regarded him as an adversary. Faiblesse had had to conclude that Hoyt had been working alone from the beginning. The younger priest's insistence some months ago that Tumulty be sent to Porta Coeli caused Faiblesse to see his own election as Hoyt's first move to ease Tumulty from the presidency and succeed him there. Did Tumulty think that Hoyt and Faiblesse had been allied against him for years? But what else could he possibly think? It was all very confusing. Not that Faiblesse did not enjoy his job. It had been exciting from the very first when he had accepted Hoyt's suggestion that he transfer his office from the campus to the house on Cavil Boulevard in Fort Elbow.

The Founder, having accepted the house as a gift from a remorseful layman who had bartered it for the promise of memorial Masses, never lived in it. He preferred the rooms in Little Sem that he had occupied as long as anyone could remember. A priest or two had been sent to live in the house, some progress had been made toward converting it to society use, though progress is not the word Father Faiblesse would have chosen. He was appalled to find that a paneled wall between the kitchen and pantry had been torn out and fluorescent lights had been installed everywhere. His first move was to have everything restored to its former condition. He claimed the second floor for himself. A sitting room was converted into a chapel for the house, other rooms on the floor were designated guest rooms and of course an especially nice room was set aside for the Founder should he ever wish to visit. When guests came they were never assigned to the rooms on Father Faiblesse's floor, however; members of the society who turned up for a meal and lodging were likely to find themselves put under the eaves, where servants had slept in a better day. An elderly couple, the Nickleses, were hired to keep house. Faiblesse's official staff was small: the assistant superior, Father Nobis, who had served in the same capacity for the Founder, Father Fogarty and Miss Liczenski, the secretary. If Nobis had harbored any hope of succeeding the Founder he never revealed it. He had, however, resisted the move to the house on Cavil Boulevard. Faiblesse insisted that the assistant superior must live with him, he needed the man's experience, but Nobis clearly thought his post had been devalued by the move from Saint Brendan's campus. He seldom pestered Faiblesse for things to do and Faiblesse himself soon learned that there was scarcely work enough for one of them. Nobis's only idiosyncrasy was to spend an hour every afternoon in chapel. Faiblesse saw him seldom, except at meals. These were served in the large dining room on the main floor, Faiblesse enthroned at one end of a very long table, Nobis at the other, a stone's throw away. Father Fogarty often and Miss Liczenski at lunch occupied the equator between the poles of the table. The secretary, an unpretty woman, was sliding into unmarried middle age but still kept up the fiction that her job was temporary, something to do until she settled down. She talked incessantly and thus was a convenient addition to the table. Her stupidity grated on Fogarty, who was a financial whiz, Hoyt's man in the house, in charge of the society's portfolio. Some months ago, Miss Liczenski had spent the greater part of a meal asking Fogarty the current values of a number of blue-chip stocks. Common or preferred? She did not understand. Fogarty grudgingly gave her quotes, then concentrated on his lunch. Kindly Father Nobis asked the secretary why she had wanted to know. It seemed that she had a significant, indeed a surprising, number of shares. They had been left to her and many indeed were original issues. Fogarty had stared at her as if she were retarded. To his credit, however, he went on with the conversation, conceding her the right to curiosity about her holdings.

If Fogarty was a somewhat infrequent companion at meals, this was because he combined his work for the society with a vice-presidency at the college. The financial affairs of the two were separate but it made sense to have one man presiding over both. Fogarty was forty. His eyes were set in pouches; his beard required shaving twice a day. Like the president, he had taken of late to wearing lay clothes, business suits, wide garish ties.

He wore a ring, too, which Nobis had tried to shame him into removing by taking his hand, genuflecting and attempting to kiss the offending bauble as one had once greeted bishops. Fogarty, a man without humor, was equally without shame.

"It's my birthstone," he explained.

Miss Liczenski said it was beautiful. Nobis said that birthstones were a carry-over from paganism, a superstition. Father Faiblesse said nothing. Like Nobis, he always wore a cassock in the house.

"You should wear a collar, Father Fogarty," Nobis had said seriously the first time the younger priest appeared in mufti.

"Dress is unimportant."

"Then why don't you dress as a priest?"

"Dressing as a priest is a comparatively recent custom. In Germany priests on the street have been indistinguishable for years."

"In Germany they gassed six million Jews."

"I don't see the connection."

Father Nobis launched into an erratic argument, the burden of which was that German priests had stopped wearing clericals so that, unlike the Jews, they could not be easily identified by Nazi persecutors.

"That's nonsense," Fogarty said. "The Roman collar is hardly on a par with circumcision."

Miss Liczenski giggled and bent over her salad. Mrs. Nickles, entering with the entrée, scowled at the secretary. The housekeeper was irked by the spectacle of an employee like herself seated at meal with the priests of the house.

"How could the society afford to clothe us all in the fashions of the day?"

"This is not an expensive suit." Fogarty's voice was defensive, and no wonder. Father Faiblesse had seen his haberdashery bills. The man had ordered suits and trousers and sport coats, neckties, socks and shoes like a bride gathering her trousseau. Perhaps Father Fogarty meant that there were even more expensive suits than those he had bought, but certainly any one of them had cost far more than a simple black suit would have. Father Faiblesse had no intention of entering the argument, however plaintively Nobis looked to him for support. Instead he complimented Mrs. Nickles on the lunch. Her eyes, magnified by the thick lenses of her glasses, sparked with pleasure. Her joy was brief. Miss Liczenski added her own praise and Mrs. Nickles walked stiffly from the room. Her husband, as usual, was perched on a stool in the pantry and from time to time, visible only to Faiblesse, craned his neck around the door to see how the meal was progressing. It was his way of helping his wife. Mr. Nickles did little else. Ah, well, his pittance of a salary was small price to pay in order to retain the marvelous cooking of Mrs. Nickles. Too marvelous, Father Faiblesse thought, sighing. Among his dreams and velleities was that of one day devoting himself to the practice of asceticism, to live on bread and water and repent his sins. It would have been more than penance enough to go back to the fare at the college or, a more likely future, to that of Porta Coeli.

After lunch Faiblesse went upstairs to his room, parting from Father Nobis at the door of the chapel. He sometimes wondered if his colleague was not too ostentatious in his devotions. Perhaps if Nobis did not take over the chapel as his private place of prayer, he himself might spend an hour or two there on his knees. In reparation for having eaten too well, perhaps, or to pray for the society whose care was in his hands. The thought was a wry one. If Fogarty was Hoyt's man, so, too, was Faiblesse. Any doubt on that score that might have survived his first term would have been delusion indeed. Faiblesse might head the society but his champion had wanted to be president of Saint Brendan's College. Naked ambition was a rare thing in the society and Faiblesse was not alone in having no defense against it. Besides, it had made perfect sense to appoint Hoyt president when Tumulty tendered his mandatory resignation. What perhaps made less sense was exempting the post from the canonical limit of six years' tenancy. Hoyt had become unrestrictedly and without time limit the president of the college. That had been necessary to his plans for Saint Brendan's. Faiblesse had been informed of these plans in an offhand way, with no suggestion that Hoyt's putative religious superior might be of another view. Faiblesse had been confronted by an almost organized opposition when he allowed Hoyt to free the college from its legal and financial links to the society, to appoint a lay board of trustees and proceed with the creation of a faculty that seemed systematically to exclude members of the society. Excellence was Hoyt's watchword, taken over from the Tumulty administration, and who could be opposed to excellence? None other than Michael Tumulty, it appeared, at least when it assumed the form of the secularization of the college. Long impassioned letters came back from the society's house on the Via Nomentana in Rome, where Tumulty had been assigned to look after the handful of student priests in the Eternal City and to do such liaison work with the Vatican so small a society required. Thank God Hoyt had thought of the Rome job for Tumulty when it fell open; the post could quite legitimately be regarded as a plum, a reward for years of service. Faiblesse had found it more difficult to justify the new status of the college to Garrity, particularly when he found himself sympathizing with Garrity's fears as to the direction the society was taking, sympathized personally, that is. He could not as father superior admit that they had collectively lost their sense of purpose as a community. That would have been to confess to gross negligence of duty. The Founder, oddly when you stopped to think of it, had taken these radical changes in stride.

"Times change," he observed when Faiblesse reported to him on the laicization of the college.

"Father Hoyt is convinced that it makes financial sense. And we, of course, will continue to benefit from the role we play in the college. We would not, however, be adversely affected should the college fall on hard times."

"There are not many of us involved in the college now."

"But now each man is paid a salary commensurate with his office and that is returned to the society. We are also paid rent for the facilities. We receive far more income from the college now."

"The college always did sponge up money," the Founder said.

"Yes. Now that it is no longer a religious institution, at least technically, there is greater likelihood that public money will be available. The trustees, moreover, turn out to be great fund raisers. Father Hoyt is certain that the college will prosper as it never has before."

The Founder's expression altered slightly and Faiblesse regretted having echoed Hoyt's confident prediction.

But the prediction proved true. The college did flourish, its star rising as that of the society set. The Founder had never chided Faiblesse, had accepted his visits and heard what he had to say without demur. Only gradually did it dawn on Faiblesse that the old man listened to him as to his religious superior. It was a dizzying realization. The man who had founded the society now owed him loyalty and obedience. But his own obedience was owed to Hoyt, who had put him in office and could likely replace him with ease when his term was up, indeed before that, should it seem to his advantage.

"First Hoyt, now Fogarty," Nobis said, his hand on the chapel door.

"Times change," Faiblesse said, grateful for the Founder's words.

"So do fashions. Will priests follow them all? Surely one of the advantages of clerical clothes is that they permit us to escape such worldliness."

"I myself have no intention of dressing like a banker, Father."

"No doubt, no doubt. But you should put your foot down, Father. Before it is too late."

Faiblesse sought and found his neutralizing smile. "I won't keep you from your devotions, Father."

"I pray for the society," Nobis said. "And for the Church." A bewildered look came into his eyes. Faiblesse patted his arm. Nobis opened the door and disappeared inside the chapel. The door hissed shut after him, squeezing a floral smell into the hallway. Faiblesse continued to his room.

Nobis is ready for Porta Coeli, he thought. Thank God Oliver Fleming built that place for us. Faiblesse had not been treasurer all those years for nothing. Now he directed as much money to Porta Coeli as he could, ensuring that the retirement home would have an ample and untouchable endowment. Fogarty did not resist this effort. Doubtless he was more concerned to conceal, ineptly as it turned out, his own expenses. In any case, Fogarty's main concern was with the college finances and he showed a remarkable intuition for the fluctuations of the market. The Saint Brendan portfolio was not confined to the tried and true; a goodly proportion of its funds went in and out of the market, increasing and multiplying as it did so. Fogarty had the touch. It was only fitting that Father Faiblesse's main concern was the society. It was not himself he was enriching. Even now the endowment he had built up for Porta Coeli would keep the place afloat in the vast unlikelihood that the college encountered rough financial seas. It is not for me, Faiblesse assured himself. A lifetime of habit had ingrained in him the demands of the vow of poverty. Did Fogarty rationalize his sartorial splendor by convincing himself that it in some way furthered the work of the society and the college?

Faiblesse had been smoking a late morning pipe and reading *Tom Playfair,* a novel by a Jesuit named Finn, a boyhood favorite of the father superior, when Tumulty called to tell him that the Founder had fallen into a coma.

"My God. Is he dying?"

"He could be, yes. It is serious."

"When did this happen?"

"Just now. Within the hour."

Silence came over the wire like an accusation and Faiblesse held the phone away from him, staring at the perforations of the mouthpiece. Tumulty had taken a distant line with the father superior years ago but communication had all but ceased since his removal to Porta Coeli. Why couldn't the man simply accept being there, relax, read, prepare to meet his God? The thought of withdrawal and the promise of peace brought a gasp of longing from Father Faiblesse. He asked Tumulty if he should come at once.

"There isn't much that can be done. He's comatose."

"I want to see him, before . . ."

"Of course."

"Michael, will you call me if there is any sudden development?"

Tumulty said he would. After he had hung up, Faiblesse sat stunned. Had Tumulty understood that he would have to see the Founder ill in order to believe it? The sense of a changing of the guard had not been strong when the Founder retired or even when he moved to Porta Coeli. Hadn't Tumulty been the one to tell the old man he must live there? Faiblesse remembered how Tumulty accepted the assignment, clearly regarding himself as a kind of executioner. I should have told him myself, Faiblesse thought. The Founder had received it as a matter of religious obedience, without complaint, in silence. None of them would ever know what the old man really felt about his removal to Porta Coeli. He seemed to like it. Why not, why not? And had his end now arrived? Faiblesse rubbed his eyes wearily. He could not imagine the society without Father Cullen. But then he had been unable to imagine anyone, least of all himself, succeeding Father Cullen as father superior. Times do change.

Faiblesse decided to wait for a further call from Tumulty and when it came the following day he decided to drive himself. Mr.

Nickles drove with the caution of a driving instructor, a caution more dangerous to others than carelessness itself. Any outing in the car became a troubled passage, accompanied by irate horns. Faiblesse took off his cassock and changed into street clothes. In order to avoid Mr. Nickles, he went downstairs by a stairwell at the rear of the house. He crossed to the garage almost furtively. He got safely out of the garage and down the driveway, but when he stepped out of the car to open the gates he heard the thin voice of Mr. Nickles calling him. He came shuffling over the lawn, pulling on a jacket as he came. From a window behind him, Mrs. Nickles watched her husband. Perhaps she was as anxious to get her husband out of the house as Faiblesse was to leave him there.

"You should have called me, Father." Nickles took hold of the still unopened gate and began to tug at it.

"Shouldn't you first lift that thingamajig?" Faiblesse put the toe of his shoe under the bolt that locked the gate in place. "I won't need you, Mr. Nickles. That's why I didn't call."

"But I'm your driver." Mr. Nickles's lower lip jutted out and he glanced toward the house.

"You can come along if you like. But I'll drive."

"But I'm supposed to drive," Nickles whined.

The man looked as if he might cry. Faiblesse revised his view as to which of the Nickleses was most set on getting Mr. Nickles out of the house. He agreed that Mr. Nickles should drive. He got into the back seat, settling deep in a corner. He had never got used to being chauffered about like this; he also wanted to be out of sight of any angry drivers who managed to pass the car. Mr. Nickles had a tendency to straddle lanes.

Down Cavil Boulevard they drove, heading south, then eastward out of the city, past service stations, hamburger stands, chicken drive-ins, franchise after franchise, more service stations. Americans were born in automobiles, Americans died in automobiles, usually violently; more and more they ate and banked and—so Father Faiblesse was told; he himself did not often hear confessions now—reproduced themselves in automobiles. Mobile beings, as O'Leary might say. The country, certainly this city, had changed before Father Faiblesse's eyes. *Motus magis est causa corruptionis quam generationis.* O'Leary again. How Latin clung to the grooves of the mind. Or did age turn up such nuggets as frost forces stones from a field? Change corrupts more than it renews. How true that seemed. The country, the Church, the society. The Founder stricken, most likely dying. Faiblesse sank back further into his corner, feeling despondency come over him. The society.

When the Founder first came from Ireland, sailing westward toward the horizon of hope, this land had seemed to spread before him like a field ripe for the harvest. How the old man had loved to describe the thoughts with which he had left Ellis Island. The natives might have been surprised to have the United States regarded as a missionary country. For that matter, so might the hierarchy. American Catholics were the humblest citizens, by and large, but they were a growing group and they were generous. Most remarkable of all, they actually took the duty of Sunday Mass seriously, but then a good many of them had come from Ireland. Priests from the Continent were dumbstruck by such fidelity and docility. Rome quickly recognized in America a faithful daughter unlike any she had had for centuries. The Founder had come after the fuss over the American heresy had been settled, though there were still signs of the struggle between Irish and German Catholics. The Germans had wanted to retain their own language in sermons, confessions, schools and in the Catholic newspapers they supported in such numbers. They had no desire to be melted down in the national pot and they blamed the Irish for wanting to become indistinguishable from other Americans. Underlying the Americanism charge had been that struggle over languages. Fort Elbow had been torn by it. In the end it was the Kaiser who settled the matter definitively, though in a way the Irish had already won by acquiring a stranglehold on the hierarchy.

69

The Irish bishops had run interference for the Founder and sped Vatican approval of the society he wished to form. But the truth was that the Society of Saint Brendan had never been taken seriously by the American bishops, however willing they were to make use of it. Much of what the society did was stop-gap, interim work, filling in until replaced by a bishop's own men—who then referred to members of the society as the S.O.B.'s, an unkind alteration of the initials signifying membership in the Society of Saint Brendan. The society had given retreats and missions, had assumed responsibility for scattered parishes, most of them rural and in lesser dioceses. The Founder had never driven a hard bargain and this made bishops suspicious of him. They could not believe that he meant to do only what he said, send in his priests to help them. Temporary, of course. Mission work is always temporary, eventually giving way to an indigenous clergy. So the society had got the short end of the stick everywhere, not that the Founder ever said so. It was doubtful that he even thought so. Was it that which made him so equanimous now when the society seemed to be dissolving before his eyes?

The brothers had been the first to go, but that was only to be expected. Under a strong man, Brother Humbert, they had secured their autonomy shortly after the Second World War. Their high school in Canton, Ohio, had gone under and was snatched up by the local school board. Vocations fell off and of course there had always been a high rate of attrition among the brothers. Ten years ago they had incorporated and then, with only a dozen left, been released from their vows as a group. They retained the corporation and went west, where they were now producing an imitation Irish Mist. And prospering. There were those, and Father Faiblesse was among them, who resented the reliance on their erstwhile religious connection in advertising their wares. The label on the bottle showed a chubby monk toasting the world with a bulbous snifter. "Brother Felix would share a cup with thee." This motto had been dreamed

70

up by an ad agency, of course. There had never been a Brother Felix and none of the owners were brothers now. They were all married or worse. California changes people.

Saint Brendan's College, which had evolved from the seminary, had been the society's single solid purchase on the future. By what seemed providential design, at least in retrospect, the Founder's early decision to admit a few laymen to the college as an accommodation to some generous local families with ungifted sons had led to a gradual, almost imperceptible rise in lay enrollment until the seminarians were a minority, though a sizable one until Vatican II delivered its body blow to priestly vocations. Today there was only one lad enrolled in the college who had expressed interest in the society and that was on a Monday, which raised the fear that it was a product of post-weekend remorse rather than of pious zeal. Father Hoyt's severing of the connection between the college and the society could thus be seen as the next inevitable step in a continuous evolution. Faiblesse assured himself that he could not have gone along with it otherwise. He would have opposed Hoyt. After all, he was Hoyt's religious superior no matter how independent the college and its presidency had become. Hoyt was still a member of the society and thus subordinate to Faiblesse. But of course there had been no reason to oppose Hoyt, particularly in the light of Mr. Fleming's magnanimous offer to build the most modern of retirement homes for the aged members of the society. Porta Coeli, debt-free and amply endowed, was the one solid earthly possession remaining to the dying society.

Mr. Nickles had turned in at the college gates and was now moving at a yet slower speed along the campus avenue. Here the car's snail pace was not only within the law but prudent as well. Students used the lawns and walks and avenues indiscriminately. Indeed a dozen or so coeds now sauntered only a few feet in front of the hood of the car, indifferent to it, their dulcet voices borne back to the father superior, huddled in the

71

rear seat of the car. Coeds. He had really meant to oppose Hoyt on that; the decision to admit women was made before the board of trustees took over ownership of the college. He had actually put some probing questions to Hoyt.

"Is it wise, Father? After all, the seminarians . . ."

"What seminarians?"

"It is true that vocations are down at the moment, but eventually there must be an upswing. We can't have our seminarians attending a coeducational college."

"Why not?"

"Rome would not approve."

"Rome has nothing to do with it, Father, and you know it. That sort of thing is past. The American bishops will never again turn over their independence to Roman congregations run by senile bureaucrats."

Faiblesse had not liked that. Hoyt was still young enough to have only contempt for age, as if he himself were immortal and immune to the ravages of time. But Faiblesse had let the matter drop. It no longer seemed important. If vocations ever did pick up again, the difficulty could be faced then. And by someone else. Father Faiblesse was under no illusions about the immediate prospects of the society.

That remembered almost altercation with Hoyt started up the stomach pains which had been intermittently bothering Faiblesse for weeks. He had had difficulty holding down his food, he seemed more than usually sapped of energy, he either lay sleepless at night or sank into an almost drugged slumber from which he awakened unrested and restless. Dear God, let it be nothing serious. He dreaded doctors. He feared the surgical knife. He was scared to death.

Mr. Nickles sounded the horn and the girls turned and slowed their pace. One girl made an odd gesture of greeting with the middle finger of her hand. Another put her hand on the hood and boosted herself onto the slow-moving car.

"Well, I'll be goddamned," Mr. Nickles said, whether at the

72

girl's audacity or at the flash of thigh her mounting of the hood had revealed.

"I pray you won't, Mr. Nickles."

"Pardon my French, Father, but look at her. Bold as brass. I've half a mind to slam on the brakes and throw her off."

"Don't do that. Please."

The other girls, delighted by the stunt, seemed ready to join their surprising hood ornament, but then one caught a glimpse of Father Faiblesse and the collar he wore. Surprise, then shame. She pulled the girl off the car. Nickles eased past them and Faiblesse lifted his hand, dismissing the incident, as a greeting, more or less as a blessing. The girl who had recognized him as a priest trilled, "Good afternoon, Father."

Father Faiblesse smiled up at her. Good girl. He returned the single-fingered wave he had received earlier; doubtless some passing campus idiosyncrasy. The stories one heard about the young could not be wholly true. That girl would grow up to be a fine wife and mother. And how surprised she had been that he had used their form of greeting.

Mr. Nickles circled the administration building and soon was on the narrow road that skirted the lake and led to Porta Coeli. He stepped up their speed to twenty-five miles an hour, getting a good grip on the wheel with both hands as he did so. Father Faiblesse looked out over the lake to where the low roof line of Porta Coeli was visible through the trees. His heart lifted at the sight of the place. God bless Oliver Fleming for giving them that house.

6

Mrs. Fleming entered the room on her motorized wheelchair, to find her husband sunk in meditation beside the fireplace. The cigar in his hand was, untypically, lit.

"Oliver Fleming, you're smoking."

She had startled him: rubber wheels on the thick pile carpet, her motor the merest murmur. Besides, Oliver was deaf in an unacknowledged way. He glared at her.

"I've had bad news."

She waited, her fingers on the controls; life had been a matter of bad news for so long: deaths, dreadful illnesses, faces one would never see again.

"The Founder has had a seizure."

"Oh." Her finger moved and she wheeled closer.

"He is in a coma. He is not expected to recover."

"I'm sorry to hear that."

"No, you're not. Be honest. You don't give a damn."

"Very well. I don't give a damn."

"They should have let me know at once."

74

"What could you have done, Oliver?"

"That's not the point. I love that man. What is that humming?"

"My chair."

"I have asked you to get rid of that damned thing."

"And I have asked you not to smoke cigars."

"What difference does it make?" he asked gloomily.

She sighed, knowing his mood. Why had they wanted to live into old age? Why did they persist in hanging on to life when there was so little left to living? Despair coiled in the shadows of the room, a feature of the afternoon, of their time of life.

"None at all to your health," she said. "Dr. Bloomer says smoking would have killed you long ago if it were going to. It is the smell I object to."

"And I object to that damnable buzzing. Can't you turn it off?"

"Of course." She did so.

"Why must you act like a cripple?"

The chair was not necessary to her. Neither was the elevator now installed in the stairwell; nor did she really need the apparatus which lifted her into and out of her bath, working on water pressure.

"You'll atrophy. Ask your Dr. Bloomer. He'll bear me out."

Bear him out. The phrase created an image she preferred not to entertain. But did she really give a damn? Oliver was right. The thought of death, the death of others, did not bother her as much as it had. It demanded only an attitude of sorrow, a pretense of grief. In Oliver's case, there would be inconvenience as well. She looked closely at her husband. More bones than flesh; his clothing hung on him like hand-me-downs. The ridged skull seemed never to have supported hair. His milky eyes glowered at the corner of the room where the shadows were. Oliver had shrunk while she had bloated. There would not be much left of Oliver to bury when the day came.

"Oliver, Father Cullen must be very old."

"He is nearly twenty years older than you and I. Is that meant as consolation? Do you imagine death means nothing to him or to those of us who love him?"

"Don't shout."

"I am angry I was not told at once."

"As an interested benefactor?"

He beat his hands on the arms of his chair. "I will not have you mocking me. Not on this."

"You would have been better advised to give money to the Jesuits or the Franciscans. Even the Dominicans. Some order a person had heard of. They would have shown you some gratitude."

"Gratitude? Is that your understanding of this? That man was a second father to me. More."

"Will you go see him?"

"Yes. I may stay there a few days."

"Another retreat?"

"Yes!"

"You're half a monk yourself, Oliver, do you know that? I am surprised you did not stay and become a priest."

He took the cigar from his month and smiled with sly malevolence. "So am I."

She flicked a switch, described a circle in the middle of the room and disappeared out the door. The rubber wheels left impermanent tracks in the pile of the rug, parallels running in the eternal hope of meeting.

Fleming, O. (for Oliver)—Flamingo to his school-day friends, since that is how his name had sounded when the roll was read in class—returned the wet and ravaged end of his cigar to his mouth. His denture rocked as he clamped down on it. Enid's badinage had interrupted the dark Irish relish with which he had been contemplating the imminent demise of the Founder. He was no longer surprised that one can take pleasure from tragedy and disaster. The wished-for tears gathered again in Flamingo's

76

eyes. O God, God, how lovely it had been all those years ago: good companions, exemplary priests for teachers, the certainties of a scheduled day: rise, Mass, eat, class, eat, class, play, study, eat, study, prayer, sleep. The wheel of the day within the wheel of the year, the whole turning on the fixed point of the Founder. He was shaping them, they the clay, his the potter's hand, the schedule the wheel on which they turned. The metaphor was hopelessly mixed, but what difference did that make? The old man in a coma now. Phelan's voice had sounded cranky and old, like Flamingo's own, two boys speaking of an adult who had fallen ill.

Enid did not understand; she could never understand. The Jesuits and Franciscans! Did she think he was buying a few prayers for his soul? A Mass stipend could go into any clerical hand. That wasn't it. Nor was it merely the loyalty of one who had been at Saint Brendan's and was now a member of the board of trustees. His heart was there, his youth, still beating in those old buildings, those grounds, that lake. His tears were no longer forced. Flamingo wept for himself and the lost boy who had not remained, had not become a priest.

Girls. The flesh. Ah, dear God, how foolish youth is. Mad dreams of pleasure entertained at night in his dormitory bed while around him others slept, the light pale at the window. From down the hallway the sound of a toilet flushing. Night and his dreams of a houri with whom to share his life; what was the priesthood to that? He had tried to reject such thoughts as sinful, dangerous, disloyal; in chapel in the morning he prayed for perseverance, for a vocation to the priesthood. But on the edges of his mind there remained the image of a faceless girl, pliant, modest, passionate, his. Enid. That is what he had been panting for, that is all it was. Fifty years and more married to Enid, a life spent accumulating riches as if money could lend some purpose to his life. A solid citizen. A machine shop, metal work, sheet metal when it came, trailers, mobile homes. Drive a Flamingo. He had become rich and it seemed a judgment on him. Money was power to do whatever he wanted now that he no longer wanted anything. Enid. All those years with her. She would outlive him; all her friends were widows. All his friends, his real friends, were members of the Society of Saint Brendan, the companions of his youth. I will go in unto the altar of God, God who gives joy to my youth. The prayer at the foot of the altar at the beginning of Mass. All changed now, of course, all English and razzmatazz, gibberish.

The Founder had expelled Oliver Fleming from Saint Brendan's one April day in 1913. The reason was unseemly conduct with a person of the opposite sex, unseemly, that is, for a boy ostensibly preparing for the priesthood and a celibate life. The girl was the girl in the orange canoe. That is how they had referred to her, the three boys who on a hike around the lake had come upon a girl pushing a canoe into Saint Brendan's Lake. The three boys were Flamingo, Phelan and Rush, who had died during the thirties of a heart attack.

"This is a private lake," Rush said to her.

Startled, she turned to look at them. Her dress was done up above her knees in some way. Her shoes were in the canoe. She stood in shallow water and the whiteness of her legs, the aquamarine extension of them under water, the doelike alarm in her eyes, filled Oliver Fleming with an overwhelming rush of feeling.

"Did you have to sneak up like that?" the girl asked.

"We weren't sneaking. We're on a hike. This lake is private."

"I suppose you own it."

"The school does. Over there." Rush pointed. "Saint Brendan's."

"Never heard of it."

"It's a Catholic school," Oliver said. His voice was oddly flat.

"It is a seminary," Phelan said precisely.

"And you three go there?"

Phelan and Rush nodded proudly. Fleming stepped away, putting a slight distance between himself and his companions.

78

"You're studying to be priests?"

Rush assured her that they were. The girl let go of the canoe and undid her dress. Her skirt dropped toward the water and she hopped ashore. The canoe drifted out into the lake but the girl was more concerned to keep her skirt dry. She stood on the grass next to them. Oliver was transfixed by her white feet against the green grass. Then she noticed what was happening to her canoe and cried out.

"My shoes are in the canoe," she wailed.

Without any hesitation Oliver walked into the lake, wading hip deep before his hand closed on the side of the canoe. He brought it ashore and beached it securely. Water was running from his trousers like rain from a roof. His shoes felt ruined, his stockings sodden lumps. No one said a word during his performance.

"Thank you," the girl said. "Thank you very much."

"That was a dumb thing to do," Rush said. "With your shoes on and all."

The girl smiled at Oliver. She did not think what he had done was dumb. "You should take off your shoes."

He obeyed. He sat on the grass and undid his laces. His shoes came off with difficulty. He took off his stockings and wrung them out. Two pair of bare feet in the April grass. He felt dizzy.

Phelan asked the girl who she was and what she was doing there. She was from Fort Elbow. The canoe belonged to her cousins, who lived on a farm not far away. They had brought the canoe over that morning. Her cousins would be along soon.

"We've never seen that canoe on the lake before."

"They said they always come here."

Rush and Phelan denied it.

She considered this. Her expression was solemn. She said to Oliver, "I think they played a joke on me. They said it was all right."

Voices were audible in the woods and five other young people came into view, laughing. The girl had guessed correctly.

79

What a joke to set a female cousin canoeing on the seminary lake. Oliver was furious with them.

That had been the beginning. The others had used the girl's name in kidding her, her given and family name; he knew she lived in Fort Elbow. He found the address and wrote to her. Innocuous, saying nothing, that letter had seemed to him freighted with significance. Her reply was equally bland. The Founder took another view of the importance of the matter. He called Oliver Fleming to his room. He demanded an explanation. Oliver had only the damning truth. He had written to a girl. She was not a relative of his. He could not say what his reasons were.

"You have broken a serious rule of this institution."

"Yes, Father."

"You are going to have to leave."

"Leave?"

"Go home. I am sorry, Oliver. Go immediately to the dormitory and pack your things. I will contact your parents. You do not have a vocation to the priesthood. There is no disgrace in that. Thank God we discovered it so early."

Oliver went to the dormitory and packed. He cried as he did so. In later life it would be those tears he remembered, the image of a broken-hearted boy being sent home from the school he loved, away from his dearest friends, into the world. The truth was that he had been delighted. And relieved. A tremendous burden had been lifted from him. He was free. Free.

7

ALMA BISHOP wondered why Father Faiblesse couldn't just slip his hand beneath the plastic when he anointed the dying Founder, but Sister Diotima had the oxygen tent off, collapsed and pushed into a corner before Faiblesse could answer the nurse's question. There were more important things than preserving the earthly life of the Founder, the old nun's action seemed to say, and giving him the last rites of the Church was one of them. Faiblesse, who would have found the plastic tent little or no impediment, admired Sister Diotima's decision. He rather hoped that she would be around when he himself lay on his deathbed. Nor did that seem wholly unlikely, though Sister Diotima was as old as the Founder. She was still spry and alert and on the job. Father Faiblesse sighed. It was unlikely that others of Sister Diotima's caliber would emerge from the present dwindled ranks of nuns. Sister Diotima had turned off the oxygen tap.

"We have to light the candles," she explained to Miss Bishop. Her removal of the tent now made more sense.

"Yes, Sister."

"Well, light them."

Miss Bishop had no matches. Father Phelan did. He struck one, then had trouble with a candle wick that had embedded itself in the wax. While he tried to pry it free the flame burned to his fingertips. He yelped in pain. "Damn," he cried. The old nun inhaled reprovingly and took the matches from Phelan. She had no trouble lighting the candle. A wise old virgin. Now they were ready.

Faiblesse had as much trouble with the last rites as Phelan had had with the candles. They had given him an old ritual book, a Latin one, but the father superior did not find it familiar. He had never done much pastoral work. His mind was distracted and went in search of the last time he had said the prayers for the dying, anointed a patient's body. It had been in a hospital in Syracuse, twenty years ago and more. Some second cousin on his mother's side. He went on reading from the book while he reminisced. That had always been an advantage of Latin; one went on praying no matter where the mind was. The thought stayed with him and found vocal expression when he closed the book. " 'My words fly up, my thoughts remain below: Words without thoughts never to heaven go.' " Only Miss Bishop was unsurprised by this addendum. Phelan made a point of complaining about it afterward.

"The Founder is a very traditional man. He does not care for the new liturgy. He especially does not like it to be made up as one goes along."

Father Phelan seemed determined to keep talk of the Founder in the present tense. Faiblesse put a hand on the sleeve of his jacket.

"Father, I was as surprised as you were."

"The stroke? I could see it coming."

"Could you?"

"It isn't that the lines you quoted did not pierce my soul. I thought of other things as we stood there, Father Faiblesse."

"What other things?"

Phelan had taken the ritual book and stole; he now draped the stole over his arm, black satin on the navy blue sateen of his warm-up jacket.

"I'd like to talk to you about it."

"Shouldn't the others have been there for the last rites, Father? Weren't they told?"

"They came yesterday."

"Yesterday?"

"We anointed him yesterday, too."

Good God. But Faiblesse said nothing. Had Phelan been humoring him, allowing him to give the last rites to the Founder a second and unnecessary time? Or was it that Phelan did not remember that such repetition was pointless? Faiblesse felt a fleeting fear of the irregularities that could crop up in a house like this, all old men, forgetful. Who knew what went on in the chapel when they said their Masses? They might easily compete with the wilder divagations of the new liturgy. Father Faiblesse told himself that he must make discreet inquiries.

"Here is my room," Phelan said.

"Well, Father . . ."

"No, no. Come in. I must talk to you."

Faiblesse looked at his watch, making sure that Phelan noticed. He had found that the sight of a superior consulting his timepiece has marvelous effects. But he had underestimated Phelan. He was tugged into the man's room and the door shut decisively behind him. "Sit down, Father," Phelan urged. He himself disappeared into the bathroom, from which soon came the sound of running water. In a moment he came out again, shaking wet fingers. "I really burned myself."

"You should have it looked after."

But there were more important things on Phelan's mind. "Father Faiblesse, what do you know of this insane plan to tear down Little Sem?"

Faiblesse looked pensive. "What do I know of it?"

"Haven't you heard!"

83

"Oh, yes." It seemed cruel to snuff out the delighted hope that had gleamed in Phelan's eyes.

"Well?"

Faiblesse sighed. "Father, you must be aware of the altered status of the college. It is no longer under the jurisdiction of the society."

"I'm aware of the fact that we gave the place away, yes."

"That is not a very accurate way of putting it."

"We no longer own it."

"True. Legally. One result of that is that decisions of the administration no longer come to me for review."

"Father, this time we can stop him. It's providential. He needs our permission. Well, he isn't going to get it. We've made sure of that. Oh, he has a Trojan Horse in the house but there are those of us who will never consent to the destruction of Little Sem. Personally, I consider it an obligation to the Founder to stop this. Especially now." Phelan's excitement had modulated into solemnity.

"I appreciate your loyalty, Father, but you really must not get upset. For better or worse—and can we really say that it is for the worse?—Father Hoyt has a free hand at the college."

"Not on this, Father. Not on this."

Father Phelan's jumbled account of an old document in the archives which vested such power in the hands of the occupants of Porta Coeli sounded like an old man's fantasy to Faiblesse. Age would veto youth. Surely Hoyt would not have let himself get caught by something as debilitating as this alleged document.

"Father Phelan, why are you so determined that Little Sem should not be replaced?"

"It can never be replaced!"

Faiblesse smiled indulgently. "Of course I do not mean replaced. But we have little need for a preparatory seminary these days. Nobody does. The college, on the other hand, needs a new student dormitory."

"For girls!"

"I think you're right."

Phelan frowned. He had played his trump and not taken the trick. "A dormitory can be built anywhere."

"Really, Father, as I've said . . ." He had to get away from Phelan. The man had an *idée fixe*. Worse, Faiblesse did not see what Phelan expected him to do.

"Think of what that building means to the society, Father. Even if the college is no longer ours, we did build it. The Founder. Us. And all those who have already died. Can we just ignore the sacrifices they made? Little Sem is the one thing we have left. We all went to school there. You were a student there yourself, weren't you?"

"Yes. I was there."

And hated it. It had seemed a cold, dour building even then: its staircases too wide, its windows too high, the corridors covered with linoleum squares, green and brown, dark colors which had seemed darker when one moved over them as over a chessboard, an insignificant pawn. Faiblesse was surprised by the cheerlessness of his memories of Little Sem. His pleasant memories, so far as the society went, came later, the last years of study doing theology in Washington, before he was assigned to the college.

"I knew you would take the college's view," Phelan said accusingly.

"Because I worked there?"

Phelan nodded bitterly.

What drove this old man? Nostalgia? His opposition to the removal of that worthless building reminded Faiblesse of the poor souls who campaign against urban renewal, the routing of new highways, any effort to replace the old. Of course one always felt a partial sympathy. The advocates of the new were usually an unsavory lot. Hoyt was no exception to that, certainly not as far as Phelan was concerned. How many like Phelan were there at Porta Coeli? Not that it could possibly matter.

"I have never heard of the document you mentioned, Father. I wonder why."

"It was only recently found, by Father Corcoran. In the archives. That's why he hasn't been able to destroy Little Sem yet. A few here have given their permission, but only a few. The rest of us will not betray the Founder."

"You have a penchant for strong words, Father. In this connection, I should say that betrayal is an extremely strong word. I have never detected, in my conversations with the Founder, any profound feeling about the fate of Little Sem."

"He had already expressed his feelings in the document Corcoran found. They seem very strong feelings to me."

"Then isn't it strange that he himself seems to have forgotten that document?"

"There is no evidence that he forgot it."

"Except that, as you tell me, Father Corcoran had to discover it in the archives."

Was Phelan's story true? Had work stopped on campus? Faiblesse felt that in entering this room he had walked through the looking glass. The air was sweet with new and old cigarette smoke, a not altogether unpleasant smell. It seemed the odor of ancient priests. Members of the society had always been immoderate consumers of tobacco, perhaps because they had not been allowed to smoke until after taking simple vows and lighting a cigarette became a symbol of initiation. Would so many have taken up smoking if the activity had not been granted such significance? Faiblesse looked at his watch and rose.

"Is Father Corcoran in the house now? I'd like to talk to him."

"I'll look."

"I'd appreciate that, Father. If it's convenient."

"I'll get him."

"Meanwhile, I want a word with the doctor."

Dr. Dowling spoke of aneurysms while trying to arrange his long legs beneath the desk in his office at Porta Coeli. He did not sound optimistic. The antiseptic smell of the infirmary wing of the building, the professional diffidence of Dowling, the image

86

of Father Cullen on his bed, brought back the stomach pains Father Faiblesse spent a good portion of his day ignoring. Pain as signal, wasn't that the theory? The body's warning. What did his own pain portend? He described the pain to Dowling, but as another's, not his own, and triggered a lecture. To stop it, he asked Dowling how long the Founder could be expected to live. Reduced to lay status by Dowling's competence, Faiblesse was reminded of the deference usually accorded priests, himself in another office with a different clientele.

"That's very hard to say. His pulse is good. He is a very durable old man." Dowling smiled. "That could be said of more than one person in this house. Do priests always live so long, Father?"

"These men are the survivors."

"Yes. I see what you mean."

But what had he meant? They were a remnant, certainly. Their fellows had been cut down about them over the years and they alone had escaped to tell the tale. Only to find that no one was interested. Faiblesse marveled, as he had before, at the facilities of the infirmary; it was a regular hospital. Fleming had been unstinting in his generosity. Why had the college trustee chosen the society for his gift? They had not been lucky of late in attracting wealthy benefactors. He must ask about Fleming. The Founder was beyond inquiries now and suddenly Father Faiblesse thought of how much would die with the old man, knowledge of the origin of various traditions in the society, memories of its first days. If only the old man had written it down or agreed to tape some of his recollections. One could only hope that the archives contained the essentials.

When he had left the doctor, Faiblesse continued to muse on the society's history. Would it really matter if it was never written? One wanted to assume a listener of insatiable curiosity, one for whom no detail would be too minor. Almost certainly, there was no one who cared. Except God, of course, and He keeps His own records. Records . . . archives . . . poor old Phelan and the forgotten document which would enable a handful of cranky old men to triumph over Hoyt. Faiblesse smiled. He wished that he had not asked Phelan to find Corcoran. There would have been easier ways to cut short the interview. Mr. Nickles and the car were behind the building but Father Faiblesse went outside through the main entrance. The peace of the surroundings settled on him as he looked out over the lake. How delightful to live here, one's work done, some time left to put one's soul in order. The Gate of Heaven indeed.

And then Father Faiblesse noticed that, across the lake, Little Sem still stood. Beside it, menacing as a prehistoric monster but immobile, rose the angled crane of a wrecker. Was it really true that an old devil like Phelan had stymied Hoyt?

8

"F<small>ATHER</small> F<small>AIBLESSE</small> has come to see the Founder,"
Garrity said, looking into the room.

Tumulty, in a chair near the window, put down his breviary. "I've phoned him twice since the attack."

"Phelan has him in tow. Perhaps we should rescue him."

"I should think you would ask Noonan to do that."

"Noonan?"

"The acting superior of the house."

Garrity almost but not quite made a face. He shut the door behind him and, inside the room, sat on the bed. "Phelan will pester him about Little Sem."

"Pester him? But you're opposed to the plan for a new dorm, too."

"Nooo. What would I care about a new building, or an old one, for that matter? It is not a matter of brick and mortar, Michael." Garrity paused. "Are you busy?"

"Go on." Tumulty laid his hands on the arms of his chair,

89

unwilling to show his relief that Garrity had at last brought the matter up. As so often in the past, patience had its rewards. The news that Phelan had been conducting Faiblesse around the house had made Tumulty want to rush from the room in pursuit of the two of them. Hoyt had indicated that Faiblesse was unaware of the difficulties created by the promise to Oscar Shively and it was clear that he wished the father superior to remain in the dark. Faiblesse has enough on his mind. No need to bother him with this, he had said, but clearly it was Hoyt who was bothered. The marvel was that Hoyt could utter remarks like that for all the world as if he really meant them. The one redeeming thing about Faiblesse as father superior, Tumulty thought, was that the man was all but inert, withdrawn into that white elephant on Cavil Boulevard, more out of things than the residents of Porta Coeli. He did not visit the campus once a month and surely even he must realize that the center of things remained on the campus, in the college. But whatever disadvantages might ensue from Faiblesse's being informed of the Shively document from so irrational an opponent as Phelan were more than offset by the chance that Garrity, the intelligent and loyal opposition, might reconsider his stand.

"It isn't just a matter of the building, is it, Michael? Not for you and not for me."

"Would Noonan and Phelan agree?"

"Forget them for the moment. They see it as a symbol, I suppose. But of what? Their lost youth, the boyhood that seems impossibly happy from this distant vantage point. Those are not mean sentiments, of course. I don't suggest that. But, after all, it is a species of sentimentality. The building is, nonetheless, a symbol and knocking it to dust means something a good deal more than knocking it to dust."

"What?"

"I wish you could help me to see what, Michael. Hoyt is, after all, your man."

90

Tumulty laughed and the irony was unforced. "Hoyt is his own man, you can be sure of that."

"But you hand-picked him as your successor."

Is that what the others thought? Is that how it had looked? My God, how distorted the view of the partially informed. Hoyt *had* given him that, the appearance of stepping aside voluntarily. If it had come to a fight, it would have been no contest; the young man had the board of trustees in his pocket. How bitter had been the realization that, in the event of a fight, the only trustee whose vote he could have counted on was Oliver Fleming. No doubt Oliver would have been as uncomfortable with that alliance as he.

"What is he up to, Michael?"

"Is it so difficult to believe that all he is up to is building a new dormitory on the site of Little Sem?"

"Yes. This is not an isolated act. It fits in with too many others, some of which go back to your own time as president of the college."

"Any administrator knows that his acts will be criticized by some."

Garrity dismissed the remark. "My criticisms of you never arose out of any doubt concerning your grasp of what the society is. With Father Hoyt I have that kind of doubt. Is he really one of us?"

"Of course he is."

"But how would he act differently if he had set out to destroy the society? What was the real point of cutting the college free of the society?"

Tumulty suppressed a sigh. Repeating the justification of making the college independent, citing the happy consequences of having done so, he remembered his own angry mood in Rome when he had got wind of it. That his opposition had been confined to letters—letters!—had infuriated him and it was all he could do not to take a cab to Fiumicino and fly home to Ohio

91

and confront Hoyt personally. But that would have been to put himself in a weakened position, an unauthorized return home to face a Hoyt who had clearly won over Faiblesse to the scheme. Faiblesse. How cunning it had been to get Michael Tumulty out of the way before giving Hoyt the go-ahead. Beware of the apparently weak opponent. He had underestimated Faiblesse for years, a quiet, pudgy man brooding over his books, performing minor miracles with the college finances, but only a cipher, a machine, a calculator without a significant self. And all along those ledgers had been in the hands of a coldly ambitious man, a character out of Dickens. And how incredibly serpentine Faiblesse had been when he sent Tumulty to Porta Coeli.

"Good news, Father. Good news." And the smile that had illumined Faiblesse's face could not have seemed more sincere. "Your long years of work for the society are now going to be fittingly rewarded. At any rate, rewarded as well as they can be in this life."

Tumulty had tensed in his chair, his mind unwillingly shuffling the possibilities of advancement. What could Faiblesse give him that he had not already had? And lost. Something outside the society? He became aware of the fact that Faiblesse had begun to speak of Porta Coeli. What did Tumulty think of the place? His mind still aloft, seeking the promontory on which he would be asked to alight, Tumulty had said the usual things about what a wonderful place Porta Coeli was, how grateful they all must be to Oliver Fleming for his generosity in building it for the society. Faiblesse opined that, with the Founder now in residence there, Porta Coeli had become the heart of the Society of Saint Brendan.

"He seems to like it," Tumulty agreed.

"He loves it. It will be a great relief to me to have you looking out for him. Not everyone at Porta Coeli is as vigorous as he once was."

"Look out for him?"

"A manner of speaking. He has suggested that he be replaced as head of the house. That seems inappropriate to me. You have always worked well with him. He has confidence in you. You will have everything but the title. Of course I cannot appoint you head of the house."

"You want me to live at Porta Coeli?"

Forming the words was like voicing an obscenity for the first time. The world, not visibly altered by the cataclysm, spun on. Faiblesse was nodding like a department store Santa. Surprise, surprise. Thus did Shakespearean tragedy veer toward farce. The numskull seemed actually to expect Tumulty to cheer his own exile.

"I gather that this is not a permanent assignment."

Faiblesse was taken aback. He murmured something about no assignment being permanent. Tumulty suggested final. Was it a final assignment? Faiblesse, as if sensing that he had already won, holding as he did the trump of Tumulty's vow of obedience, called the appointment temporary. They would see. They would see. Thus parents put off the importunate questions of children. Tumulty had never felt so shattered in his life. Faiblesse of all people was informing him that his life was over. This was infinitely worse than being shipped off to the somnolent quarters on the Via Nomentana, half a mile from Mussolini's old mansion. Like il Duce, Tumulty felt that he was destined for an ignominious end, his Milanese piazza the enervating tranquillity of Porta Coeli. Dear God, how he wished he could accept this as the Founder had, as Garrity apparently had. But he could not. It was not in his nature. That is why he must make his moves with consummate caution now, why he must win over Garrity in a final success that would mean he would be out of this house and back in harness again.

He said to Garrity, "I share your concern at the direction the society has taken."

"I knew it. Then how can you act as Hoyt's agent now?"

"Only on Little Sem."

"But that is the only way we have to stop him. A small obstacle but a real one."

"I agree that it is small. I doubt that it will stop Father Hoyt, in the sense you have in mind."

"Then what can we do?"

And there before him, clear as day, was the tack he must take with Garrity in order to win his consent to the razing of Little Sem. Of course. Tumulty could not restrain himself from getting up from his chair. He must not blurt it out. Garrity, too, had stood and Tumulty saw that the other man's question had been meant as a rhetorical one. There was a sad look in Garrity's eyes, blue agates emergent from sagging pouches. Garrity's hair, still more gray than white, fell like eaves from a high part. He looked old but he had aged with dignity. The network of wrinkles on his face, the wide, slack mouth created, with the accumulated sadness of his eyes, an impression of truce with a confusing world.

"I have an idea," Tumulty said, opening the door. "I think it is a good one."

Garrity turned, the flicker of interest in his eyes. Unqualified hope was hardly more than a memory to him, but Garrity clearly had not despaired.

"Another time," Tumulty said. "You're right. Let us find Father Faiblesse. We must rescue him from Leo Phelan."

Mr. Nickles grew tired of sitting in the car. That could be interesting when he parked on a busy street where there were curious passers-by to ignore or kids to shoo away from the car. He kept it gleaming, loved to be out in the garage rubbing it with a chamois cloth, humming as he did so. He had not the faintest idea what went on under the hood of this magnificent car; indeed there were buttons and gauges within whose function he did not know. What he did know was that the car was

94

extremely expensive, consumed gasoline at a furious rate and elicited admiring and covetous glances from those who knew the least thing about the market value of automobiles. So it could be pleasant, parked in the city, to sit behind the wheel and wear a disdainful proprietary expression. He would imagine himself a man who had succeeded in life. The great car was only a toy and he drove himself as a whimsical indulgence. Retired now, it was his wont to wing away in winter to Caribbean cruises: a few months in the sun, warming his bones, the wearying years of acquisition behind, his pleasures well earned and thoroughly enjoyed. Mrs. Nickles? If she gained a foothold in his reveries it was as the cantankerous housekeeper he kept on for reasons of sentimentality. The old girl could really not cut it anymore. He had always been generous with employees. Treat people right; it paid. No point in rubbing their noses in the fact that he was boss. It takes all kinds. Nonetheless, he would have to have a talk with Mrs. Nickles. (Odd that they bore the same name; perhaps she is a relative. Ah, that's it. His brother's widow. He could not abandon his brother's widow so he supported her, gave her a home. She puttered about the house a bit; it gave her the illusion of earning her keep.) Such imaginary flights from under his wife's thumb usually filled Mr. Nickles with pleasure. Today, unfortunately, daydreaming did not come to alleviate the boredom of waiting in the car behind this nursing home for aged priests.

By God, the clergy had it soft. Look at the way Faiblesse and Fogarty live. The fat of the land. And what did they do all day that could be called a job of work? Did they worry about the future? Ha. Why should they? They had this place to look forward to. Just move in. He would bet they each had a private room, and there must be a great view of the lake. Sit and fish all day, that would be their life.

Curious, Mr. Nickles got out of the car and stood beside it, stretching his legs. Then, hands behind his back, just strolling, he walked along the back of the building. Where were the old birds anyway? Out front? In their rooms? Sleeping one off? Mr. Nickles grinned. He had never realized before that priests were allowed to drink, but now he knew they did their share. He had learned that from the number of bottles he toted from the house to the trash can. Of course Faiblesse was the big cheese and Fogarty was some pumpkins, too. He had never understood the setup, though. When he and the Mrs. got the job, Mr. Nickles had been leery of the priests, figuring they would talk religion all the time. The topic had never come up. Miss Liczenski was Catholic and should understand such things, but when he asked her about it she answered with a question of her own. How many doctors insisted on talking medicine with him? That made sense to Mr. Nickles, not that he knew many doctors. Of course he had never approached a priest professionally. He was not a Catholic. He was not anything else either. Did he even believe in God? He wasn't sure. He could not claim to have given the matter much thought, but he had a right to his opinion.

"At your age you shouldn't talk so foolish," Mrs. Nickles snapped, when he raised the topic with her. "Of course there's a God."

"How do you know?"

"Everyone knows."

"*I* don't know."

She sniffed. What did his opinion matter? Since that conversation, Mr. Nickles was sure he was an atheist. Women.

If priests drank, which had surprised him, they didn't seem to fool around with women, no matter what you read in the newspapers. At least Father Faiblesse and Fogarty didn't. Mr. Nickles was certain he would have noticed if anything like that was going on. He had kept his eyes open. When he questioned Mrs. Nickles about it, edging up to it discreetly, she answered with her cold-fish stare. Reminded that, after all, she made the beds, Mrs. Nickles snorted with disgust and left the room. She had always been a prude. Sometimes Mr. Nickles thought that his wife was on the way to becoming a Catholic herself. She might have done it already if Miss Liczenski wasn't one.

When he reached the end of the building, Mr. Nickles stopped and peered around the corner in the direction of the lake. There was an old fellow on the lawn, but he did not notice Mr. Nickles. The man wore a straw hat whose brim was turned down all around. Shirt sleeves, black trousers, slippers. He was slightly stooped and was holding out his hand, palm cupped, trying to coax a squirrel toward him. It was an old squirrel with a yellow underbelly; on its hind legs, it was holding something, some kind of nut. Mr. Nickles thought it strange that the old fellow should try to coax an animal with food when it was already eating.

"Come here," the old fellow said, his voice impatient. The squirrel perked up. The man began to move toward him. The squirrel, motionless, watched him approach. The man's tone became gentle, wheedling. His pace was stealthy. Mr. Nickles watched, fascinated. When the man was only six feet away, the squirrel put what it was holding in its mouth and dashed for a tree. It was up it and out of sight before you could say Jack Robinson. The old fellow threw what he had in his hand after the squirrel.

"Scat," he cried. "Get out of here. Go."

And then he turned and saw Mr. Nickles standing there.

"Who are you?"

"I drive the car," Mr. Nickles said, taken aback. The old man was madder than hell to have been observed. "For Father Faiblesse. Are you feeding squirrels?"

Wary eyes studied Mr. Nickles for a moment. The man shuffled toward him as if he were afraid of losing his slippers. Mr. Nickles saw that they were ancient, crushed, the color faded. They looked very comfortable.

"My name is Nickles." Like the squirrel before him, Mr. Nickles was thinking of flight, but then the old man smiled.

"Did you see that squirrel run?"

"He really moved."

"Crazy animal. I think he's rabid. Most squirrels eat right out of my hand. Birds, too. Land on my shoulders, head, all over me."

"I don't know one bird from another."

"Is that so?" A tolerant smile. "They're easy to identify, once you get the hang of it. Like airplane spotting. You remember that?"

"Of course."

"I was a chaplain briefly. Before the war."

Mr. Nickles wondered what war the man meant.

"And now you're retired?"

"Retired?"

"Don't you live here?"

"Oh, yes."

"Looks like a nice place."

"I've been in worse. Some of my colleagues are not exactly *compos mentis.*"

Mr. Nickles did not understand.

"A little touched. Like that old squirrel."

"I know what you mean. I have a wife."

"So you're a married man."

"We all make mistakes."

The old man laughed. He seemed to have shaved only one side of his face. The skin that hung loosely on the jowl jiggled in merriment. Mr. Nickles wondered if this old bird was compass menthol himself. He did not have the look of a priest.

"You said you drive Father Faiblesse?"

"I manage the house on Cavil Boulevard," Mr. Nickles said carefully. "From time to time, I accompany Father Faiblesse in the car."

"Do you live at the generalate?"

Mr. Nickles said that he and his wife had an apartment there, three rooms, very nice.

"Thank God you're still active. You seem to be in good health."

"I am."

"So am I. But what does it matter? Age is the thing. You reach a certain age and they put you on the shelf."

Another old man was approaching from the lake; the slight breeze lifted the white wisps of his hair and gave him a strange look. The old squirrel reappeared at the same time, its inquisitive rodent face peering around the trunk of the tree it had climbed. The newcomer wore baggy pants and a baggier coat sweater, whose pockets bulged. The squirrel, on the grass again, hopped along after him.

"This is Father Faiblesse's driver," the prewar chaplain said. He was not pleased at the interruption. "Father Ucello." He winked significantly at Mr. Nickles.

"I suppose Father Faiblesse has come to see the Founder," the newcomer said.

Mr. Nickles mumbled something noncommittal. He had no idea what the reason for the boss's visit was. The squirrel had hopped to within inches of Father Ucello's foot. Mr. Nickles pointed this out, wondering if he should pass on the prewar chaplain's judgment that the animal was rabid. Ucello stamped his foot but the squirrel did not move. The prewar chaplain was red with anger. He turned his back on Ucello and again winked at Mr. Nickles, this time looking as if he might squeeze his eye from its socket. Ucello took a piece of stale bread from his pocket and dropped it on the grass. The squirrel put it in his mouth and scampered up Ucello's body. Ucello closed his sweater pocket and the squirrel continued to his shoulder, where it perched.

"Shouldn't you be careful?" Mr. Nickles asked, worried.

The prewar chaplain threw a murderous glance at the squirrel. A guttural sound escaped his throat.

Ucello said, "The animals here are a terrible bother. They won't leave us alone."

Mr. Nickles noticed that the trees about were now alive with birds; they darted and swooped and fluttered to the ground at Father Ucello's feet. Absent-mindedly he scattered the contents of his pockets upon the lawn. A pair of bluejays tried to monopolize the food but Ucello stepped into the fray and restored peace. A magnificent redbird alighted on his unoccupied shoulder. The prewar chaplain's face was a mask of rage.

"Come," he said to Mr. Nickles. "Show me the car you drive."

9

Sister Diotima told them that Father Faiblesse
had gone away with Father Phelan right after they had anointed
the Founder. Aghast, Garrity asked her to repeat what she had
said. The old nun came over to him and, half on tiptoe, repeated what she had said in a shout.

"But we already anointed him, Sister."

The old head rocked like a metronone and Sister Diotima
pushed her hands up her sleeves. "I didn't know."

"It's not your fault," Tumulty assured her. "But Father
Phelan knew. Did you see where they went?"

She hadn't noticed. Tumulty saw Alma Bishop come out of
Dr. Dowling's office and cross to the nurses' station. Did he
imagine that her step was springier? His promise emerged once
more from memory. Tomorrow, soon, he would go see the
girl's mother. Girl! It was ridiculous. Why couldn't Dowling
make a move? Why couldn't they simply act like adults? With

101

Alma, piety had become a vice, but what was wrong with Dr. Dowling? A morbid loyalty to his dead wife, perhaps. Perhaps a word with the doctor was in order, too, but delicately, delicately. Tumulty had had enough experience with such matters to know that too often a woman's perception of a man's intention was the product of wish rather than reality. He sighed but of course he enjoyed the thought that the fate and happiness of others might depend, however partially, on what he said and did. Garrity suggested that they go to Phelan's room.

"It would be just like Leo to drag him there."

"Not to Noonan?"

Garrity considered the suggestion. "It's possible."

But Faiblesse was in neither room. Noonan lay on his bed, flat on his back, out like a light, his breathing a deep, measured nasal snore.

"Our leader," Tumulty could not resist saying as Garrity eased the door shut.

Garrity smiled. "The sleep of the just."

They found Faiblesse outside, in front of the building, looking across the lake toward the campus. He turned at the sound of Garrity's voice and a smile came and went. The smile for Garrity, its erasure occasioned by Tumulty. Tumulty took a certain satisfaction from the realization that he had introduced a chilly propriety into his dealings with the father superior. With the remembered reflex of days of power, he opened with an accusation.

"Sister says that you gave Father Cullen the last rites."

Faiblesse's eyes rolled upward. "It was only afterward that Phelan told me it had already been done."

"It doesn't matter," Garrity said. And of course it didn't, not really, but the situation put Faiblesse at a disadvantage. Sensing this, Garrity's instinct was to lead away from the cause of distress. He pointed across the lake.

"It still stands."

"Father Phelan told me the most remarkable story."

"It's true," Tumulty said curtly. If Faiblesse were what a father superior ought to be, such news would not reach him through such channels as Leo Phelan.

"And you men really hold veto power?"

"There has been some opposition," Tumulty said. "Not all of it wise."

"And who is opposed?" The question was addressed to Tumulty.

"Phelan, of course. And Noonan."

"I am opposed, too, Father," Garrity said quietly. He continued to look across the lake. There was a faint smile on his face. "Do you know, looked at through half-closed eyes, that scene hasn't changed in fifty years."

"What was on this side of the lake?" Faiblesse asked. "I was just trying to remember."

"A pasture, some woodlands, a bathhouse for a time, until the Founder put an end to it. That was after my time. You can imagine the distraction it must have been, people romping in the lake while the boys sat in study hall."

"Surely the society owned this land then."

"All but a narrow strip which had access to the lake. The Founder bought it in order to close the beach. Paid through the nose for it, too."

"The poor man," Faiblesse said, glancing toward the house.

"Yes."

"I spoke with Dr. Dowling. He seems unsure how long Father Cullen will live."

"I pray that he recovers," Garrity said.

"Apparently there has been brain damage. Survival seems hardly desirable."

After a decent pause, Garrity said, "Michael and I have been discussing the college, the society, the future of Little Sem. Could we talk about that with you, Father?"

"Father Phelan told me that you are in favor of its destruction, Michael."

Tumulty said, "I favor construction, not destruction. The new dormitory will be built there. It is the ideal locale. As soon as those who have celebrated their golden anniversary give their consent, the work will continue."

"And you oppose it, Father Garrity?"

"Father, I do not like the way things have been going in the society. Please don't take this as criticism of you personally. Frankly, my doubts center on Father Hoyt. The college is in his hands now, not the society's. I do not understand his attitude toward the society. Is it to be sacrificed for the sake of the college?" Garrity inhaled sharply. "Nor do I care for the way Father Hoyt dresses. Who would know that he is a priest?"

"I know, I know," Faiblesse said sadly. "I have much the same situation with Father Fogarty." He looked at Tumulty. "The man has become a fashion plate."

"Have you forbidden the dress he wears?"

"Oh, heavens, no. I regard it as a fad."

"It is not a fad, Father," Garrity protested. "We have been tolerant of too many things, saying they are only fads. There are revolutionaries in the Church. It is painful enough to read about them in the paper, in magazines, but to think of them in the society itself . . ."

"You mean Father Fogarty?" Faiblesse's brows shot up.

"I mean Father Hoyt. If I oppose his building plans, Father, it is for wider reasons. Perhaps there is something providential in the fact that we old men can still do something about controlling the way the society is evolving. It is not a pleasant thing, sitting here and seeing the society to which we have given our lives repudiated by the college the Founder built."

Faiblesse nodded. "Father Phelan said much the same thing."

Tumulty noticed that it was impossible for Garrity not to be annoyed at having what he said reduced to the level of Phelan's plangent approach to the world. Garrity said, "I felt it my obligation to say these things to you, Father."

"Of course. And I appreciate your frankness."

"These things must be said."

Faiblesse nodded vigorously, sensing that Garrity did not intend to press him further. "Well," he said, looking about with vacant benignity. "Isn't this a lovely place? Gentlemen, I envy you."

And that, Tumulty thought, was the unkindest cut of all. They said good-bye and Faiblesse turned toward the house. As he did, Phelan appeared and the father superior hesitated. He glanced at Tumulty and Garrity, squared his shoulders and moved across the lawn toward Phelan. It was difficult not to pity him.

"He doesn't understand," Garrity said.

"No."

"Or he doesn't care. How can Hoyt act without his consent?"

Because his consent consists in his failure to forbid. But there was no point in saying that. Whatever Faiblesse's condition, it was unlikely to commend itself to Garrity. If anything was providential, it was Garrity's realization that, if Hoyt was to be controlled, Faiblesse was not the man to do it. That realization must be allowed to settle deep in his mind. Like others in the house, Garrity hugged the hope that eventually, before things went too far, the father superior would step in. Prior to the Founder's stroke, that hope had been turned on the old man, too. Surely he would not stand by and permit the society to be spurned by its own college.

They sat on a bench, looking down at the mottled surface of the lake, and while Garrity spoke of the accomplishments of the Founder, of the society, told the litany of the years of effort that now seemed threatened by repudiation, Tumulty found it easy to submit to the rhythm of the lamentation. It was a vision of events congenial to the old: the past with its virtues sinks from sight and the present which replaces it seems by contrast bogus and threatening. The new is a product of jaded shallowness and even the current continuation of what has always been takes on an unreal air, an adult drama enacted by children. Surrendering to Garrity's outlook, Tumulty could almost take it for his own.

Phelan had been unable to find Corcoran. He was not in his room, he was not watching television. He was not in chapel. The chapel was empty. Phelan remained there a moment, kneeling at the back. The afternoon sun threw patches of color on the smooth white plaster walls. The stained-glass windows seemed a child's imitation of the real thing: large pieces of glass, all primary colors, their arrangement vaguely reminiscent of objects in the real world. Those windows were a favorite object of derision in the house. Now, in the afternoon, they had the simple appeal of a color chart. Along the unwindowed wall of the chapel were the alcoves in which they said their morning Masses. The main altar, a thick slab of marble under a suspended crucifix, was contained by the curved parentheses of the pews. Phelan thought about God, a species of mental prayer, then rose to go.

It was absurd to expect help from Faiblesse. The man was the creature of Hoyt and everyone knew it. And how can you carry on a conversation with a man who insists on replying with interrogative versions of what you have just told him? Faiblesse could not possibly be unaware of what Corcoran had found in the archives. Phelan was certain that the discovery had thrown the enemy camp into consternation, as witness the effort to infiltrate Porta Coeli through Tumulty's wretched agency. Doubtless this visit of the father superior, conveniently camouflaged by the illness of the Founder, was only another move in their campaign. Phelan felt surrounded by conspiracy. Tumulty's activities might be merely diversionary, drawing their first energy and leaving them vulnerable to a *coup de grâce*. Phelan, lost in thought, went back to his room. Visiting chapel had been a wise move, a recharging of batteries against a godless assault. He did not notice the figures on the lawn when he passed the main entrance and, when he arrived at his room, was surprised that Faiblesse was no longer there. He went immediately to his desk and opened the drawer. The slip of paper on which he was keeping a tally of the house was in plain view. If Faiblesse had snooped around he would certainly have seen that. Too late, Phelan put his tally at the bottom of the drawer, under a jumble of papers. He had underestimated his adversary. Now Faiblesse would know how meager the opposition was. Worse, he would know the identity of the loyalists. Phelan smiled grimly. One veto was enough. However unsure he might be of the others, he knew himself to be as rock. But where had Faiblesse gone?

When he came outside, he saw the three figures on the lawn. What was Garrity doing with those two? Father Founder lay on his deathbed and already the vultures circled. Phelan snatched up his binoculars and trained them across the lake. It came as almost a relief to see that Little Sem still stood. The crane was still there, too, the wrecking ball dropping like a plumb line from its arm. It looked like an Erector set. Destructor set. Tinker Toys. Phelan felt his mind wander, as if consciousness were being pulled into the widening cone of his magnified vision. The binoculars were a time machine, zooming him across the lake to his youth. The Founder was over there, not behind him, a frail failing body under an oxygen tent.

"Bird watching, Father?"

It was Faiblesse, speaking at Phelan's elbow. Phelan dropped the binoculars and they bounced painfully on his stomach. There was an amused look in the father superior's eye. Had it been put there by a peek at the tally sheet?

"I keep an eye on things, Father."

"I was just saying how pleasant it must be to live here." Faiblesse inhaled, closing his eyes as he did so. His eyes were bright when they reopened. "So peaceful."

"Did you have a nice chat with Father Tumulty?"

Faiblesse seemed puzzled by the implications in Phelan's voice.

"I gather that you were unable to find Father Corcoran."

"He must be on campus."

"In the archives?"

"Perhaps."

"Well."

Phelan accompanied Faiblesse through the house to the parking lot on the other side. The car was empty. Faiblesse was annoyed.

"Now where is Mr. Nickles?"

The object of the inquiry appeared a moment later but Phelan was distracted by the arrival of another car. The sight of the little figure behind the wheel made his heart leap with joy.

"Flamingo," he cried.

Oliver Fleming brought his car to a stop with a bang; he had misjudged his turn as he swung toward the building to park and his front bumper grazed some trash barrels. Faces of kitchen help appeared at the windows. Mr. Nickles shook his head at this recklessness. Fleming pushed open the door of his car and the two priests went to greet him. Oliver seemed alarmed at the fact that Faiblesse was there.

"Am I too late?" He got his feet onto the asphalt of the parking lot.

It was Phelan who understood that Oliver referred to the Founder. He assured him that the old priest was still alive. Father Faiblesse had given him extreme unction within the hour.

"I'll take you right to him," Phelan said. "He could go any minute."

"Or last for weeks," Faiblesse said. "The doctor isn't sure."

"My bag can wait," Fleming said but, hands in pockets, he stopped to look at the house he had given the society. A satisfied smile played on his thin lips.

"Then you are staying," Phelan said with delight.

"I thought I would make a short retreat."

"I'll tell Sister Diotima. She'll make up a room."

"Are you leaving, Father?" Fleming asked Faiblesse.

108

"I'm afraid so. You must come see me, Mr. Fleming. At the generalate."

"You mean the house on Cavil Boulevard?"

"Yes."

"I will."

Phelan took his old friend's arm. Thank God he would have first shot at Oliver. By the time Flamingo talked with the father superior he would know the lay of the land. There would be little need to explain to Oliver how important it was that Little Sem be saved. But first things first. A visit to the Founder's sickbed. The good-byes in the parking lot were ragged and prolonged —Faiblesse had to go into their gratitude for the gift of Porta Coeli and who could blame Oliver for wanting to hear that?— but finally Phelan had his guest inside the building. They had not gone three steps before he was informing Oliver that the Founder was being betrayed by his own society even as he breathed his last.

10

WHEN THEY had come round the lake and were on the campus road, Father Faiblesse, on an impulse, had Mr. Nickles stop the car in front of the administration building. Going slowly up the steps to the entrance, he found himself half hoping that the president would not be in or, if in, too busy to see him on this unscheduled visit. It was the wan hope of a boy expecting punishment and willing to bargain almost anything for its postponement. His pace was glacially slow as he went down the hall to the president's office. "I am a weak man," he told himself, but he gained no strength from enunciating this simple truth.

The president, alas, was in and, again alas, he could see Father Faiblesse immediately. The father superior entered the office, hesitated a moment, then advanced over the carpet toward the great desk behind which an unrisen Father Hoyt sat.

"I have just come from seeing the Founder," Faiblesse said.

"How is he?"

"I gave him the last sacraments."

"Sit down, Father. Please."

Father Faiblesse sat. How large the presidential desk, how expensive its furnishings, how uncluttered its surface. Hoyt had a genius for administration which, Faiblesse felt, was akin to a genius for acting. Not action; acting, the thespian art, indulged in vicariously. A director's talent.

"How are they taking it?"

"They?"

Father Hoyt sat forward in his chair and placed his angled elbows on the desktop. His once lean face had become full, emphasizing the dimples that never went completely away. Cool gray eyes, unblinking, watchful, assessing, in command; one half expected the lower lids to lift, like a bird's. Father Hoyt wore a gray chalk-stripe suit and a floral tie. His collar was soft as if to stress its comfort compared with the throttling rise of the starched Roman collar that Hoyt wished to dethrone as the sartorial mark of the priest. The fingers of his hands interlaced: narrow hands, long fingers, no ring. Fogarty was farther along than his mentor in matters of dress. The president's hair was combed forward and his sideburns had perceptibly lowered.

"The old men," he said.

Faiblesse assumed a thoughtful expression. He felt more affinity with the old men in Porta Coeli than he did with Father Hoyt. Even Hoyt's name was new; it had been Heute when he joined the society. It would be more accurate to say that the society had joined him, its fate conjoined with his. And what was Hoyt's fate? Excelsior, success, putting the college on a solid foundation. The secular board of trustees, coeducation, government grants: these moves had indeed put the college on the map. His success left his critics little room for maneuver. Father Faiblesse realized that he should feel more identified with what Hoyt had accomplished. He had been the senior partner. The phrase was Hoyt's, used often during the father superior's first term in office. He employed it infrequently now. Faiblesse knew that he had become the president's creature and, through him, so had the society. If the college was free of the society, the society was inextricably dependent on the college, its income derived in great measure from the salaries paid its few members who were still on the college payroll. Faiblesse's own salary as a member of the board of trustees was not a negligible item in the society budget. Fittingly, no doubt, Hoyt's salary was far less negligible. He turned it over ungrudgingly; his expense account alone enabled him to live in a manner difficult to reconcile with the vow of poverty he had taken.

The old men. That is how Father Hoyt had once summed up the society to Bishop Brophy and Father Oder in the episcopal mansion in Fort Elbow. Faiblesse had been taken along to the dinner by Hoyt, the occasion more than the usual fence-mending with the local bishop; Hoyt had wanted to explain to Brophy and his vicar-general the reasoning behind severing Saint Brendan's College from the society. With the accession of Brophy to the see of Fort Elbow and the ascension of Hoyt to the presidency of the college, the latent animosity between bishop and religious community within his diocese had disappeared. Faiblesse could remember the almost icy encounters of the Founder and Bishop Caldron. The Founder had not got on with Caldron since their first meeting, when he had cited the arrangements he had entered into with Caldron's predecessor on first locating the society in northwest Ohio. Caldron had not liked the suggestion that his own freedom of movement was restricted by the previous decisions of others. The Founder, as usual, had documentary evidence. The matter had been dropped; candidates for the diocesan priesthood would not be educated at Saint Brendan's. In those days, the society had had its hands full training its own aspirants. Caldron had never forgotten what he seemingly regarded as a churlish response from a guest in his diocese. He had not liked the Founder; he did, however, admire him, even revere him. For years he had spent his monthly day of retreat at Saint Brendan's, on that day going to confession to the Founder. It was difficult to imagine Bishop Brophy, or Father Oder, having recourse to Hoyt to confess their sins and receive absolution. The three men understood one another so well Faiblesse felt like an outsider with them. He wished Hoyt would not insist that he come along on such visits. He had thought of pleading illness but actually to make the excuse would have made him really ill. It was at table that Brophy asked Hoyt what the greatest problem facing his plan was.

"The old men," Hoyt said unhesitatingly, and set the table aroar. Faiblesse had joined in the laughter, feeling himself a traitor to his kind. His attempt a minute later to say something about the traditions of the society dwindled into silence. No one was listening to him. Now, seated beside Hoyt's desk, he said, "Of course they are taking the Founder's illness hard."

"Was he able to talk?"

"He is in a coma."

Hoyt's brows lifted, recognition that this was serious indeed. He sat back in his chair and his face went into shadow.

"How old is he, Father?"

"In his nineties."

"I hope to God I never live that long. I've never understood the scriptural obsession with longevity. A man should be snuffed out in full flame, not gutter into darkness."

"Perhaps you'll feel differently later."

"No doubt. When my mind has decayed and survival at any cost seems desirable. Do you think the Founder thanks God for the length of his life?"

"I am sure he has submitted himself to God's will."

"But one does that in the case of evil, too. Granted that he has accepted his advanced age, can he be truly grateful for it?"

"You would have to ask him that."

Hoyt looked thoughtful. "I must confess that it has often crossed my mind that the society has had a rougher row to hoe with the Founder still among the living. The older orders have their founders safely dead and canonized but other congregations have flourished with something less than a saint behind

113

them. The process gets started, biographies are written, legends developed. We've been deprived of all that. Our Founder could always be produced in person and there isn't much mythical about an ordinary-looking elderly priest."

"Newman lived a long life."

"He died at eighty-nine and for his last decade they kept him pretty well hidden from the public. You must have seen the photographs of him in his old age. A crumpled old woman, with that horrendous beak besides. Few saw him like that. The Newman that existed spoke through his writings."

"I had no idea you were a Newman scholar."

"I'm not. He wrote on higher education. Lovely stuff, completely impractical. I doubt that he could have run a college."

"I thought he had."

"He tried to." The president laughed. "In Ireland."

There was, Faiblesse reflected, little similarity between Newman and the Founder. The Founder had written nothing but letters and there was little chance that they would be collected; most of them were pleas for funds, or haggling with creditors and bishops. Quite often of late they had been written to reprove a wayward member of the society.

Faiblesse said, "The doctor doubts that the Founder will emerge from his coma. Nevertheless, death is not necessarily imminent. He could hang on."

"For how long?"

"Days. Weeks."

"God bless him."

After the callous thoughts he had just expressed, Hoyt's prayer for the Founder filled Faiblesse with sudden tenderness. Hoyt must feel some affection for the old man after all.

"In my view, he is a saint."

"Because he founded the society?" Hoyt's facetious smile returned.

"Few men have done as much."

"God is merciful."

Faiblesse had never been able to tell which Hoyt was the genuine man. There was what he preferred to believe was the surface Hoyt, the sleek, glib, worldly administrator of Saint Brendan's who had made the pages of *Time*. Though he regarded it as a weakness in himself, Faiblesse agreed with men like Garrity and preferred the college as it had been. Oh, it had always been changing, evolving, but there had been continuity in its alteration from a seminary to a college for men and, more recently, a coeducational institution. It was not change he objected to, but the quantum jump the institution had taken with Hoyt, the surface Hoyt. The real Hoyt was hidden beneath the facetious self he wore like a mask; underneath were depths where his motives dwelt. Those motives, so Faiblesse had argued to the president's critics, the old men, were actually quite similar to those that had driven the Founder. The good of the society, of course, but, more importantly, furthering the work of the Church. The Church and the world in which it was placed had changed; the society, too, had changed. They should thank God that in His providence He had given them a Father Hoyt to guide them through these troubled times. Faiblesse had often convinced himself with such arguments, but it was difficult to retain conviction when faced with the teasing mockery of the putative savior of the society and college.

"You think I'm hard to say that he has hung on too long, don't you? Banquo's ghost, the ghost at the banquet, whatever it is. I owe the idea to the Founder himself. My question earlier was rhetorical. I do not think he thanks God for preserving him so far beyond the normal span of life. He would have preferred not to see what has happened to his work. What had to happen; he was willing to concede that. I have never made a major move without consulting him, Father. I am carrying on his work. He knew that." The sly grin returned. "It was the cross he carried during these last few years, knowing that."

115

"I never heard him criticize you."

"I'm sure you didn't."

Faiblesse's eyes drifted to the window behind Hoyt. "Did he ver say anything to you about Little Sem?"

"What do you mean?"

"Did he object to its being taken down?"

Hoyt sat forward again, coming into the light. "That's what s really bothering them over there, isn't it?"

"Some of them connect the razing of Little Sem and the Founder's seizure."

"That's nonsense."

"I notice that the wrecking has not begun."

Hoyt smiled, unhappily. "And you've learned why."

"Do they really have veto power over it?"

"They do. I'm sure it gives some of them a heady sensation. The delay is temporary. And costly. You know that the board agreed that that location is the ideal one for the new dorm."

Had they agreed to that? No doubt. The agenda for the trustees' meetings was a script sedulously followed. Didn't they all feel that Hoyt was simply keeping them informed on what he was doing? As he had kept the Founder informed, apparently. Of course they must have endorsed Hoyt's judgment that where Little Sem stood was the only logical place for the new government-financed coed dormitory.

"Then the document is genuine?"

"Absolutely. Every man in the society who has celebrated his golden jubilee must agree to the use and disposition of the original building."

"That's an odd provision."

"Who knows what circumstances made it seem sensible at the time?"

"The Founder would know."

"Yes, of course."

"Odd."

"How many are still holding out over there?"

"I don't know." Faiblesse stood. "If the Founder dies, when he dies, they will have to elect a new superior of Porta Coeli."

"Not a very demanding post. The doctor and nurses run the place."

"Still, it must be done."

"That's your concern."

On the way home, Faiblesse brooded in the back seat, reviewing his conversation with Hoyt. It had been foolish to drop in on him, demeaning. How grand of Hoyt to concede him some functions as father superior of the society. The election of a new superior at Porta Coeli was his concern, meaning that it was unimportant. Was his resentment due to personal vanity alone? He knew that he should stand up to Hoyt, represent the society, not report to him as if Hoyt were the superior and he the subordinate. In bitter truth, that was their real relation, no matter his title and Hoyt's vow of obedience. Even the Founder had been reluctant to invoke the vow as reason for submission. That was the last card to be played. And, as between him and Hoyt, the bidding had hardly begun before he had thrown in his hand.

"That's a nice place out there, Father." Mr. Nickles's eyes were framed in the rear-view mirror. "That home for old priests."

"Isn't it, though?"

"It must be nice for you, knowing that you'll end up living there."

Gloom lifted with the prospect of a time when responsibility would be taken from his shoulders and he could retire to the peace and contentment of Porta Coeli. He more than shared Mr. Nickles's assessment of the place. To go there would mean the last remnant of ambition and vanity could be shed. What could the aspirations of an old man, a retired man, be, at least in this life? Life in Porta Coeli would be a continuous pleasant retreat, the distractions of the world set aside at last forever. And there would be the mild delight of reminiscing with congenial friends, recalling the old days, better days. An almost cherubic smile es-

117

tablished itself on Father Faiblesse's lips. How could anyone at Porta Coeli be really upset by outside events? The fate of Little Sem was, on the long view, the merest bagatelle.

Tumulty. He was a strange man, wanting to go on as before, struggling, arguing, winning. Didn't he realize that he was retired, out of the battle at last? Faiblesse wondered if Tumulty would still be living at Porta Coeli when he himself moved there. It was an unwelcome thought, but the alternative was ghoulish, callous in the manner of Hoyt.

"There was one old fellow feeding birds and squirrels. Right out of his hand. They landed on his shoulders, ran up his leg. Who was that saint?"

"Francis?"

"That's the one."

Faiblesse resumed his smile. He could see himself at Porta Coeli, awaiting his little brother death, at one with the world and God.

Mr. Nickles was thinking that with a knack like that, a person could tame wild animals and birds and sell them for pets. He would have to mention that if he ever saw that old priest again. Lots of people might be interested in having a redbird or even a bluejay rather than a common canary or parakeet. Imagine a robin in a cage. There would be real money in it. Of course one would keep it small. No sense in making it seem like work. Like Father Faiblesse in the seat behind him, Mr. Nickles was intrigued by the image of himself festooned with birds and other wildlife. Senior citizen tames forest, teaches squirrel to count to ten. A photograph of himself on the first page of the second section of the Fort Elbow *Tribune*. Does your wife help you in your work, Mr. Nickles? My wife? I'm afraid not. The poor woman is a cripple. Besides, she frightens the birds away. A regular scarecrow. Better not quote that, son. Mr. Nickles remembered the first priest, the one who had been unable to coax the squirrel to come. It was an unsettling thought that he himself might have that effect and Mrs. Nickles be a magnet attracting brightly plumed birds and frisky squirrels. Turning a corner, Mr. Nickles ran the rear wheel over the curb. They bumped into the street again and proceeded up Cavil Boulevard. In the back seat, Father Faiblesse had lurched out of his reverie and now wore his customary petrified expression as they drove.

Father Fogarty, dressed to go out, stopped Father Faiblesse on the stairs as he was going up to his room.

"How is the Founder?"

"Are you going out there?"

"Is there any point?"

"Perhaps not. He's in a coma."

Fogarty's face gave a preview of what it might look like when he grew old: his forehead wrinkled, his eyes went dim, the corners of his mouth sagged. But it was a professional response to another's sorrow, the priest at the wake or graveside, bringing a more transcendent comfort than the funeral director could provide.

"I'll remember him at Mass," Fogarty said. And then, because each member of the society prayed for the Founder at every Mass, added, "A special commemoration."

"Will you be back for dinner?"

"I'm afraid not. I accepted an invitation."

"Did you tell Mrs. Nickles?"

"Gosh, I forgot." Fogarty glanced at his watch; Faiblesse appreciated the expertness of the ploy. "Would you tell her, Father?"

Faiblesse said he would. Not that hearing this late would be of much help to the housekeeper. After he had telephoned Mrs. Nickles and received, as he had known he would, the information that she had already prepared a meal for three, Faiblesse wondered if there was anyone he could invite to dine with himself and Nobis on such late notice. Oliver Fleming would not have minded, but he was at Porta Coeli. Oder? Out of the question. Well, there were worse things than dining without Fogarty. Fogarty was one of the young.

Seated by a window, Faiblesse opened his breviary. The sounds of Cavil Boulevard came to him as from a great distance. This house was well insulated, comfortable, pleasant. He would miss it. Miss it? He smiled. His daydreaming on the drive back from Porta Coeli, looking ahead to retirement. He was not yet sixty-one and there was no mandatory age for retirement. He could continue in active life another six or seven years. A twinge of pain in his abdomen brought him back to the troubled present. His eyes dropped to the open book and he began to mumble Vespers. As he prayed, on the edge of his mind he thought of ways in which he could increase the endowment of Porta Coeli without arousing Fogarty's suspicions.

In the kitchen Mr. Nickles was telling his wife what a cushy life those old priests had out there, right on the edge of a lake. Retired, though what they were retired from he didn't know. Most of them probably hadn't lifted a hand in labor during their whole lives. Mrs. Nickles looked at him with a cold, contemptuous glance.

"Miriam," he said. "We ought to get a bird."

"A bird!"

"A pet. It would be nice having one, wouldn't it? Singing. Companionship."

"Hmph. I have enough birds to look out for as it is."

11

*I*N THE REFECTORY the elderly men sat at the long table with their guest, Oliver Fleming, placed in the chair at the head, Phelan at his right. Tumulty had drawn comfort from the fact that Noonan had not taken the opportunity of his selection as interim head of the house to usurp the Founder's chair. He had simply moved the prayer card to his usual place. Now they stood for a moment in silence until, automatically timed, electronically tolled, the six o'clock Angelus sounded. Noonan led them through the prayer and they sat, the scrape of their chairs a signal that brought waitresses streaming from the kitchen with trays.

Through the babble and the plunking sound of ice water being poured, Tumulty could hear Leo instructing Fleming on the impending fate of Little Sem.

"They cannot tear it down," Oliver said with finality.

"Just what the Founder would have said." Leo banged the table with his palm.

"Would have said? Wasn't he told?"

"Oh, they told him all right," Leo said. He added ominously, "Before his attack."

121

"Michael Tumulty was there when the Founder had his seizure," O'Leary interrupted, centering the attention of the table. "Isn't that so, Michael?"

Tumulty nodded. There was an unintelligible murmur from Harrington, whose wheelchair was pushed up to the table. Hadn't he been told of the Founder's illness?

O'Leary said, "He wants to know if it was serious."

"Of course it was serious. The man's in a coma."

"What exactly happened?"

O'Leary was a hypochondriac whose curiosity could be morbid. A hush had fallen over the table. They all leaned forward, even Leo Phelan.

"It seemed quite a serious seizure to me. The nurse says the future is uncertain." Tumulty addressed himself to Fleming. These were things the others knew, unless they had forgotten. "He had some difficulty breathing, then fell back on his pillow. I called Miss Bishop and she and Sister Diotima came on the run. They had no need of Leo or myself."

"Leo?" Father Garrity, on Tumulty's left, looked down the table at Phelan. "Were you there, too?"

"Of course I was there."

"Of course? You never mentioned it."

"Leo was talking to the Founder when I came into the room," Tumulty said. "What may very likely be the Founder's last words were addressed to him."

Phelan was both pleased and alarmed at the attention this brought him. He looked angrily at Tumulty but dismayingly it was Noonan who asked what the Founder had said.

"He was in a bad condition. Breathing badly, as Michael said. It was difficult to understand him."

"But what did he say?"

"I don't think it would be fair to repeat it," Leo said primly. Nothing could have been better calculated to fuel the curiosity of those at table.

"Fair?" Noonan was startled.

"Unless it was something personal, you must tell us what the Founder said." Garrity spoke calmly but it was clear that he would suffer no nonsense from Leo.

"Good Lord," Phelan cried. "It was nothing important. I had asked him a question." He looked brightly down the table, as if that might suffice. But he could see it would not do. Even Harrington seemed attentive.

"I asked him about Little Sem," Phelan said.

There were groans along the table. Garrity hushed them. "And what did he say?"

"The man was practically babbling. He didn't know what he was saying." He fell back in his chair. "Ask Tumulty if you want to know."

"What did he say, Michael?" Garrity asked.

Tumulty hesitated. He had hoped Leo would tell them. He felt again as he had beside the sickbed. The Founder's words were what he had hoped for and now poor Leo had given him an opportunity to broadcast them to the house. But it was Garrity he wanted to persuade. If Garrity should give his consent to the taking down of Little Sem, Tumulty was sure the others would follow. For decades Garrity had been the conscience of any community or house he lived in. His career in the society had not been brilliant but those in authority had always looked to Garrity for necessary support. It would not do to try to use the Founder's words as an emotional trump with Garrity.

"He was in obvious pain. His breathing had become a rattle. Just before the stroke he advised Leo to let go."

"Let go?"

"To sever all connections with the world."

Old heads nodded approval, Garrity's among them. He said, "And Little Sem?"

"He was speaking at the time of Little Sem. It is only a building, he said. Let it go. It doesn't matter."

Garrity nodded again, more deliberately. "Good advice," he said. He looked at Michael. "For all of us."

123

There were murmurs of agreement. Phelan's voice was heard. "It was only that. Advice. Not an order, not a matter of obedience."

"Is that true?" Garrity asked Tumulty.

"Yes, that's true. He spoke as a spiritual father but it was advice he gave."

Phelan approved this turn in the conversation. "They were the words of a saint," he said. "A holy man. I had told him that building was a shrine, his first achievement, a symbol of the society he had founded. He dismissed these suggestions. Out of humility." Phelan's voice trembled with interpretation. "He was too humble to want the building kept as a shrine to himself." Leo sat upright and glared at Tumulty. "But that does not mean we must share his judgment or be humble for him. What kind of loyalty would we show by tearing down what that great old man has built up?"

"Little Sem is *falling* down," Tumulty said patiently. "It is a hazard. Architects have made studies—"

"What architects?" Phelan wanted to know. "Hoyt's paid minions. We are treated like babies who can be put off by appeal to the opinion of nameless experts. I doubt that there ever was such a study. They want our consent. They need our consent. Well, they shall never have mine and that is enough to stop them."

The waitresses were putting plates before them and Phelan lost his audience. Not that he really needed to persuade. He was right. His opposition alone would suffice. For a moment, Tumulty wondered if even Garrity could convince Phelan to relent. He looked at his plate. Swiss steak. It was not a dish he cared for, but he ate it almost with gusto, as propitiation, as a prayer. Please God, let me be successful in gaining consent to the college building plan. Let me prove that I am still a leader, an achiever, a man of action.

At the far end of the table, Phelan was refusing his meal.

"But that is the menu, Father."

124

"I cannot eat it."

"Cook says it can be cut with a fork. It is not at all tough."

"Young lady, these are my own teeth. That is not the problem. I do not care for Swiss steak, tough or tender."

The girl took the dish away. Tumulty watched her exchange a look of exasperation with another waitress.

"We should have wine with our meals," Trask said.

"An excellent idea," Phelan agreed. He replaced the water glass he had picked up.

"An expensive idea," Garrity said. "It has never been the custom in the society to have wine with meals."

"It is the civilized way," Trask said. His eye rose to the wall as if seeking there the corroboration of vinous cathedral towns, monastic refectory tables laden with tankards, the alehouses of Western culture. "The Christian way," he said more boldly.

" 'At least I've always found it so,' " Huff quoted. " '*Benedicamus domino.*' "

"Christian Brothers brandy with our Wheaties," Tumulty murmured to Garrity. Garrity, perhaps thinking of Brother Felix, frowned.

"Perhaps we shall have wine with our meals," Phelan said brightly. "In the Noonan regime."

Tumulty felt that he had been housed with fools, senile fools. He shared the waitresses' estimate of his tablemates, and that included Oliver Fleming. Oliver was pledging to Leo his undying opposition to any plan to knock down Little Sem.

"I went to school there," he said querulously. "I love that old building."

Could he really love something that had long since outgrown its usefulness? Was Little Sem a metaphor of themselves? That could explain the opposition. This guess at latent motives made Tumulty feel vaguely superior to the others. Foolish old men. But Garrity was in the opposition, too, and Garrity was no fool.

12

"FATHER CULLEN is still in a coma, Alma says."

"I'm afraid so, Mrs. Bishop."

"Surely he won't come out of it alive? You should be thankful."

"I think I see what you mean," Father Tumulty said dubiously.

Mrs. Bishop sighed. "It is a cruel thing to grow old, Father. A cruel thing."

"Well, as the saying is, consider the alternative." They seemed to be trading the wrong kind of consolation.

"Father Cullen lived a long, useful life. Founding the society, the college, so much. I envy the accomplishments he can carry with him into the next world."

"Not everyone is so appreciative of what he has done." To his own surprise, Tumulty heard something of Phelan's plaintive tone in his voice. It was a hazard of living at Porta Coeli; one came to regard the young as ignorant of what had gone before and made the present possible. Not a good line to take with Mrs. Bishop if he was to do Alma any good.

Before coming on this visit to Mrs. Bishop, Father Tumulty

126

had tried to smoke out Dowling's intentions, but without much success. The man had a photograph of his dead wife on his desk still and, though it was all but buried under papers and cartons and other medical debris, it seemed a bad sign. The woman had been dead for over a year. It was not that Dowling looked to be the morbid sort; if anything, he was far too blasé about the difference between the quick and the dead. And he insisted on quizzing Father Tumulty about his own health. Did he have trouble keeping food down, did he have sharp pains in his abdomen, did he find himself weary before the day began?

"I have never felt better in my life," Tumulty assured him.

"Your superior is concerned about it."

"My superior!" Whom would Dowling mean? Good God, was Noonan spreading the rumor that he was ill?

"Father Faiblesse. You must let me take some tests."

"For what? I assure you I am in perfect health."

Dowling's brows rose. Clearly perfect health was a mythical state to one in his line of work. "You are being foolish, Father."

"When did Father Faiblesse say that I was ill?"

Dowling's face assumed an expression of exaggerated prudence. "I hope you won't mention this to him. He was careful not to mention your name."

"Then what makes you think he was speaking of me?"

"I put two and two together."

Tumulty stared at the merry mask of wisdom Dowling now put on. What in the name of God did Alma Bishop see in this man? Ah, the harbors into which loneliness drives people. He turned the conversation to Dowling's children. Dowling said that they were thriving. He unearthed another photograph from his desktop, as if to remind himself of what his offspring looked like.

"They should have a mother."

"They do."

"I mean now, to look after them."

"I tell them their mother is looking after them. Up there." Dowling's eyes contemplated the ceiling.

"Of course. Are you afraid that she would disapprove if you married again?"

"Father, even if I were inclined to marry again, and I'm not, I am too busy to go courting."

"Perhaps you needn't go far."

"What do you mean?"

"Doctors and nurses," Tumulty mused. "It's an old story, isn't it?"

Dowling grew angry. "Libel. Filthy talk. Don't you believe that stuff, Father. Take my word for it, a hospital is more like a monastery than a bordello."

"I meant more permanent unions. Doctors do marry nurses, don't they?"

"If they're crazy they do. Nurses have a way of poking their noses into your practice, prescribing on the phone, that sort of thing. You wouldn't believe some of the stories. I knew a man whose wife kept certain patients from him, dealing with them herself, forging his name on prescription blanks. A nurse knows just enough medicine to do real harm. This woman would have operated if she could have gotten away with it. As it was, she delivered half a dozen babies on the excuse that her husband was busy. He was home in bed. Of course she knew how to order interns around." Dowling's ceiling-seeking gaze displayed the whites of his eyes.

"Surely that is a unique case."

"Ha."

Tumulty stood. "Well, thank God we have Sister Diotima here."

"A wonderful woman. It's amazing how she has kept up."

"And Alma Bishop."

"How old is Sister Diotima?"

"Nearly three times Alma's age."

"How old is that?"

"Well, how old would you say Alma is?"

"I'm never sure with fat women."

128

Tumulty fled. Did Alma have a ghost of a chance with Dowling? It was difficult to wish that she did. In any case, she must be freed from the clutches of her possessive mother.

"Sometimes I think you priests and nuns had the right idea," Mrs. Bishop said to him now.

"How do you mean?"

"Children are ingrates. They have no idea what parents went through for them." Mrs. Bishop made an unconvincing gesture of resignation. "I won't bother you with my troubles, Father."

"Thank God for Alma, Mrs. Bishop."

She looked at him for a moment. "Perhaps you know a different Alma than I do."

"She is a dedicated nurse. Almost too dedicated. She should have a life of her own."

"A life of her own! She *has* a life of her own. And she does not have to work as a nurse. If she must be a nurse, I am patient enough for her."

They were seated on a balcony overlooking an artificial lake around which were grouped the condominiums of Shively Court. A brace of ducks drifted on the untroubled surface of the water. It was pleasant and restful. Father Tumulty drew Mrs. Bishop's attention to the view, to the weather, to the world outside herself.

"Yes," she said. "It is lovely."

"How long have you lived here?"

For a moment she seemed not to understand. "Oh, you mean in this apartment. I was one of the first occupants."

Father Tumulty could not remember when these buildings had gone up and studying the dappled brick wall behind Mrs. Bishop did not help. The bricks had a distressed used look to them, doubtless baked in when they were made, age feigned, an ersatz oldness. These buildings would have crumbled before they reached the age those bricks suggested.

"It was foolish to put up three-story buildings without elevators." The Bishop apartment was on the third floor of its building. "I feel stranded up here, like a plane circling an airport."

Mrs. Bishop did not look stranded. Small-boned, weightless, she sat like a little stick figure in her chair as if the only significance of her body was to support the iron will within it.

"You must let Alma go, Mrs. Bishop. She has to lead her own life."

"Has she complained of me to you?"

"You know her better than that."

"I know her inside and out, Father Tumulty."

"Young men are interested in her." After a conscientious caesura, he added, "There is a Dr. Dowling at Porta Coeli."

"A doctor," Mrs. Bishop said, and snorted.

"Alma is a nurse."

"Against my wishes. She said she wanted to help people. People! I'm people, too, Father Tumulty. Does it only count when the help is given to strangers?"

It occurred to Father Tumulty that he would be one of the strangers Mrs. Bishop meant, he and the Founder and the rest of them. He said, "Alma should have her own apartment."

Mrs. Bishop was shocked. "She is a single girl, Father. She still has a family." Tears started up in Mrs. Bishop's eyes, genuine tears. "I mean she still has me."

"She has been a good daughter to you."

"And have I been such a terrible mother?"

"We are old, Mrs. Bishop."

The plural helped, establishing a kinship between them as they sat in the sun staring down at the manmade lake and its pair of ducks trailing rippling vectors over the water. Fifteen, twenty years Mrs. Bishop's senior, Father Tumulty felt much younger than this self-centered woman whose purpose in life had come down to squelching her only child. What did she gain from her unwillingness to let Alma go? How silly and unseemly the purposes of mankind seemed that sunny afternoon. Father Tumulty felt a personal moral move toward him over the water, as accusative as those quacking ducks.

130

"Can't she wait?" Mrs. Bishop asked softly. "It won't be long."

"It has been far too long already. How old is she?"

Mrs. Bishop had to think. "Only thirty-four."

"And how old were you when you married?"

"Twenty. I had just turned twenty." The memory softened her. She closed her eyes and spoke as if in a trance. "Mr. and Mrs. Oscar Shively announce the marriage of their daughter Florence—"

"Shively?"

Mrs. Bishop's eyes opened. "Yes. My maiden name."

"Oscar Shively?"

"My father."

"And this is Shively Court."

She followed his gesture, looking out over the railing of the balcony. "I can remember when this was pasture, Father. That lake was just a little swampy thing in those days, full of reeds and sword grass. Real ducks, wild ducks, lived on it."

"Your father donated the land on which Saint Brendan's College stands."

"I know."

"He is our principal benefactor. We pray for him daily. He is buried in the chapel of Little Sem."

Mrs. Bishop nodded, not really interested. She did not gauge her father's importance by such criteria as those. She did say that she was glad that the society remembered her father's generosity. "It is a virtue others might learn."

"And Alma is an only child?"

"I was lucky to have her. It seemed that I would never have a child at all. Years passed. It was awful." She peered at him. "Did you know my husband?"

"No, I didn't."

"He is still alive."

"I see."

"He deserted me."

131

For the first time Tumulty felt pity for her. Bishop, Bishop. He was sure he had not known the man. That he might have wished to escape from Mrs. Bishop was not difficult to imagine, perhaps, but to leave his child as well . . .

"Alma never told me."

"I doubt that she even remembers him."

It was one of those minor tragedies that have a way of emerging whenever a priest spoke to the laity. Father Tumulty's thoughts went suddenly and without warning to his own family. His father and mother, long since dead, his brothers and sisters scattered about the country, grandparents themselves now with multiple progeny, names on Christmas cards, little more. Of course he remembered them all in his prayers, calling the roll of the names, but if any images came to him they were of long ago, of a frame house in south Minneapolis, the grass in the yard trampled bare, kids everywhere, neighbors, his brothers and sisters. How happy it seemed. Both his parents had been blessed with happy deaths. Quick, painless, at least relatively so, attended by the rites of the Church. God rest their souls. He should have known that Mrs. Bishop would take on dimensions when he visited her. A grass widow, a poor little rich girl, a mother after years of anxiety and then abandoned by her husband. No wonder she clung to Alma now. And to think that she was actually Oscar Shively's daughter.

Father Tumulty moved his chair out of sunlight and into shadow, closer to Mrs. Bishop. Not only had she ceased to seem a spoiled old woman, she now spelled potential trouble. Think of what Leo Phelan would try to do if he knew that Oscar Shively's daughter lived within binocular range of Saint Brendan's College. How easily she might be maneuvered into thinking that Hoyt was threatening to desecrate her father's grave. What provisions had been made for the transfer of the tomb? Instructed in the plain facts of the matter, unvarnished, uninterpreted, a simple statement of what was at issue, she might become as outraged as Phelan. Mrs. Bishop's large-knuckled hands gripped the arms of her chair as she stared unseeing over the lake. A will of steel there that could be turned against Hoyt as it had been turned against Alma's desire to have a life of her own. Phelan must never learn that she was living here. Excited by a tingle of dread, Father Tumulty wondered what Garrity would do if he learned of Oscar Shively's daughter. His own eyes drifted over the balcony railing and, staring at a swaying cottonweed, he was lulled into a pensive mood. Garrity. The time drew near when he must play what he hoped would be his decisive card, gaining Garrity's acquiescence to the destruction of Little Sem. That was a small price to pay to gain Michael Tumulty's release from Porta Coeli and return to a position from which he could influence Hoyt and help preserve the original conception of the Society of Saint Brendan. He was certain this approach would win Garrity over. And he would present the plan in all sincerity. Hoyt was a missile hurtling aimlessly into the future, insensible to the good of the society. That energy had to be harnessed as it had been harnessed while Michael Tumulty was president of the college.

"Will you talk to Alma, Father?"

"Talk to her?"

" 'Honor thy father and mother,' " Mrs. Bishop quoted.

"I came to talk to you."

"And I appreciate it, Father. Not everyone would understand."

And that, he thought while he went down the three flights of stairs to the street, was all too true. To understand all is to forgive all. Alma would have to be more decisive but in such a way as to spare her mother's feelings. He sighed. Her task seemed scarcely more difficult than the one he had set himself: to persuade Garrity that the only way to control Hoyt was temporarily to give the man his head.

13

FLAMINGO HAD INSISTED that they drive his car over to the campus to take a look at Little Sem. Phelan offered to let Oliver use his binoculars and was rebuffed.

"I want to *see* the place. Last night, in bed, I thought how long it had been."

"You often visited me in my room there."

"But that was on the first floor. What are the upper floors like now?"

"All changed. That building has been used for so many things."

"What happened to the dormitories?"

Dormitories. How long had it been since the third floor had been four huge dormitories, one for each year of the high school? Partitions had later turned them into classrooms. He explained this to Flamingo, to no avail. Oliver wanted to see for himself. On the drive over, Phelan wondered if this trip was a mistake. If Little Sem no longer looked like the building Flamingo remembered, would he still be as indignant about its being torn down?

"When are you going to talk to Father Hoyt, Oliver?"

"I tried to call him twice. They told me he wasn't in. Don't worry, I'll add my veto to yours."

They parked the car behind the building and then walked around to the side in order to examine the wrecking apparatus standing there. The huge angled arm of the crane rose higher than the roof of Little Sem; from it hung a cable and the wrecking ball. Phelan stopped and tugged at the bill of his cap. No need to say anything. This engine of destruction was eloquent in itself. Flamingo, bless his heart, walked up to the monster and disdainfully kicked a tire. The tire stood higher than he did and its treads were inches deep. Seen this close, the wrecker was intimidating, seemingly unstoppable. They walked silently around to the front of the building.

The next hour and a half was almost maudlin. Flamingo began before they entered the building, pausing on the front walk to survey the great wooden porch that ran along the front of the building. He remembered standing on that porch at the age of thirteen, feeling homesick and afraid. He had worried that he would not make any friends among the other new boys.

"You had lots of friends," Phelan said.

"And here I am now." Oliver's voice choked.

"Let's go inside."

"All right, all right."

The main hall on the first floor was dusty and deserted. Where pictures had hung there were now only rectangles paler than the rest of the plaster. The doors had been removed from their hinges. In what had been the Founder's rooms, someone had turned up a corner of the carpet for reasons neither could guess. The windows had not been removed and they were closed. The building was hot and airless and Flamingo recalled the uncomfortable heat of early autumn and of May before the school year ended.

"We had air conditioners in our rooms in recent years."

135

But there was no sign of an air conditioner having been installed in any of the windows in the Founder's rooms.

"I thought he had one," Phelan said. "Apparently not."

Above the first floor it was dirtier still. Bolls of dust blew across the linoleum, the stair treads were gritty with sand, the heat increased. Flamingo bounced up the stairs as if he were a boy again. Following, bent over, his binoculars dangling from his neck, Phelan marveled at Flamingo's sentimentality. His own was such a familiar companion that surprise was out of the question, but Flamingo had been expelled from this school, he had lived a full and successful life; there seemed little reason for his nostalgia, or at least for the degree of it. Indeed, confronted by an attachment to this old building that rivaled his own, Phelan saw it as he had not before. Little Sem was very old, there was no doubt of that. The odd smell of the place was not sufficiently explained by its being closed up and the weather warm. There was the odor of decay and rot. The banister wobbled under his hand; the glue where it was joined had dried and flaked away. It had become a hazard rather than a help. Phelan stopped and looked over the railing, down the curved drop to the basement, lost in shadow below. Of course saving Little Sem did not mean preserving it as it was. The place needed repairs, but the job could be done for far less than the cost of tearing it down; he was sure of that.

His confidence in that estimate wavered when they reached the third floor. The walls that had been put up to make classrooms were of some pulpy material. One could dig holes in it easily with the fingernail, as hundreds of students had proved to themselves. The blackboards were gone and the bulbs had been removed from the light sockets. Not much had been considered salvageable and it was difficult to disagree. Flamingo chattered on merrily, his mind flying back over the decades, trying to recall how the dormitories had been laid out; one had only to seek for permanent walls. The hallway had once been the

136

center aisle of the sophomore dormitory. Flamingo located the spot where his bed had stood.

"My locker was right there." He pointed at a wall filled with penciled slogans Phelan could not quite make out. When he went up to the wall and read, he scowled and turned his back on it, shielding Flamingo's eyes from the graffiti. It was incredible how filthy-minded young college men were. Every summer in recent years they had had to sand down the tops of student desks to rid them of lubricous messages and the sketches of genitals with which bored scholars whiled away the lectures.

Flamingo had gone in search of the place where the student prefect's bed had stood. It took him into another classroom. Phelan stayed where he was. He was tired. Those stairs had always been a steep climb. Flamingo's reedy voice came to him, unimpeded by the flimsy wall separating them. "Here it is. I am sure this is where it was."

Depressed, Phelan went to join him. The scene of the past had altered beyond recognition. He thought of the unearthed forum in Rome. What would Caesar or Cicero make of that mile of rubble? The only constants seemed spatial coordinates, longitude and latitude, imaginary gridded nets wound round the globe. If Little Sem were knocked to the ground, the space it had occupied would remain forever. Phelan shook the thought away. That was not permanence enough. This building was a symbol.

Oliver stood trancelike, lost in the past. "Have I ever told you my real grudge against Michael Tumulty?"

"He has given you much cause for concern, I know that."

"No. This was personal. I once asked him to include my name on the roster of alumni of Saint Brendan's. Not the college, the seminary. After all, I did go here."

"Yes."

"He refused."

137

Phelan shook his head, but his sympathy was false. Of course Tumulty had been perfectly right. Only the ordained were considered alumni of the seminary. Those who left were in their way nonpersons.

"I threatened to go over his head."

"To the Founder?"

"Yes."

"But you didn't."

"I still may. I still may."

Before they started down again, they sat on the stairs. Phelan was really bushed, his mind abuzz; his legs ached. He wished he were back in his cool and pleasant room in Porta Coeli. Flamingo was babbling about events of long ago, of a walk around the lake, something about a canoe. The musty air seemed to have filled Phelan's lungs; he felt that if he inhaled deeply he would surely sneeze and he had a dread of sneezing. Once he had dreamed of losing his soul and the life it gave him by sneezing too violently. Flamingo's talk had shifted inexplicably to his wife. Phelan had never liked listening to husbands complain about their wives or wives about their husbands. He was prepared to believe that spouses were as annoying as they were claimed to be, but he did not like the unstated implication that his own life was free of such petty vexations. The married had no idea how difficult it could be to live in a religious community, no matter the vows and motivation. And after all, marriage is a sacrament; a man and wife had supernatural aids which should help in overlooking the shortcomings of the other. Perfect love can make it a joy. Words from the marriage ceremony.

"She is the girl in the orange canoe," Oliver said. He had put his hand on Phelan's arm.

"What?"

"Enid. She is the girl in the orange canoe."

"What are you talking about?"

138

"Surely you remember. We were walking around the lake. It was spring. You and I and Rush."

"Rush is dead."

"I know Rush is dead. That isn't the point. That girl we met. She is Enid."

"I don't remember."

"Of course you remember! She had a canoe. An orange canoe. I can see it as plainly as if it were right here before us. We stopped and talked."

Phelan tried to summon the memory but could not. Flamingo became quite angry. He rose and thumped down the stairs in silence. In the car he sat behind the wheel, his hands on it, as if he were trying to push it away from him.

"Enid," he said, his tone insistent. "My wife. She is the girl in the orange canoe."

Phelan nodded in pretended comprehension.

"I married her."

"A very touching story."

It was not the right thing to say. Flamingo glared at him, started the motor and drove recklessly back to Porta Coeli.

14

*T*UMULTY'S INTENDED TACTIC with Garrity was to
convince the other priest that, by allowing Tumulty to secure the
agreement of the house to the destruction of Little Sem, he
himself would be reassigned and would then be in a stronger
position to affect if not control the future acts of the head-
strong young president of the college. Would Garrity be per-
suaded of the feasibility of the plan? The importance of the
move was such—lose Garrity and all was lost—that Tumulty reviewed it many times in his mind, plotted it out, imagined the
conversational exchange in which he would carry the day, and
did not act. In anticipating what Garrity would say, however,
he found doubt begin to nibble at his soul. It was not simply
that if his future ability to influence Hoyt was questioned he
could not guarantee the malleability of the president. That was
admittedly chancy, as all future events are. The real trouble
was that Tumulty began to wonder if he did indeed want to be
the instrument of Hoyt's success on the matter of Little Sem
itself.

He was not overcome by nostalgia or sentiment. The sight

140

of that old building did not stir his pulse or bring back memories too sweet to bear. For every golden moment in the past there was at least one balancing leaden one to be summoned from memory. Nonetheless, it was a building in which he had lived as a boy and worked as a man, it was, as he heard a dozen times a day, not merely brick and mortar but a symbol. And a symbol of what? Of the Society of Saint Brendan. It was there that they had all been schooled by the Founder in the ideals of the society, there that first fervor had been cultivated, directed, shaped beyond the desire for personal triumph and success. Had he not fallen far from that ideal, not only in much of his active life, where it was the career of Michael Tumulty that had been paramount, but now, in recent months, in the twilight of his life? Worse, did not his eagerness to get out of Porta Coeli bespeak a self-assertion that contradicted the spirit of obedience? What pride it was to think —and in his heart of hearts he really believed this—that the very future of the society depended on his deeds. Learn a lesson from the Founder, Michael, he instructed himself. Allow the young to carry on. No matter that you may be too conscious of their mistakes. Their actions were often good ones and, in any case, the issue was in the hands of God.

This salutary thought subtly became its own kind of temptation. Sit tight and let Hoyt and Faiblesse bring the society to ruin. Say nothing, do not lift a hand, enjoy the apocalypse. *Après moi le déluge.* Such were the thoughts that insinuated themselves into Michael Tumulty's mind and it was all too convenient to have Garrity's principled doubts with which to disguise these less than noble sentiments. It was possible, he found, to look across the lake at Little Sem and the destructive crane beside it and wish for the work to begin. Reduced to rubble, that symbol of the spirit of the society would be a judgment on Hoyt and, less directly, on Faiblesse. Let them bear the responsibility for it. When he became conscious of such thoughts and repudiated them, he decided once more to be the whole-

141

hearted agent of Hoyt's project, but was not that simply another and worse temptation? Reflection became a tennis match he could not win and he sat one day despondent on a bench, looking at the lake and seeing nothing. What should he do? What did God want him to do?

Praying for light had always in the past been a search for further justification of what he already intended to do, a matter of seeing his own will as one with God's. Now he found himself genuinely confused. No matter what he did, aided Hoyt or remained inactive, he would be acting badly. It was a dilemma he did not welcome. He had never understood those who spoke with seeming pleasure of anxiety and doubt and ambiguity. Michael Tumulty liked things clear and they had become bewilderingly confused.

"Having long thoughts?" It was Garrity.

"That is the province of youth," Tumulty said, covering his first reaction at having been discovered in the doldrums. "Sit down."

Garrity sat, sighing as he did so. "Well, I see that Little Sem still stands."

"Yes."

"Is that why you are sad?"

A flash of pique was gone as soon as it came. Garrity was not taunting him. "No."

"This has become a foolish business."

"I know. I have been wondering how I might end it by persuading you to give your consent."

"It is odd to have become important again. I don't mean personally. Any one of us can stop Hoyt in his tracks."

"If you agreed, the matter would be settled."

"Oh, I doubt that, Michael. But how were you going to persuade me?"

"My trouble is I'm not sure that I want to."

"Perhaps you should try. I do not enjoy being intransigent. The more I think of this opposition, the more unsavory it

142

seems. A group of old men asserting themselves. We are like children, stamping our feet at the weather."

"Father Hoyt is not a natural force. He is simply a man with ideas that may be right or wrong."

"It is not a crime to wish to replace an old building with a new one."

"If only it were that simple."

"The only thing that makes it complex is that document Father Corcoran turned up. I wonder if there would have been any lasting rancor here if we had simply looked across the lake one day to find Little Sem no longer there."

"And I wonder if Oscar Shively is resting peacefully through all this turmoil."

"Oscar Shively?"

"The man to whom the Founder gave the assurance. He is buried in the chapel of Little Sem."

Garrity's eyes narrowed in recollection and then that rectangular slab in the middle aisle of the chapel took shape before his mind's eye. "Surely the body will be moved."

"Of course. Before the wrecking begins."

"If Oscar were still alive, I doubt that he would smile on Father Hoyt's project. I doubt that he smiles at it now. Not that he can do much about it from where he is. Did he have a family?"

Tumulty hesitated only a moment. "Yes."

"I wonder if Father Hoyt has consulted them."

"No."

"You're sure?"

"I'm sure his daughter would have mentioned it if she knew."

"Then you've talked with her?" Garrity was truly surprised.

Tumulty settled back on the bench, enjoying this turn in the conversation and not certain why. Partly, of course, it was the usual pleasure at being the repository of information of a more or less arcane kind. But partly, too, he sensed that it was

143

a dangerous thing to put such information in the hands of an opponent of Hoyt. If it had been anyone other than Garrity he would have remained silent, but he was sure that Garrity could be trusted with the knowledge that Oscar Shively had living heirs. So he told Garrity about Mrs. Bishop, garnished the tale by mentioning that Oscar Shively's granddaughter was a nurse at Porta Coeli. Garrity nodded through the tale, interested enough but not really excited by it.

"I suppose it is arguable that a promise to Shively does not amount to a promise to his heirs."

"The promise was to Shively himself."

"I must say I don't like the idea of breaking that promise, Michael."

"Is it clear that it would be broken? He continues to be commemorated in our Masses, along with our other benefactors. That is what was promised to him."

"Wasn't the place of burial mentioned in that document Corcoran found?"

"Yes."

Tumulty felt a strange buoyancy, almost a kind of innocence. He need not have told Garrity this but, having done so, having put what could conceivably be a powerful weapon in Garrity's hands, he had the strange sense that he had delivered the whole thing into the hands of providence. Whatever Garrity did now was acceptable to him. He had been freed from his dilemma by this unlooked-for conversation.

"You must tell me how you mean to persuade me to agree to the taking down of Little Sem."

That easily Garrity seemed to put the heirs of Oscar Shively from his mind. So be it. Tumulty felt carried along by the drift of this exchange. He told Garrity of the terms of his agreement to help Hoyt. If his success meant the tearing down of Little Sem, it also meant his release from Porta Coeli and an opportunity to exercise a restraining influence on Hoyt.

"You're that anxious to leave this house?"

"Yes."

"You've earned the right to a rest, Michael."

"I have no wish to rest."

"No. You're younger than your years. There is still much that you could do."

"Hoyt would be indebted to me for clearing his way on this. I know him. I have known him well for years."

"And then he turned against you."

"What do you mean?"

"It doesn't matter. I believe you could be a good influence on him. Yes. It is a good argument, Michael."

Tumulty waited. Should he press now for Garrity's agreement? He was so close to getting that agreement that he could almost hear the words issuing from Garrity's mouth. Go ahead, Michael. I give my consent. But they sat in silence, under the constant rattling whisper of the leaves above their heads. Finally Garrity said, musingly, "Yes, it is a good argument. Let me think about it."

"I only wish that Father Hoyt were a patient man."

"I won't keep you waiting long."

Garrity stood and looked intently across at Little Sem. "I had forgotten that tomb in chapel. Imagine, all those years of walking across the mortal remains of Oscar Shively. It doesn't seem respectful."

Tumulty got to his feet, too. "It's what Oscar wanted."

"He must have been a strange man. What is his family like?"

"Well, you know Miss Bishop."

And when they went inside, Alma Bishop was visible in the hallway near the nurses' station. Garrity, with a faint smile on his face, walked toward her and Tumulty went along. She turned as they came up and Garrity took her hand ceremoniously.

"I had no idea you had such distinguished forebears."

145

"Neither did I. Who do you mean, Adam and Eve?"

"The granddaughter of Oscar Shively." Garrity might have been a butler announcing a guest.

"Does that make me distinguished?"

"In the Society of Saint Brendan it does. He was one of our first and most generous benefactors. He gave us the land across the lake."

Alma's eyes crossed and she exhaled impatiently. "Believe me, I am fully aware of that. My mother likes to calculate how much it would be worth now."

"I suppose you have visited your grandfather's grave?"

"No. I don't even know where it is."

"Surely your mother knows. It is in the chapel of the first building Father Cullen put up. In the middle aisle."

"Mother never told me that. I must go see it."

"Perhaps you shouldn't put it off too long."

"Why?"

"The building is the one we call Little Sem. There is some thought of taking it down."

Did Tumulty hear a sound behind them or was it only some psychic perception that caused him to turn and see Noonan standing there, listening to the exchange between Garrity and Alma Bishop? There was no question that Noonan understood the import of what was being said. His head was tipped back and he greeted Tumulty with a lidded look. Garrity, too, became aware of Noonan and a pained expression came over his face.

Noonan said, "I have been taking a look at Father Cullen. He seems unchanged."

"That's true," Alma said. She had no idea of the discomfort of Tumulty and Garrity.

Noonan, his head still tipped back, moved off down the hallway, perhaps on his way to spread this interesting news among his cohorts. Good God, when Leo Phelan got hold of this!

"I'm terribly sorry, Michael," Garrity said. "I had no idea he was there."

"It's not your fault."

"I had no right to babble like that."

"Is something wrong?" Alma asked.

They assured her that nothing was wrong and succeeded in rousing her apprehension. It would have done no good to explain. All too likely she would be hearing from others about her grandfather Oscar Shively.

Tumulty and Garrity walked slowly back to the residence wing and, before they parted, Garrity put his hand on Tumulty's arm. "I am sorry, Michael. I needn't tell you that Noonan may well make mischief with this."

"There was no way you could know that he was there."

"My agreement, Michael. My consent. You have it. I agree to the destruction of Little Sem."

"No. I don't want you to decide like this."

"I have decided. You have my agreement."

Tumulty nodded. It would have been insulting in the circumstances to thank Garrity. Moreover, the victory might very well be Pyrrhic. Now that others knew of Oscar Shively's heirs, it was no longer certain that Garrity's agreement would carry the house. He was conscious of Garrity's eyes on him when he continued to his room.

15

AFTER THEIR RETURN from Little Sem, Phelan accompanied Oliver to the guest room and left him there. The truth was that Oliver more or less sent him packing. Ah, well, allowances must be made for age. Running up and down the stairs at Little Sem had no doubt tired him. For that matter, Phelan himself was exhausted. He went to his own room, where he lay on the bed, arranged his binoculars carefully on his chest and fell asleep.

Half an hour later he awoke fresh as a daisy and bounded from the bed. There was work to do. Going in pursuit of Noonan, he met him in the hallway. Noonan wore a self-satisfied smile that was the twin of the one that Phelan smiled.

"We have an ally," Phelan announced.

"Oh?" Noonan seemed to be speaking from some eminence. "And who would that be?"

"Flamingo. I took him over to Little Sem. You should have seen the man, Noonan. He was overcome by emotion. He loves that building. He is enraged at the thought of its being torn down."

"Then why did he agree to it?" Noonan asked sweetly.

They had reached Noonan's door. Phelan pushed through after Noonan. He did not want a repetition of the rebuff from Oliver. Noonan took a bottle from beneath his shirts and suggested that Phelan get glasses from the bathroom.

"What do you mean, agree? Oliver Fleming would never agree to the destruction of Little Sem."

"He is a trustee."

Phelan stopped. That was true. He looked at Noonan. "You don't think that Hoyt actually asked permission of the trustees, do you?"

"He says he did."

"Ha."

"I am sure he did. But more or less in the manner he used with us before we learned of that document from Corcoran. I am sure Oliver Fleming didn't realize what he was agreeing to."

"Oliver said he never heard of the project."

"I can believe that, too."

Such condescension toward his old friend annoyed Phelan. He got the glasses from the bathroom. Noonan poured their drinks and Phelan found his own niggardly. The elation with which he had come to tell of Flamingo's promise to read the riot act to Hoyt had fled before Noonan's incomprehensible attitude. Noonan seemed determined to regard bad news as good. What earthly satisfaction could he take from the thought that Hoyt might have wormed an agreement from the trustees without their knowing it?

"Cheers," Noonan said, and he actually sounded cheerful.

"You're happy."

"Well, you bring good news. We are fortunate to have Oliver Fleming as our ally."

"He is a good man, Noonan."

"Indeed he is." Noonan drank. Phelan felt completely deflated. "You should have brought Oliver along for a drink, Leo."

149

"I'll go get him."

"Wait. I don't want to distract him. He's here on retreat, isn't he?"

"An informal one."

"I never knew him well."

"He admires you, Noonan."

"Whatever for?"

Phelan thought for a moment. "Because you are a priest. He has a tremendous respect for those of us in holy orders. That is a rarity in laymen today, as you well know. That is why he built this place for us, that is why he likes to visit here."

"The guest room is nice."

"He likes the spiritual atmosphere, Noonan. It reminds him of when we were boys together. And of course he remembers you as head prefect."

"Doesn't he have a wife?"

"Of course he has a wife."

"I simply asked. Have you met Mrs. Fleming?"

Phelan nodded. There was no need to say that he did not particularly care for Enid Fleming. If Oliver showed an exaggerated respect for the clergy, she more than balanced it with her undisguised contempt. She doubtless thought all priests were trying to pry money out of Oliver.

Noonan put down his drink and, standing beside his desk, looked contentedly at Phelan. "Leo, I have solved our problem."

"Have you now?"

"I have. The man to whom the Founder made the promise that gives us veto power was Oscar Shively. You didn't know his name? Well, that is it. Up to this point, we have taken great comfort from our ability to veto Hoyt. But think about it, Leo. Hoyt has shown remarkable patience, and he is not a patient man. Within days, perhaps even tomorrow, he will just go ahead, with or without our consent."

"But he can't do that."

"Who would stop him? Leo, think of it. Can he really fear a houseful of old men? The paper Corcoran found put him off balance, the Founder's stroke prolonged the delay, but take my word for it: he will go ahead whether or not we agree."

"But we could sue him."

"Yes, we could. And we would all be dead before the courts settled the matter. In the meantime, Little Sem would have been swept away and a new building put in its place."

Of course Noonan was right. That is precisely what Hoyt would do. It was a cause for wonderment that he had delayed this long. But why in the name of God was Noonan so calm about it?

"I refuse to give in," Phelan cried. "You may be a fatalist, but I am not. It is possible to stop him." He paused and groped for a word. "Injunction. We can get an injunction."

"Good idea. But fortunately I think it won't be necessary."

Phelan stared at him. "You said you had a solution. Is this what you meant, giving up?"

"Not at all, Leo. I had recalled the name of Oscar Shively. It has just come to my attention that his daughter and grand-daughter are alive. I have reason to believe that they will be shocked to learn of the proposed desecration of their father's grave and the society's unilateral dismissal of its solemn obligation to his memory."

Phelan sat down on the bed. A grudging grin of admiration lifted the rounds of his cheeks, narrowing his eyes. Good old Noonan. Good old Noonan. How could he have doubted him? The man had not been head prefect for nothing.

"How did you learn this?"

Noonan pulled out the desk chair and placed one foot on it. "It doesn't matter. Leo, I'm putting you in charge of this. Go immediately to Miss Bishop and find out how you can contact her mother. You must see the mother today if possible."

"Miss Bishop?"

151

"Oscar Shively's granddaughter. Ask Alma to come see me. You will know what to say to the mother. Do you have money enough for a cab?"

Phelan got off the bed. "I'll ask Oliver to drive me. He will be delighted to have a hand in this."

Noonan agreed. Phelan went immediately to the guest room and knocked on the door. There was no answer. He knocked again. Oliver would never forgive him if he allowed his old friend to sleep through this. Phelan opened the door and saw that the sitting room was empty. So was the bedroom. He tapped on the closed door of the bathroom.

"Are you in there, Oliver?"

No answer. Phelan put his ear to the door and listened. He opened the door. Nothing. Where in the devil had Oliver gone?

When he came out of the guest suite, Phelan was unsure whether he should go first to Miss Bishop or find Oliver. He looked into the recreation room, then wandered outside. He came upon Ucello, surrounded by a cloud of birds. Flamingo's car was no longer parked behind the building. He turned to Ucello.

"Have you seen Oliver Fleming?"

"He drove away a few minutes ago."

I have offended him, Phelan thought. But how? He went to his room, sat on the bed and recalled the afternoon with Flamingo. There had been something at Little Sem when they were sitting on the stairs, something about Oliver's wife. Phelan removed his baseball cap and massaged his temples. The girl in the orange canoe. Oliver had married her. What nonsense. Apparently it meant something to Oliver. How angry he had been when Phelan said that he did not remember the girl. He searched his memory now, in vain. He should have encouraged Flamingo to go on, to tell him more about this girl and her orange canoe. It would not do to have him angry. Had Oliver remembered to call Father Hoyt and add his voice of protest to the wrecking of Little Sem? Phelan put on his cap and checked the parking lot again. Could Oliver have cut his visit short and gone home? Phelan went back to the guest suite and saw no baggage there. He picked up the phone.

"Yes?" It was a woman's voice, weak, remote.

"Mrs. Fleming, is Oliver there? This is Father Phelan calling."

"Has he started home?"

"I cannot find him here in the house." Phelan cleared his throat, then chuckled. "We had a nice conversation about you today."

"Father Phelan, I do not feel well."

"I'm sorry to hear that. Oliver tells me that you are the girl in the orange canoe."

"The what?"

Phelan chuckled again. "The orange canoe. Oliver told me all about it."

"I don't understand."

Phelan was confused. Perhaps Oliver had not said that he had married the girl in the orange canoe. Had he been lamenting some lost love? If so, this conversation was indiscreet.

"Perhaps I didn't understand either, Mrs. Fleming."

"I would like to know if Oliver is coming home."

"His car is gone. His bag is gone."

"I have fallen. I am frightened."

"Yes, my child." Her voice seemed to be coming to him through the grille of a confessional. Why had Flamingo brought up that nonsense about an orange canoe? Phelan felt that he had made a fool of himself. And now Mrs. Fleming confessed herself a fallen woman. "I can do nothing over the phone, of course."

"If Oliver has not left yet, tell him I need him at once. And he must not call an ambulance."

Phelan returned the phone to its cradle. The woman was senile. Flamingo had suggested that his marriage was a cross. Poor man. His wife must be demented.

There was nothing for it but to go see Miss Bishop. It was a

153

shame that Oliver could not be part of this. There was no one at the nurses' station. Phelan continued to the Founder's room. Sister Diotima was there.

Father Cullen had not changed. The tip of his nose looked white. Had the blood drained from it? He asked Sister Diotima. She ignored him. She was changing the bottle of fluid that hung from the stand beside the bed. The plastic of the oxygen tent was clouded as if with steam. The Founder was still alive. Sister Diotima took his pulse, extracting a watch from a pocket beneath her bosom. She squinted at it, her fingers on the Founder's pulse. When she put away the watch, she secured the tent and left the room. Phelan remained behind, gripping the metal railing of the bed. *In manus tuas, domine, commendo spiritum meum.* Not mine, his. Father Phelan felt suddenly tired. He was confused and worried by the way Oliver Fleming had left and the call to Mrs. Fleming had confused him more. Things slipped so quickly out of control. How secure a grip on the mind did one have at this age? Until a few days ago the Founder had been lucid and alert and look at him now. Phelan thought of Noonan, his senior by five years. No loss of mental agility there. Imagine, finding out about Shively's relatives. Miss Bishop.

Phelan left the room and trudged down the hallway. "Miss Bishop," he called. "Miss Bishop."

The door of Dr. Dowling's room opened and Miss Bishop, somewhat distraught, looked out.

"What is it, Father? Is something wrong?"

"I'd like to talk with you."

"Talk with me?" Miss Bishop, half in, half out of the doctor's office, glared at Phelan.

"About your mother."

Miss Bishop drew the door shut behind her and stepped into the hallway. She nodded in the direction of the nurses' station, then led the way. An odd girl, Phelan thought. What will her mother be like?

154

16

WHEN ENID CALLED to tell him she had taken a
fall in getting out of the tub, feared she had broken something and
had crawled naked to their bedroom and the telephone, Oliver
told her he would be home within the hour. He had been piqued
by Enid's summons and the late-afternoon traffic changed his
mood to wrath. She could not be in serious trouble if she could
use the telephone. Perhaps that was not fair. She had said she
was lying unclothed on the bedroom floor while she made the
call. Extraordinary. Enid had ceased caring about her weight and
had puffed up like a dirigible. What a crash she must have made
if she had indeed fallen. It was not right to make fun of her. One
day—who knew how soon?—some fatal illness would take her
from him. Oliver frowned with the seriousness of the thought
but his mind moved beyond it to what he would then do. How
wonderful if he could stay permanently at Porta Coeli among his
old friends, growing close to God again. As a widower he would
even be eligible for holy orders. He could be ordained a priest
and say Mass with the others.

The slowness of the traffic ceased to bother Oliver. He was

gripped again by the vision that had gripped him as a boy, himself at the altar as a priest. The girl in the orange canoe had altered all his plans but the vision was as fresh and vivid now as it had been then. Oliver Fleming, priest. He was savoring this thought when he recalled Phelan's reaction to the revelation that Enid was the girl in the orange canoe. Surely he must remember the episode. Or was it the code of the society which dictated that Phelan erase from his mind the cause of another's leaving? That must be it. Or Phelan was losing his memory. The man was as much of a nag as Enid, harping on that call to Father Hoyt. Well, Oliver had made the blasted call.

"What is this nonsense about Little Sem?" he demanded without ceremony when Hoyt came on the line.

"Who is this?"

"Oliver Fleming. I am on retreat at Porta Coeli and am told you have plans to knock down Little Sem."

"The plan is to put up a new dormitory, Oliver. The best site, as it happens, is where Little Sem now stands. We discussed this at the last meeting of the board."

"I remember no such discussion."

"I believe the minutes were sent to you."

"I never read them. My memory is source enough. I am adamantly opposed to taking down that building."

"Have you seen it lately?"

"I just returned from inspecting it. It is in solid condition. Work could and should be done on it, but it must be preserved."

"This is a difficult matter to discuss on the phone."

"There is nothing to discuss. I am against it."

"Perhaps I could come over and we can exchange ideas."

"I am on retreat, Father."

"Afterward, then. How long will you be staying there?"

"My plans are indefinite. I should tell you that I intend to canvass the other members of the board on this matter."

"I wish you wouldn't do that. At least until we have talked."

"Very well. I will call you again when I have finished my retreat."

"Remember me in your prayers, Oliver."

But there were to be no prayers and no retreat. Enid called.

As soon as he entered the house, Oliver began to shout Enid's name. Mounting the stairs, he heard water running. It was thundering into the tub. Oliver shut it off. In the silence that followed, he heard Enid moan.

The vulnerable look in her eyes when she stared up at him convinced Oliver that Enid's plight was serious. She lay on her side, pathetically trying to conceal with the spread from the bed the mountain of flesh she had become.

"Oliver, I am in pain."

He knelt beside her, his knees cracking as he bent them. "Now then, what happened?"

"Call the doctor, Oliver. Call an ambulance."

Oliver reached for the phone to call the ass who had encouraged Enid in the purchase of self-propelled chairs, staircase elevators and bathtub seats for easy entry and exit. The woman who answered said she would have Dr. Bloomer call back.

"I must speak to him. This is an emergency."

"He is with a patient now."

"If you do not call him to the phone immediately I promise you that a suit for malpractice will be filed against Dr. Bloomer in the morning. I repeat, this is an emergency."

The woman asked him to wait. Enid was moaning. Oliver patted her head, brushing the hair back from her face. Unintelligible sounds from Bloomer's office entered his ear. Oliver had once endured some hours in the man's waiting room when he accompanied Enid on one of her many appointments. The man was either greedy or an optimist; his overcrowded schedule ran at least an hour and a half late.

"Dr. Bloomer speaking."

"Oliver Fleming. My wife, Enid, is your patient. She has

157

fallen and fears she has broken something. I was not at home at the time and do not know the details. She is in great pain. It happened in the bath."

"She is in the bathroom now?"

"No. Somehow she crawled to her bedroom and the telephone. I suspect she was thrown from the bath by the device she uses to enter it. I believe you recommended this device."

"Where is the pain?"

"Where is the pain?" Oliver repeated to Enid.

"My leg. My head."

Oliver relayed this to Bloomer. The man became efficient. He instructed Oliver to keep Enid warm. He would have an ambulance sent for her. He would notify the hospital that she was coming and arrange for a room. He himself would be at the hospital when Enid arrived.

From the closet Oliver got a blanket and put it over Enid. He propped a pillow beneath her head. Would she like some water? No. He went back to the bathroom and studied the ridiculous plastic chair. It was swung away from the tub. He could not reconstruct what had happened. Best to leave things as they were. The scene of the crime. Oliver went downstairs and lit a cigar. He was pacing the living room when the siren screamed up the driveway.

He sat in the back of the ambulance with Enid during the unsettling ride. He felt that they were being sped through town in a showcase to amuse the curious. Enid began to babble and he leaned toward her in order to make out what she was saying.

"Someone phoned about an orange canoe."

"What!"

"I don't know what he was talking about. I told him I had injured myself. He insisted on talking about an orange canoe."

"Phelan."

"I told him I could not talk, that I was injured." Enid began to cry. Oliver soothed her mechanically. What callous trick was Phelan up to, phoning Enid? He is mocking me, Oliver thought. He pretended not to remember and then phoned Enid in order to tease. Oliver did not like that. He did not like it at all.

They rode on as if in silence, the scream of the siren radiating from them. Oliver looked at Enid, strapped to the stretcher, her eyes wild with fright, her hair every which way on her head. Her cheeks puffed with her breathing. The girl in the orange canoe. O God, God.

17

"F ATHER, what on earth is going on?"

Tumulty was lifted from his chair by the surprising appearance of Alma Bishop at his door. When he called "Come in" he had assumed it was another priest who had knocked. Alma came into the room and Tumulty crossed to her and opened the door again. Nice as these rooms were, they were not meant for receiving guests, particularly women. Alma agreed that they should talk in the office. To Tumulty's relief, the office was empty.

"Father Phelan is sometimes here," he said, to explain why he had first peered inside.

"That man. Why is there suddenly such interest in my grandfather?"

"Father Phelan asked about him?"

"He has gone to see my mother."

"Sit down, Alma. Please."

"I don't want to sit down. Father, you have to stop him. If Father Phelan gets her all upset, well, I don't know what I'll do."

"When did Father Phelan speak to you?"

"Fifteen, twenty minutes ago. But he left already. By cab."

Tumulty drew the telephone toward him. Alma gave him the number and he dialed it. The phone rang and rang. Alma told him to be patient. Her mother refused to hurry to answer the phone.

"Perhaps she is on the balcony."

"She can hear the phone from there."

Tumulty let the phone continue ringing, though he began to doubt that Mrs. Bishop was at home. Which was good enough. Alma said that she doubted Phelan had phoned before leaving. Suddenly the ringing stopped and the querulous voice of Mrs. Bishop spoke in his ear.

"This is Father Tumulty, Mrs. Bishop. I hope I haven't disturbed you."

"How are you, Father? You brought me off the balcony."

"I'm sorry. Mrs. Bishop, I have something unusual to say to you."

"Is it about Alma?" Excitement, apprehension, vindication—the catch in the old voice might have meant many things.

"No, no. Nothing like that."

"Thank God." Surely that was a sigh of disappointment.

Father Tumulty restrained himself, avoiding Alma's eyes. "Mrs. Bishop, one of my fellow priests, Father Leo Phelan, is on his way to see you."

"Do I know him?"

"I don't think so. He is an old man, Mrs. Bishop, older than his years." He covered the phone and asked Alma how Phelan had been dressed. It was as he had thought. "I do not say that he is senile or wholly without the use of his faculties. In many ways he is quite alert."

"Is he crazy?"

"He is wearing a windbreaker, a baseball cap, and will have a pair of binoculars slung around his neck."

"Good Lord."

"Now he is perfectly harmless. Physically. However, he does

161

have an unhappy knack of upsetting others. I fear that he may say things which will trouble you."

"About Alma?" Despair springs eternal.

"About your father."

"My father! I doubt that he could say anything about my father I haven't heard before." An edge had come into Mrs. Bishop's voice.

"I am sure of that. Nonetheless, I thought it best to call you. Father Phelan should arrive at any minute."

"I won't let him in."

"Then he will return. He is a tenacious man. You have nothing to fear from admitting him. I would advise listening to whatever he has to say, agreeing with him and, above all, not showing that you find him at all strange."

"I don't think so, Father. I would be afraid."

"Don't be. As I said, he is quite harmless."

"Are you coming for him?"

"I could. Yes. I will do that. Admit Father Phelan and I will be there as soon as I can."

"Well . . ."

"Please, Mrs. Bishop. This is a delicate matter. There are few people with whom I could be so frank."

"Oh, very well. But you come right away."

He assured her that he was on his way. He put down the receiver and got to his feet. Alma Bishop wore a squinty smile.

"You made him sound like some kind of nut."

"I thought I denied that he was."

"That's what I mean."

"I'd better get over there."

"What is Father Phelan up to?"

"Alma, he is trying to preserve an old building on campus. The one in which your grandfather is buried. I suspect that he will tell your mother that we intend to desecrate her father's grave."

"If it were *my* father, she would probably want to help."

"Is he dead?"

She shrugged. "I don't know."

"Good may come of this, Alma. For you."

It was an empty reassurance. Phelan was stirring up trouble to no purpose. He was indeed mad if he imagined Hoyt would not have checked the legality of moving Oscar Shively's tomb. Tumulty decided that he should let Hoyt know what was going on. Alma left him, to call a cab from the nurses' station, and he dialed the president's office. Hoyt was not in and he spoke to Deely, his assistant. Deely merely took the information, no comment or reaction. Tumulty wished that he had not called.

The old woman who opened the door regarded him with half-frightened eyes and when Phelan told her who he was it did not seem to help.

"May I come in?"

"Oh, yes."

She pressed against the wall when he went by her, then closed the door. "Go out on the balcony, Father. It's lovely there. And you'll be able to use your binoculars."

Phelan had forgotten that he was wearing the glasses. He took off his baseball cap. Behind him, the woman seemed to be giggling. Good Lord, was she another Enid Fleming? She was certainly old enough to be dotty. They went out onto the balcony, exchanging doubtful glances. Phelan told himself to proceed with care. He had imagined he was coming to see a woman to whose piety he could appeal, transforming her into an avenging goddess. He wondered if he would be able to get through to Mrs. Bishop at all. She slumped into a chair and he, too, sat. Looking out over the little lake, he realized that he was not a mile from the campus, less from Porta Coeli. The taxi had cost over two dollars. If he had known the location of Shively Court and the price of the cab he would have walked.

"I notice this development is named for your father."

"All this land was once ours."

163

"He was generous to the Society of Saint Brendan."

"Did you know him personally?"

"I regret to say that I didn't. He must have been a remarkable man."

"In his way, I suppose he was."

"You must miss him greatly."

"After all these years? I miss my mother a great deal more."

"Yes, I suppose you would."

"What do you mean?"

"Aren't daughters always closer to their mothers?"

"My daughter isn't."

"Alma?"

"Alma. She resents having an old mother to look after."

"Oh, I'm sure that isn't true."

"But it is. Ask her."

Father Phelan thought the conversation was off to a bad start. Mrs. Bishop's manner had become normal only when she spoke of her daughter. Prior to that, she seemed to be watching him and she smiled a strange little smile. If she were seriously senile would she be living alone like this? Now that he thought of it, he was surprised that she had let him in. How could she know that he was a priest, dressed as he was? It was stupid not to have changed first. He apologized now for the way he was dressed.

"You look comfortable anyway."

"Do you know Oliver Fleming?"

"I know who he is."

"I recently showed him around Little Sem. That is what we call the building in which your father is buried."

"Oh, yes."

"Then you knew he was buried there?"

Mrs. Bishop's eyes narrowed. "He should be lying with my mother. Why did he have to be buried in a church?"

"He wanted to be remembered in our prayers."

"And what about my mother?" The old eyes sparked with

164

anger and Phelan sat back in his chair. No matter what he said, it seemed to lead to troubled territory. What an old crone the woman was. His hope of stirring her to indignation now seemed silly.

"Are you so sure your mother hasn't been in our prayers all these years?"

"Has she?"

"Wouldn't you say that your mother was a benefactor of the society?"

"She was more a victim than a benefactor. My father became impossible to live with after his conversion. Once he decided to lay up for himself treasure in heaven, he put his whole mind to it. Father Cullen should not have encouraged him as he did."

Father Phelan bristled. Criticism of the Founder was unthinkable in the society. Phelan had never before heard a contrary word. Who did this shriveled old woman think she was?

"Where is your mother buried?"

"In a proper cemetery."

"It is an honor to be buried in a chapel, Mrs. Bishop."

"Well, my father paid for the honor."

"I'm sure you don't mean that."

"I most certainly do. Why, sometimes I think your society drove a wedge between my father and mother. If it is such an honor to be buried in church, you should have made room for her, too."

Father Phelan dearly wanted to escape. This woman was utterly irrational. And then, without fanfare, she subsided.

"May I try your binoculars?"

Phelan handed them over. Mrs. Bishop tried them while still wearing her spectacles and Phelan explained that they were not necessary. She put her spectacles in her lap. Focusing the glasses, she became enthralled.

"Why, this is marvelous. I must get a pair."

Mrs. Bishop stood and her spectacles dropped on the floor

and bounced through the railing. Phelan stood and saw that they had landed on the grass below. To his surprise he saw Tumulty looking up at him.

"Pick up her glasses, Michael," Phelan called. "She dropped her glasses. There, on the grass."

"Hello, Father Tumulty." Mrs. Bishop leaned over the railing and pointed the binoculars at Tumulty. "Oh, you look so close." She took the binoculars away from her face and turned to Phelan. Her gaze was vague and unfocused and she smiled ecstatically. "I shall get a pair, Father."

"They are good for bird watching."

"Is that what you do?"

"Sometimes."

It was a relief to hear the bell ring. Phelan offered to let Tumulty in. What luck that Michael should be passing by. Tumulty looked quizzically at him when Phelan opened the door. Mrs. Bishop's glasses dangled from his hand.

"Having a nice visit?"

Phelan whispered, "Michael, she is not all there."

"You don't say."

"She's crazy."

Tumulty smiled in a way Phelan did not like. "Bring my binoculars back, will you? Tell her I had to go."

And Phelan slipped through the door and hurried down the stairs. In recent years there had been much talk of the difficulty and hardship of celibacy. Phelan had never been happier to be unmarried. Imagine living out one's days with someone like Mrs. Bishop. Or Enid Fleming, for that matter.

He walked back to Porta Coeli. He was in no hurry to talk with Noonan. He skipped rosary and dinner, getting a snack in the kitchen while the others were at table. Throughout the evening he holed up in the Founder's office, with the light out. He was down to two cigarettes when he finally crept to his room. The house was asleep.

He had a final cigarette after cleaning his teeth, the smoke

166

tart and tasteful. He said a decade of the rosary, sitting in his chair. To bed, to bed. How good to slip under the covers, to settle his head on the pillow and push his feet down into the dark papoose of the bed. His toes encountered something. He raised his knee swiftly, like a racing cyclist. Imagination. Carefully he sent his foot back to where it had been, slowly, slowly. Ugh. Whatever it was was wet and cold. He threw back the covers and turned on the light. His binoculars lay on the top of his dresser. He had to dig before he found the thing in his bed. A toad. Tumulty! Phelan got out of bed with the creature in his hand, more dead than alive. A toad in his bed! He had always hated practical jokes, a mainstay of dormitory life in Little Sem. In the bathroom he flushed the toad down the toilet. All right, Tumulty. From now on it was war.

18

TRASK, his slippers in one hand, an empty bottle in the other, tiptoed down the hallway and into the refectory. It was a moonlit night and he had a hazy but adequate view of things. Or so he thought until he collided with a table. He froze as several pieces of silverware clattered to the floor. His breathing was shallow and sharp and his ears probed the dark like antennae. He had to get rid of this bottle. The trash cans outside the kitchen door were his and the bottle's destination. Certain he had waked the house, he hurried through the kitchen and pushed against the outside door. It was locked. Suddenly this seemed an insurmountable obstacle and he felt self-pity well up within him. The universe, reduced to a locked door, was as usual against him.

He looked around for a place to put the bottle. If he left it on the sink drainboard, the cook might be accused of drinking on the job. Trask pressed his eyes shut, imagining the cook. The man wore a white hat and a dirty apron and his face was the face of Father Trask. His expression was the practiced one with which

Trask had, over the years, confronted those who could no longer overlook his drinking. He had preferred anger to patient understanding and talk of his illness. Infrequently he had accepted that interpretation: he was the plaything of physiology, no more responsible for his drinking than for his fallen arches. He had never really believed this. It was important to see his weakness as responsible and thus corrigible, his and not his body's. His fingers found the hook and eye. He let himself into the night.

The parking lot glowed in moonlight, a twice-reflected hidden sun. The low plane of the building was punctuated by the deeper shadows of windows. The house was asleep. Trask, too, longed to sleep but he did not want Sister Diotima to find another empty bottle in his room. She never scolded him, simply slipped the telltale bottle into the huge plastic bag attached to the cart she wheeled from room to room on her morning rounds. She had the mercy of a mother, which is a sterner form of justice. He had let her down but she would suffer in silence.

Why did he drink? He had pondered this question so many times that asking it had the roteness of prayer. Once the physical explanation was rejected, only the moral answer remained. It was vanity. Just that. Why shouldn't the answer be simple? Urged on by a therapist, he had once thought back over the history of what he called his toots and had found some real or imagined snub at their origin. His pride had been hurt and he retaliated by humiliating himself with drink. If that was the answer, it changed nothing. Whenever he embarked on a toot he felt suddenly liberated, as if nothingness itself yawned before him, promising solace, forgetfulness, vindication in deeper failure.

He was startled by a sound near the trash cans. He pressed back against the closed door. The fear he had felt in the refectory was but a prelude to what he felt now. He was being watched. A small ghostly face looked up at him, eyes whitely rimmed. Repeated medical warnings rang in Trask's ears. The beast moved menacingly. Trask screamed and threw up his hands. The bottle flew free and bounced across the parking lot. The raccoon lum-

169

bered into the light and stopped to look back at him. Identified, the beast no longer frightened. He was real, out there, not a projection of alcoholic terror. The harmless, inquisitive animal enraged Trask. He feinted toward it, shouting. He still held his slippers. He threw one at the animal. "Go. Get out of here." Trask threw the other slipper but the raccoon remained where it was, staring at him with those absurd ringed eyes.

"What are you doing?"

Trask wheeled. It was Ucello in the window of his room.

"Nothing. I'll take care of it."

"I heard glass."

"Some animal is in the garbage."

"That's a raccoon."

"Of course it's a raccoon. He won't go away."

"Why begrudge him our garbage?"

"He'll make a mess."

The bottle, unbroken, lay on the asphalt, sparkling in the light of the moon. Trask was certain it would catch Ucello's eye but Ucello was making enticing noises, trying to coax the raccoon to his window. Trask told him to be still.

"Everyone is sleeping."

"You're right. Wait there. I'll come out."

Ucello disappeared. Trask looked at the raccoon, which had dropped to four legs but did not go away. Circling the beast, Trask moved toward the bottle on the parking lot. The raccoon turned like the hub of a wheel, keeping his eye on Trask. When he stooped to pick up the bottle, Trask heard a crash in the refectory. Ucello, too, had walked into the table. A moment later Ucello came outside. Trask hid the bottle behind his back and walked toward the kitchen door. Ucello's attention was on the raccoon. He was speaking soothingly to it. Trask slipped the bottle into the trash can whose top had been moved aside by the animal.

"These cans need better covers," he said. But he noticed that

170

the covers were made to fit over the cans. He asked aloud how the raccoon had got it off.

"I loosen them before I go to bed. He has a prehensile hand of sorts; he doesn't need much help."

"You uncover the garbage for raccoons?"

"When I remember. I like to watch them from my window."

"Wouldn't it make more sense to leave food out for them?"

"How would I know when they come? I can hear them on the cans. Sometimes they overturn them. They are intelligent creatures. Perhaps we should go in. He is wary of us."

"Why doesn't he run?"

"They are slow." Ucello opened the door. "Did he wake you?"

Trask liked the thought of himself roused from honest slumber by a noise outside, then going to satisfy his curiosity and mild concern. Ucello seemed to have forgotten the sound of glass or to have attributed it to the scavenging of the raccoon.

"I wondered what was going on out there." They were passing through the refectory now. "I've never heard them before."

"You would have, if your room was at the back of the building."

"Yes."

"You must be a light sleeper."

"I was still awake."

"It doesn't bother me when I can't fall asleep. What difference does it make? It is interesting to stand at the window and listen. There is a whole night world around us and I know very little of it. I feel like an eavesdropper. All that life going on in the dark. It is wonderful."

"Yes."

"*Benedicite omnia opera domini domino.*"

Trask nodded. They were in the hallway now, which was illumined by a dim night light.

171

"I have some wine," Ucello said. "Would you like a glass?"

"No," Trask said, too quickly. He added, "Thank you."

"It would help you sleep."

"I don't think I'll need it."

"You're lucky."

Trask nodded, occupying the field of fortune Ucello ascribed to him. "All I have to do is close my eyes and I am asleep."

Ucello shook his head, marveling at this capacity. "Well, good night, Father."

"Good night, Father."

Walking to his room, Trask became aware of the cool tiles beneath his feet. Good Lord, his slippers were outside in the parking lot. He stopped, wondering if he should go back for them. But he would surely be observed by Ucello. All his stealth had been in vain. He would get his slippers in the morning. If that damned raccoon had not made off with them.

A door opened and Noonan stood pajamaed in the doorway of his unlit room. Flustered, Trask said that he had heard a noise outside.

"I have been hearing them inside. Crashing noises in the refectory, whispers in the hall."

Noonan flicked on the overhead light in his room and was suddenly silhouetted. Tall, his baldness emphasized by the fringe wild from sleep, he tucked in his chin as if to get a better sighting on Trask's bare feet.

"You're discalced."

"I threw my slippers at a raccoon."

"You threw your slippers at a raccoon."

"He was in the trash."

"And in need of slippers."

"Ucello and I chased him away."

"I am relieved. Are you through banging about in the refectory?"

"Ucello walked into a table. Good night."

"I wish it were."

172

Trask walked with what dignity he could muster down the hall. The floor was cool beneath his feet. He would catch cold. If only he could have a nightcap against that possibility. But the bottle he had been so anxious to dispose of had been his last. Such pacifying effects as its contents had had on him were gone, fled before the fright of that damned raccoon, the intervention of Ucello and now the lofty, half-humorous disapproval of Noonan. What did it matter? They all treated him with the demeaning deference due a drunk. If he had another bottle he would open it. In default of that he got into bed and lay listening to the night world Ucello professed to find fascinating. He can have it, Trask thought, yawning, seeking sleep. When he closed his eyes, their twins, white-ringed, watchful, formed upon his lids.

19

"Someone put a toad in Phelan's bed."

"Ha."

"Phelan thinks it was Tumulty."

"That's ridiculous."

"Phelan resents the way Tumulty has acted since coming here. He says Tumulty pretends to be here on a different basis from the rest of us. Assistant to the Founder or something."

"Perhaps he is."

"He has been helpful to Father Cullen."

"A toad in his bed. Remember short sheeting?"

"Phelan's real concern is that Noonan be elected superior of the house when the Founder dies."

"I'm not sure I would want that."

"Toads in the bed."

"Bats in the belfry."

From behind a door Phelan listened to the brittle laughter. He wished that he had kept quiet about the toad. Still, it was important that others see how underhanded Tumulty could be. The man would be kept in place when Noonan was superior of the house. Noonan. The name no longer filled Phelan with admiration. Imagine Noonan actually scolding him for what had happened, or had not happened, because of his harebrained scheme for enlisting the aid of Mrs. Bishop. Phelan had been unable to convince Noonan that the woman was crazy.

"Ask Tumulty if you don't believe me."

"Perhaps I will."

And how had Noonan himself done with Alma Bishop? Quite understandably, the girl did not feel strongly about her grandfather's grave. From the way Noonan brushed the question aside, Phelan suspected that Noonan had fared no better than himself. Noonan came back to Tumulty. Why would Tumulty be able to bear out Phelan's wild story?

"Because he was there."

"While you spoke to the woman?"

"No, no. He came along and I asked him up and then got out of there."

"He was just passing by?"

"He was beneath the balcony when the woman dropped her glasses."

"Beneath the balcony? Was he playing a guitar, perhaps?"

"That's not funny, Noonan. If you don't believe me, go visit the lady yourself."

"I wish I had, before you ruined matters."

Phelan stomped away, so angry he could have cried. Noonan had a cruel streak, there was no doubt of that. And he was ungrateful. Didn't he realize that he owed his position as acting superior to Leo Phelan? As he would owe his election to Leo Phelan, when it came to that. If only Leo Phelan could view that prospect with more joy. Added to his troubles was the memory of Oliver's mysterious departure. He must telephone.

"My wife has broken her leg," Oliver said curtly. "She is in the hospital."

"I'm sorry to hear that."

"She tells me that you phoned her."

"I telephoned, yes. I wondered what had happened to you."

"I was summoned home. You spoke to her while she was writhing in pain. She will be in bed for some time."

"Did I upset her? I had no idea."

"You spoke to her of the orange canoe."

"Yes, I did. To cheer her up. Earlier, when you talked of it, I did not remember."

"But now you do?"

"It was an orange canoe, wasn't it?"

"I would prefer that you forget that canoe."

Phelan pondered this remark. Oliver seemed of several minds on the matter of the orange canoe. Phelan could believe now that he did remember that vessel. A vessel of election. One might have joshed about it in a clerical way, but of course Oliver was a layman and might not understand.

"Tell your wife that she is in our prayers."

"Thank you."

"Meanwhile, you should stay here, Oliver. It is not good to be alone at our age."

"So my wife discovered."

"Come back, Oliver."

"I may." Reserve seemed to depart Oliver's tone. "I will let you know. Now I must go visit Mrs. Fleming."

After he had hung up Phelan thought that he should have asked what hospital Mrs. Fleming was in. He might visit her. Visit the sick, comfort the sorrowful. A priest's work. Not to be confused with putting toads in a man's bed and acting like a schoolboy. Fifteen minutes later, Phelan was telling Garrity of the stunt Tumulty had pulled.

"Why do you think it was Michael?"

"He had been in my room. To return my binoculars."

"That is scarcely proof. It sounds like something Noonan might do."

"Noonan!"

"He was always a practical joker."

This was true. Doubt ate at Phelan's soul. But this was no way for the future superior of Porta Coeli to behave. Nor should he turn on an ally in the matter of Little Sem. He felt he could confide his hurt to Garrity.

"I have given my consent to the destruction of Little Sem," Garrity said.

"No!"

Phelan felt some inner edifice crumble further. The past twenty-four hours had been a nightmare. Oliver Fleming's petulance about that damned canoe, Mrs. Bishop, Noonan's cruel reaction. And a toad in the bed besides. Now Garrity said quite calmly that he had given in on Little Sem.

"Have you told anyone else?" Phelan asked.

"Michael Tumulty."

"But why?"

"Not now, Leo. It is a long story. I have been speaking to Goudge. I think he is ready to agree as well."

Phelan felt suddenly old and he did not like that at all. The others were old, visibly old, but he did not see age when he viewed himself in the mirror. The jaunty baseball cap helped, and the jacket with *Saint Brendan* emblazoned across his shoulder blades. He gripped his binoculars and went outside to his favorite bench. Training his glasses across the lake, he reconnoitered enemy territory. The wrecking crane still stood immobile. So much for Noonan's theory that Hoyt would simply go ahead. He and Noonan were now the only holdouts and he could imagine even Noonan giving in. Garrity. How could he be so treacherous? It was difficult to think that the enemy was only across the lake. After all, Tumulty was right here in the house, spreading his poison. What argument had the man used on Garrity? Phelan still stared at the wrecking crane. What a monstrous machine it was. He remembered Flamingo disdainfully kicking its giant tire. Phelan laughed. Figures of students came into sight as he moved the glasses. Girls. A damned shame. The girl in the orange canoe. Would things be different now if he had been able to remember what Oliver was talking about? Someone sat down beside him.

"Phelan, you have become a voyeur." It was Trask.

"Have you heard that a toad was put in my bed last night?"

"No!" Trask wore a delighted smile that did not go away when Phelan glared at him.

"Yes. Last night. Who do you suppose did it?"

"I didn't."

"Then who?"

"Surely you don't suspect me?" But Trask was clearly flattered.

"Guess who would have done it."

"I don't know. Noonan?"

"Why would Noonan put a toad in my bed?"

"Was it still alive?"

"Eh?"

"The toad. Was it alive?"

"It had been all but smothered to death when I found it."

"Did you keep it?"

"I flushed it down the toilet. I think Tumulty put that toad in my bed."

"And not Noonan?"

"No. What is your opinion of Noonan as next superior of the house?"

"It is not a job that requires any talent."

"The Founder has been our superior," Phelan reminded Trask. "To succeed him in any post is a responsibility. I favor Noonan for the job."

"Well, we will vote on it, won't we? Perhaps soon."

"I haven't looked in on the Founder today. Last night his condition seemed unchanged."

"Perhaps you yourself will be elected, Leo."

Phelan was stunned. He had never thought of himself as head of the house. The jobs he had held over the years had been minor ones and he had never been troubled by ambition. For himself. He was content to remain in the role of kingmaker. Whatever Noonan's behavior now, it would change when he was elected superior and he realized the debt he owed to Leo Phelan.

"Noonan is the man. Remember, he was head prefect."

"What has he done since?"

"A man the Founder himself selected as head prefect of the school has qualities of leadership."

Trask shrugged. "That was a long time ago."

Phelan tapped his fingertips on the stippled cones of his binoculars. "This house should be a festive place. A place of joy and relaxation. Our work is done. These are years of leisure. There is no need for us to live as in a perpetual lent. For example, our drinks should not be doled out to us as if we were children. If a man wants a cocktail, why, he should have it. If he wants a cool glass of beer against the heat of the day, the decision should be his."

"The Founder always kept the liquor cabinet locked."

"His successor could change the practice. Noonan likes a drop."

"We need an experienced man," Trask said. "A man who has been head prefect."

Phelan stood and squinted with unaided eyes across the lake. "I believe you have already given your agreement to Hoyt on Little Sem."

"I didn't realize the importance of what was being asked."

"I will stop them. Noonan and I. Of course we had hoped for a greater show of solidarity. We have been made to look like cranks."

"Your stand is admired, Phelan. Be sure of that."

Phelan frowned with pleasure. He left Trask on the bench, his head abuzz with dreams of easily accessible alcohol. It was a weakness with which Phelan had never been able to sympathize. An Irishman should recognize the proclivity of his race and guard against it. Thank God, he himself could hold his liquor. But he

179

would keep his word to Trask. The liquor cabinet would remain unlocked. Reduced to minimal contents, of course. Phelan felt his spirits revive. The defection of Garrity had been a blow. It was possible to believe that Little Sem actually would be destroyed. But there were other things and the election that would be held when the Founder died might very well be the most important thing for all of them, affecting the rest of their lives. What greater motivation could a man require? Tumulty beware.

Father Trask sat on, brooding over the lake. He knew that he had been recruited by appeal to what was most odious in himself. It was humiliating to have Phelan make so obvious a play to his weakness. Do I really want an unlocked liquor cabinet? Trask wondered. The truth was that he had not felt this safe in years. He was protected from himself, no matter that virtue consisted of a flimsy lock and a little key. It was demeaning, of course, to have to wait until the Founder, or more recently Noonan, remembered to unlock the cabinet and let them have a drink, perhaps even purloin a bottle. Yet Trask felt better than he had in years. His liver should have given out long ago. During his last stay in that place in Wisconsin the doctors had marveled at his constitution. His skin was peeling and had taken on a dangerous yellowish cast when he committed himself. If drink is a disguised type of suicide, as a psychologist had once tried to convince him, it proved to be a singularly slow method. The psychologist had chain-smoked while he spun his theory. Finally even breathing is fatal, wearing out the heart. Did one have an obligation to learn a way of breathing that would reduce the wear and tear? Trask did not know why he drank, only that once he started he did not wish to stop. If nothing else, alcohol had taught him humility. When he placed himself in the presence of God it was as a pitiable creature, without will or worth. My Jesus, mercy. That was his prayer. On those occasions when he had managed to go weeks, months, a whole long year once, without drinking, he had been puffed up with pride. Then he

180

stumbled again and the self he had been congratulating himself on lay in ruins. Small loss. He knew how unacceptable to God that dry, self-satisfied self was. His salvation seemed to lie hidden in his failure. *O felix culpa,* something like that. It was all very confusing. In any case, he was what he was. Perhaps no adult is capable of a truly radical change of character but certainly at his age he was pretty much what he would be when he stood before the throne of God. My Jesus, mercy.

Ucello approached across the lawn. As usual birds fluttered around him. Trask gritted his teeth. Ucello sat in the place vacated by Phelan. A large crow strutted before them with an odd jerky motion of its head. Restless nervous creatures, birds. Wrens, sparrows, finches, the antisocial jay. The area around the bench was now alive with them. Ucello dug in his pocket and scattered feed to his friends.

"What do you feed them?" Trask asked.

Ucello said that he had several bags of feed in his room, sunflower seeds, round oily ones, he didn't know the name; the mixture contained something for nearly any species.

"We should put up a feeder on the lawn."

"I like to do it personally."

"How do you attract them?" Trask asked desperately.

"What do you mean?" Ucello and the bird on his shoulder both looked quizzically at Trask.

"You attract them. It's not the feed. You attract them." He paused. "The way Phelan attracts toads."

"What do you mean?"

"One was put in his bed last night."

Ucello was appalled. "Was he injured?"

"By a toad? Don't be silly. It is not a vicious beast."

"It is a marvelous creature. Was it harmed?"

"Phelan flushed it down the toilet."

Birds rose in alarm when Ucello threw up his hands in horror. In a moment they were back. Ucello shook his head.

"That was a cruel thing to do."

181

"Putting it in Phelan's bed was cruel. He suspects Tumulty."

"Flushing the poor little thing down the toilet! That is awful." He peered at Trask. "Was it still alive?"

"Phelan is furious with Tumulty."

But Ucello was not to be distracted. The thought of a living thing pointlessly killed was painful to him. People were heedless and cruel because they were busy about too many things. There was a homily here.

"Why won't Leo settle down?" Ucello asked. "Doesn't he realize our lives are over? We are here to prepare for death."

"We must not despair."

Trask spoke as one who had kept vigil at the deathbed of hope. What a crazy quilt his life would seem when it was over. It seemed so now. The patient had survived though the operation was a failure. Maybe Ucello was right. *Lasciate ogni speranza.*

Ucello looked at him with surprise. "I said nothing of despair."

20

FATHER NOONAN and Mr. Deely, assistant to Father Hoyt, sat in a parlor near the front entrance of Porta Coeli. When Sister Diotima had summoned him to the parlor, she had said only that there was a gentleman to see him. This had caused a minor flurry in the recreation room, but any elation Noonan felt at this evidence of his continuing importance disappeared when he saw who his visitor was. Was some further pressure to be put upon his flaccid will? Perhaps he should have taken Phelan's advice and had Sister bring the visitor to him in the office. Deely had a funeral director's smile which at once sympathized, chided and suggested a brighter future. The young man was disappointed in Father Noonan. Noonan was unmoved. He had spent a lifetime failing to measure up to the expectations of others.

"Mrs. Bishop has contacted us."

"Oscar Shively's daughter."

"Yes." Deely paused to observe the pleasure Noonan took from the identification. "It was enterprising of you to discover the woman."

Noonan turned a palm upward.

"And pointless," Deely added. "She is pleased by the thought that now her parents will be buried together."

"Father Phelan felt that she should be told."

"Of course he was right. Father Hoyt is grateful to him, and to you, for correcting his oversight."

"That is one of the advantages of belonging to a religious society. The brethren make up for one's deficiencies."

"Esprit de corps?"

Noonan nodded.

"You have not shown that with respect to Father Hoyt's building plans."

"Would that be for the good of the society?"

"Father Noonan, the opposition here has crumbled. Father Garrity has given his consent. And there is another."

"Goudge."

"That's the man. Which leaves you and Father Phelan."

"One of us is enough."

"One of you is too much." Deely meant it as a compliment. From behind Noonan sun slanted through a window, its bar, bright with particles of dust, coming to rest on the arm of Deely's chair. "Father Phelan will follow your lead, will he not?"

"He feels very strongly about Little Sem. His stand is much admired here. And not only here."

"You mean Oliver Fleming."

"Has he contacted Father Hoyt, too?"

"Father Noonan, you must know that these are mere annoyances. That building is coming down, the new dormitory is going up."

Noonan guessed that Deely was in his late thirties. No doubt he thought the residents of Porta Coeli were aging fools. How absurd that some old priests should have the power to thwart the plans of Father Hoyt. Perhaps it was absurd. It was more absurd that he himself had been flattered when Hoyt had called him in. At the moment, Noonan felt in full sympathy with the bullheaded

Phelan. Why should they humbly acquiesce to Hoyt's removal of all relics of the past, of everything that suggested an era earlier than his own?

"Would you like to speak to Father Phelan?"

"I only wish I had the time," Deely said, not quite controlling a shudder. "What kind of man is he? There must be something he would be willing to trade for his agreement."

"I can't imagine what."

"A man opposes one thing because he is for another. What is Father Phelan for?"

"Youth."

Deely moved his hand impatiently on the arm of his chair. How translucent his flesh was in sunlight. Look at your hand, Mr. Deely. You will see your own mortality there.

"I mean his own youth. The past. Leo Phelan is that most irreconcilable of sentimentalists, the outwardly crusty man. He is against the wrecking of that building because it contains his past. The ghost of his youth is there. How would you bargain with that?"

"What sort of work did he do while he was active?"

"Oh, many things. Parish work. Mission work. Some teaching, I think. He was never a great shaker and mover in the society. He is my junior by several years. When we were at Little Sem, I was the school prefect."

"So he was your subordinate?"

"You could say that. You could say he still is."

"Oh?"

"I am acting superior now that the Founder is ill."

"I see."

It was a foolish thing to mention. Had he expected to impress Deely? Belatedly, he let his eyes rise comically, to counteract his words. The ceiling was made up of acoustical squares; there were lights embedded in it, squares of the same dimensions as the others.

"I will most likely be elected superior when the Founder dies.

185

Once the school prefect, now superior of a home for dying priests." He lowered his eyes and looked at Deely. "It is some-thing to ponder, Mr. Deely. Ambition does not die, not even when a lifetime convinces you of the vanity of ambition. Nor does age dilute conviction. Father Phelan will never be per-suaded to give his consent to Father Hoyt's plan. Father Hoyt should not be deluded. Tell him that."

"He won't accept it."

"I'm afraid he will have to."

"How about yourself, Father Noonan?"

Noonan smiled brightly. "I am adamant."

"I'm sorry."

Noonan remained in the parlor after Deely left, warming himself in the sun. He cared little for the old building one way or the other. He did not regard it as the scene of his triumphs. It was equally the place where he had been surprised by little Michael Tumulty one Sunday morning and had looked into the boy's scandalized eyes. How Tumulty's accusation had seared his soul. He had scandalized one of the little ones. For the first time in his life he learned what a withering experience that can be. From that day he had dreaded positions of eminence; height only measured the distance of the inevitable fall.

How pathetic his mention of being acting superior of Porta Coeli seemed in retrospect. It seemed somehow meant to counter his reaction to Hoyt's overture that day in the president's office. He had found then that he was not beyond flattery. Did the fact that he was not beyond ambition either balance that? Yet what he had said to Deely was true. He did want to be elected superior of Porta Coeli when the Founder died. The position meant little: special places in chapel and refectory, the key to the liquor cabinet, control of two automobiles. A ceremonial post. The finances of the house were handled by Faiblesse. Pomp without power. But perhaps ceremonial pomp is the greatest power of all, controlling the imagination. He could not campaign for the position, of course. He did not have to. Phelan would do that for him.

"Noonan wants to succeed the Founder as superior here."
"What makes you say that?"
"Phelan has started to campaign for him."
"That is against the rule."
"He says Noonan is a man of responsibility."
"Not if he has chosen Phelan to campaign for him."
"The two of them have stood up to Hoyt."
"So has Garrity."
"No longer. He has given his consent."
"I will have to hear that from Garrity himself. Noonan has already usurped the post, taking over as he has. That is worse than campaigning. Who asked him to take over?"
"We did."
"There was no election."
"Of course not. As long as the Founder lives he is superior. He has not resigned, he has not died, he has not been removed by Father Faiblesse. He is still our superior. We asked Noonan to carry on temporarily."
"There is no precedent for that."
"Noonan was school prefect. He was the obvious choice."
"School prefect! That was fifty years ago. We are not schoolboys. This is a serious matter."
"Noonan will be elected when the time comes."
"Tumulty will not vote for him."
"Only a majority is required."
"Others may prefer Tumulty himself."
"Do you?"
"I consider it an open question."
"And so it is. While the Founder lives."

21

> The leaving leaves have left
> Stark trees bereft
> Of green

AMBROSE HUFF considered himself in the mirror over his desk. Aging priest, seventy-two years old, works on unfinished poem. Yeats wrote fifteen lines a day, not waiting for inspiration and the muse; poetry a craft. The poet at his typewriter—a phrase in an essay of Eliot's. Huff had been shocked when he read it, preferring to think of poets in terms of quill pens and scroll-like paper. He himself wrote with a ballpoint pen on lined tablet paper, if two lines and the beginning of a third can be called writing. His lifelong gift for doggerel had not deserted him; if he turned his tablet over and paged from there he would find the quick jingles that all but wrote themselves. He was ashamed of them; they seemed a monument to the killing of his youthful gift for the sake of an easy laugh.

> Where reside its last remains,
> Flushed as they were into the drains

> And through the labyrinthine mains
> Of sewage pipes? Strange Styx,
> Strange Charon and stranger fix,
> When lying Leo toed
> Thee, bedded slimy toad.

At first he had comforted himself with the example of Belloc, but verse had been an avocation of the English writer, whereas Ambrose Huff dreamed of becoming the American priest-poet of the twentieth century. What he had become was an instructor of English at Saint Brendan's College, doing the breast stroke through a sea of student compositions, themes, essays. Criticism had numbed him, dulled his mind, killed his imagination. How foolish to try to resurrect it now at seventy-two. *Ars brevis, vita longa.*

Corcoran had brought him Xeroxed copies of the poems he had published in the Saint Brendan school magazine during the year of his editorship. He had put them in a drawer unread. He remembered his early efforts as light, bright, perfect; he was not anxious to test his memory against the reality. Corcoran sat down, draping his cassock over bony knees.

"What's this nonsense about Phelan?"

"You'll have to be more specific. He has made a great fuss over a toad in his bed."

"And he accuses Tumulty. No doubt correctly. I am told that some are promoting him for superior here, should the Founder die."

"There's not much doubt of that, is there?"

"Of the Founder's death?"

"I had meant to stop by his room today. Somehow it seems ghoulish. I am told that one can live on and on in that comatose condition."

"Yes."

"A horrible thought. I pray that my end will be definitive and swift."

189

"Better pray that it will be holy. Sooner or later the end will come. He is not expected to regain consciousness. Even if he did, the damage to his brain is such that—"

"Please." Huff raised a hand to stop that line of talk. He still held the ballpoint. His fingers were smudged with ink. "Why not Noonan?"

"Are you for him?"

"I have no thoughts on the matter one way or the other. Noonan would be diverting at least. Surely the duties are minimal."

"They are."

"It is strange. I had thought the Founder was our superior because he is the Founder."

"It is not a canonical position, that of Founder, nor is it provided for in the rules of the society. Of course the Founder always held a canonical office among us." Corcoran sat forward, a dry light in his eyes. Such trivia were close to his heart. Who but he would have recognized the document in the archives for what it was, an opportunity to thwart Hoyt?

Huff had signed the waiver without hesitation. He found it difficult to imagine the world surviving his death. What did it matter if a few buildings were knocked down?

"Thank you for photocopying these pages for me."

"I realize that you will want to peruse them in solitude. Those are precious documents. And to think they had simply been left in the attic of Little Sem to rot. Or to be lost in the rubble when it is torn down."

"When? I thought you were opposed to its destruction."

"I have no doubt that sooner or later madness will be victorious. It always is."

"Then you also predict victory for Tumulty in the election?"

"It is possible. Noonan's temporary accession was most irregular. Were you consulted about it? I was not. Goudge and Phelan presented us with a *fait accompli*. It is bad enough to be treated like a senile buffoon by others, but within the house! It is too much."

When Corcoran had gone, Huff pressed his knee against the closed drawer containing the copies of his poems. He should destroy them without reading them. *In pulverem reverteris.* He turned his tablet over and leafed to an empty page.

> In youth he cast his lines about
> In lyric and in sonnet,
> Now beached with age, at rest with gout,
> They down upon him plummet.

22

FATHER TUMULTY boarded a bus at the campus stop, wanting to get away from Porta Coeli for a time, and nearing downtown, hearing a siren, he decided on a busman's holiday and got off at Saint Jude's Hospital. Hoyt had asked him to visit Enid Fleming and talk to Flamingo. An old Fort Elbow friend, Father Mitleid, had parlayed a series of minor heart attacks into the chaplaincy of Saint Jude's, where, prepared to answer the final summons at any moment, he had survived for years. There he said daily Mass, brought Communion to bedridden patients, made frequent rounds and, for the rest, read and reread the complete Dickens, which, apart from his breviary and a few devotional books, was the only reading matter he retained from his more leisurely days as a pastor when membership in a dozen book clubs had kept him wallowing in the latest fare. When Tumulty looked in, Mitleid laid *Nicholas Nickleby* down and lifted a hand in greeting.

"You're still alive."

"Of course I'm still alive."

"Of course? Perhaps you're right. Our exit has been unconscionably delayed. I hear you've retired."

"Not quite."

"Oh?"

"I am living at Porta Coeli and acting as assistant to Father Cullen. Our Founder."

"And how is he?"

Tumulty told him and Mitleid seemed reassured that someone at least had the grace to be ill. He urged on Tumulty the merits of retirement.

"But you're busier here than you ever were."

"Busy, yes. But free. No assistants whining about the work they must do, no laymen nosing about the parish house, wanting a look at the books, eager to meddle in the school. The switch to English was a great mistake. I had a woman who wanted to read the lessons from the pulpit. The truth is she wanted to preach. Oh, how she would have loved to harangue the parish from the altar. For all I know, she has been allowed to do it."

"You're probably right."

"I don't care. Let her. The laity are tyrants. Give them a foothold and they insist that the whole parish live its life in the church. They complained of the Sunday obligation but now that they are swarming in the sanctuary with their guitars and banners and balloons and God knows what else they would like to make daily Mass a duty. Pope John has a lot to answer for."

It was like listening to Phelan. Mitleid warmed to the subject, screwing a filter-tipped cigarette into a lengthy holder, then holding it unlit while he joyously recounted the signs of the Last Days which had brought on his cardiac condition and the chance to retreat honorably to the hospital. When he got going on Bishop Brophy, Tumulty brought the conversation back to the Founder.

"If he is ill, why isn't he here?"

193

"We have complete hospital facilities at **Porta Coeli**, a doctor, resident nurses. There's no need."

"Very wise."

"We're fortunate."

"Saint Jude," Mitleid murmured. "Patron of lost causes."

"You're flourishing here."

"For my sins. You people seem to be thriving. New buildings at the college, a fancy retirement home."

"Porta Coeli was a gift."

"Who was the repentant sinner?"

"Oliver Fleming."

Mitleid's brow furrowed significantly. He lit his cigarette. "I used to resent the hold you had on him. He never gives a cent to the diocese. Perhaps he could be persuaded to donate something to Saint Jude's now that his wife is here."

"Perhaps."

"I suppose you've come to visit her."

Tumulty rose. "I'll drop in for a moment."

"Come back," Mitleid said, reaching for his Dickens. "We'll talk over old times."

It seemed an added reason to go. At the desk, Tumulty asked for Mrs. Fleming and boarded an elevator. He was surprised that Enid Fleming was not in a private room.

"I prefer the ward, Father. Here I have company."

She indicated her companions. There were two other old ladies on high beds. The ward did not seem particularly hygienic: the furniture was chipped and used, the curtains that could be drawn around the beds were beige with age, the walls needed paint or at least a hosing down. A cheerless place. He hoped Mitleid could interest Oliver in a large donation. In the fourth bed was a middle-aged woman who stared unblinking at the ceiling. She did not respond to Father Tumulty's hello.

"Cancer," Mrs. Fleming whispered in Father Tumulty's ear.

"I'll pray for her."

194

"Do. Say a Mass. Hand me my purse. I will give you the stipend."

"There is no need for a stipend. I will do it as a favor. How do you feel?"

"Numb. Yesterday I was terribly frightened. I have never felt so helpless. That was the worst part."

Tumulty looked sympathetic, or tried to. He did not know what had happened to her. She had represented only an opportunity to calm Oliver Fleming as Hoyt had requested. He had not wanted to tell Hoyt that there was bad blood between Oliver and himself. Or did Hoyt already know that? Life had become Byzantine and Tumulty was suddenly weary of intrigue. An effect of the hospital, perhaps. The end of the road made the journey seem, in retrospect, silly.

"I still feel helpless," Mrs. Fleming said. "But here I am looked after."

"Ah. The good sisters."

"Few of the nurses are nuns now. I haven't seen a nun since I came."

"That is odd."

"Oliver says they have all run off to live in sin with hod carriers and dope addicts." She chuckled. "Oliver has become bitter."

He told her that age did that, then wished he had not said it. Yet he felt the two of them had been exempted from the melancholy of age. A mixed blessing, that; others seemed to enjoy complaining.

"Do you expect Oliver?"

She said yes and he resolved to wait. A word or two across the sickbed of Oliver's wife could be most effective. Why should Fleming care for the fate of Little Sem? He had more serious worries now. While he waited, Tumulty was given more details than he cared for on the illnesses of the other two old ladies. The middle-aged woman rolled onto her side, facing away from

195

the chatter. Whenever he glanced in her direction, Tumulty felt an urge to apologize for this inane banter. It was no way to die, if that was what she was doing, one occupant of a noisy ward. When he heard of people dying in the hospital, the image he formed was of failure on the operating table or of a patient motionless on a snowy bed in a hushed and reverent atmosphere, attendants hovering nearby. A black girl peeked into the ward, then disappeared. No one else put in an appearance. It was criminal. He would bring this to Fleming's attention. His wife should be in a private room, no matter what she said. If she craved companionship, she could have television.

When Oliver arrived, he seemed surprised to see Tumulty there, and grateful, too. There was no sign of animosity, of the old enmity between the trustee and the president of the college. It all seemed too long ago. Oliver leaned over the bed and put his dry lips briefly on his wife's forehead.

"You look better."

"I am on the mend." She threw back the covers to show her husband the cast on her leg. Tumulty looked away. His eyes met the eyes of the woman who had cancer. She seemed to look right through him. Did she resent that he had lived so long while she lay dying young? He walked to her bedside.

"This talking must disturb you."

She shook her head.

"I shall say a Mass for your intention."

She looked up at him in her unnerving way. She nodded. "Thank you." Her lips were white and cracked and it seemed to be painful for her to speak.

"Would you like a drink of water?"

"No."

"Are you Catholic?"

"No."

"The Mass is a prayer. A memorial of Christ's death. I will offer a Mass for you tomorrow. What is your name?"

"Won't God know?"

196

Tumulty smiled. "You needn't tell me your name."

"Is there a God?"

Her question lifted to him, arising from pain and despair. It was not an undergraduate's mindless inquiry. Neither was it impassioned.

"Yes, there is a God."

"I wish there weren't."

"I understand." The problem of evil. O'Leary would have a dozen arguments for the woman, each making it crystal clear why God permits evil. The arguments never helped when you had the problem. Tumulty put his hand on the woman's cheek. "God bless you."

"I am dying."

"We are all dying."

She ignored him. "At least my children are grown."

Children? Where were they? Why was she left alone like this? Anger welled in him. Someone else might have directed such anger to God but Father Tumulty was angry with the children. They should be here with their dying mother. He was suddenly thankful that he had not had to keep vigil at his mother's deathbed. The news had come to him after the fact, something that had already happened. He patted the woman's cheek.

"Try to rest now."

He told the Flemings he was going down the hall to have a cigarette. He wanted to get out of that ward, at least for a minute. He walked to the end of the hall and an alcove where some nurses were. There was no nun there. He asked an extremely buxom woman why this was. She listened distractedly, asked him to wait a minute. She was holding several metal-covered records; she was obviously busy. Tumulty made a dismissing gesture and went back to the waiting room he had passed. The place was a wreck. Steel-tubing chairs, plastic cushions, cracked, sprung, uncomfortable. Magazines and newspapers, very old and dog-eared; they might have interested a collector. Corcoran. The window was covered on the outside by grilled metallic mesh. Tumulty smoked half a cigarette and went back to the ward.

As if reading his mood, Fleming said, "This is a depressing place."

His wife hushed him: a guest whose adverse comments might insult the host. Tumulty agreed with Oliver.

"As soon as Enid can be moved, I shall take her out of here."

"Home?" she asked.

"Someplace where you can have adequate care. This place is crawling with Zulus."

"Oliver, hush. Please."

"It is not prejudice. They are not trained for this work. They do not care about the patients."

"You can't know that."

"I suspect it. I will not leave you here one moment longer than necessary." Oliver was warming to the subject. He turned to Tumulty. "This place is no different than General Hospital. Where are the nuns?"

"There don't seem to be any."

"They have all absconded. This is what their damned Renewal comes down to, an abandoned hospital full of fuzzy-wuzzies. Abandoned schools, too. Why do they leave?"

"Have you met Father Mitleid? He is the chaplain here."

Mrs. Fleming knew him, of course, he had been in to see her, but Oliver did not. He was irked by what he considered an interruption. Father Tumulty took the occasion to leave. This was no time to discuss the politics of the society with Oliver. In his present mood, he was likely to connect the removal of Little Sem with the paucity of nuns.

Father Tumulty decided to walk down. The stairway seemed seldom used. The steel door closed behind him and he found himself out of the uncomfortable heat of the hospital. Plaster walls, high, unwashed, but cool; steel stairs on which his steps echoed. From far below odd sounds lifted. Tumulty suddenly felt all alone. The stairway had an allegorical air, connected with but

198

separated from the building, limbo, purgatory. He could imagine the stairs continuing down and down without end, a descent in a bad dream. Nonsense. He stopped on a landing to look out the cloudy window. Below him was the staff parking lot. The ledge of the window was ample and inviting. He sat.

His ears seemed full of Oliver's lamentation and of Mitleid's earlier one. The remembrance of things past became so quickly bitter. Of course they were right to be critical. No one had imagined that things would go as they had, least of all, Tumulty was sure, good Pope John. He had wanted people to get off their duffs, out of their routines; he certainly had not meant for religious to go over the wall, for tradition to be ridiculed or the old to be despised. The old. He still thought of them as They. He stood. The point was not to whine about change but to direct it.

Mitleid caught him before he left the hospital, breaking away from a middle-aged couple he had been reassuring or consoling.

"I meant to ask you. How is Father Faiblesse?"

"Just fine."

Mitleid looked relieved. "Thank God."

"You seem surprised."

"Oh, no. I am beyond surprise. Give him my regards."

Tumulty would have liked to find the source of Mitleid's enigmatic concern for Faiblesse, but the chaplain was drawn back to the couple he had left. Outside, Tumulty dismissed the odd exchange. Did Mitleid ever get away from the hospital? The downtown skyline of Fort Elbow was visible from the high ground on which the hospital stood. Tumulty was not dismayed by the sooty pall hanging over the city. He saw it as a reassuring mark of the industry of men. He inhaled deeply, then started for the bus stop, his exhalation audible, half musical, almost a whistle.

23

THE COST of a cup of coffee at the lunch counter of the Fort Elbow airport, a plastic-coated paper cone set in a more permanent plastic holder, was fifteen cents. The paper cups were thrown away, the holders returned immediately to use, no need to wash them. Efficient, perhaps, though the coffee had an alien taste, more noticeable as it cooled. Father Stokes thought the price exorbitant. He was a frequent customer, not that the waitresses acknowledged it. The bulk of their clientele was transient, seen once and that was all. Surly women in any case. Stokes could not imagine having a conversation with any of them. He felt on duty himself. One read of air crashes so frequently, but how often was there a priest on hand to send the departing souls shriven on their way to heaven? It bothered Father Stokes, the thought of souls unattended to. He was not a good companion on a motor trip because of this. The sight of a car pulled to the side of the road drew him as pollen does the bee. An accident, a cardiac case, some disaster where he could be of priestly help? He had provided conversation to dozens of motorists while they changed a tire or waited for a wrecker to haul them to the next town. Still, you never knew. Other priests were full of stories when they had arrived in the nick of time, some soul *in ictu mortis,* and given absolution. Father Stokes liked the image of a cleansed soul flying to meet its creator, all further opportunity for lapsing into sin gone. It was one of the greatest glories of the priesthood, that delegated power to absolve sins. Father Stokes had loved to hear confessions. He was not interested in the catalog of sins, he did not embarrass the penitent with urgent homilies; the moment he liked was when he raised his hand in benediction and pronounced the formula of absolution. But, having closed the grille, listening to the penitent stumble out of the box, into the church, too soon into the world beyond, he had known that, human nature being what it is, he or she was returning inevitably to sinful ways. Of course the divine mercy was inexhaustible. Back they would come and once again he would give them absolution. How much better to do that tremendous deed at the moment of death when it could not again be undone.

The waitress began to wipe the ebony surface before him with a damp cloth, swooping around the base of Stokes's coffee cup. His coffee had grown cold. He pushed it from him and immediately it was borne away by the waitress. Time to go. Father Stokes got carefully down from the stool. The circulation in his legs was not what it had been; he stood for a moment before sensation returned fully to his feet. The edge of the counter stool had acted like a tourniquet under his thighs, it always did, but he did not like to occupy a booth alone and order only coffee.

The waiting room was jammed with people. Outside, an airplane waited on the ramp. Threading through the excited voices was an amplified announcement that boarding was imminent. Movement began. Father Stokes had started around the edge of the crowd when his attention was caught by a stir near one of the couches. An old woman had lost her balance, a young man reached for her but she eluded his grasp and fell back upon the couch. A woman screamed. Father Stokes pushed his way through to the couch. Several people were bending over the old woman, obscuring her. The woman who had screamed looked around in a bewildered way; her eye alighted on Father Stokes, noticed his collar. He discerned a summons in her anxious look.

Now he was at the couch, pushing aside a man and woman who bent over the old lady. Stokes knelt next to the couch, more agile in his heedlessness. The old woman lay uncomfortably, one shoulder propped up by the arm of the couch. Her hat had slid over her forehead and her hair was mussed. Her eyes were closed. Father Stokes felt hands on his shoulders but he ignored them.

"Have you true contrition for your sins?" he whispered in the old woman's ear.

The eyes popped open. Father Stokes was prepared for her surprise. Relief would follow. He repeated his question. Her eyes dropped to his collar.

"I will give you absolution."

"Hey, whatcha doing?" The hand on his left shoulder got a grip, tried to pull him away. Father Stokes lifted his hand in blessing. The old woman slapped it away.

"I'm not dying!"

His hand still in midair, Father Stokes said, "Where is the pain?"

"The pain? In my ankle. I tripped. Some idiot left a suitcase in the way."

Father Stokes was pulled to his feet. The man turned him around, angry. His anger did not diminish when he saw the collar.

"You trying to scare her out of her wits? She tripped is all."

"I thought she had had a heart attack."

"She's all right. You're all right, aren't you, Mom?"

The old woman nodded. "He meant no harm."

"Maybe you want a priest when you die. I'll remember that." The man laughed. His jaw was blue with a heavy beard. Others were laughing, too.

"You think he's a rabbi, Mom?"

Father Stokes smiled, shrugged, excused himself. They let him escape. He went through the people, aware that many were staring at him. From behind, the jolly Jewish laughter mounted. Father Stokes was moving at a fast pace when he got to the steps leading to the observation floor. It did not matter that she was Jewish. It did not matter. He would have given her absolution in any case, conditional absolution. But halfway up the stairs he stopped. He hadn't the heart to go higher. He should go home, home to Porta Coeli.

24

FATHER HOYT, with elevated rear, head and shoulders bent low over the handlebars, guided his ten-speed bicycle along the campus street, headed for the lake. A prudent finger of either hand hooked the brake levers, an all-service smile was affixed to his face in response to the startled then delighted looks of recognition of students past whom he shot in effortless speed. This bicycle as much as his daily hour of yoga, practiced during the noon hour when the staff was out to lunch, had kept his tummy down, his step springy, his ex officio youthfulness intact. *Iuvenis intactus.* He smiled at his joke, necessarily private; one's knowledge of Latin was best kept concealed nowadays.

He swept by the church, an octagonal edifice, one of his first projects; it had replaced a yellow brick monstrosity, all nave and steeple and discomfort, which for decades had tested the faith of the students. Not that students were seen much in church anymore. The Sunday obligation, like so many things, was being tacitly ignored. Eventually church law would conform to custom, of course. Better Mass three or four times a year, praying with sincerity, than a weekly drudgery done under duress and half asleep. Hoyt himself had stopped preaching at the Sunday Masses. The sight of all those empty pews seemed a personal rebuke and an effort to pack the house by means of a poster campaign had failed. No matter. He had other ways of reaching the kids. An interview in the campus paper, a release to the Fort Elbow *Tribune,* a cameo appearance in the interview slot during the morning cook show on local television. And he was accessible to them. Saturday nights he held court in the student union, a real bull session. He spoke their language. At least he understood it. The campus chaplain's suggestion that he let this session evolve into a late evening Mass had been quickly squelched by Father Hoyt. That would break the spell, destroy the rapport. He wanted them to respond to him as a man, a human being, not as president and priest. That was why he had stopped wearing clerical dress. Someday he intended to look into the history of the Roman collar, do a little piece for the *Brendandelion,* the precious but glossy and expensive literary quarterly he continued to find room for in the presidential budget after the students objected to being dunned for it at registration time. Forced feeing, they had called it. The *Brendandelion* contained verse, photography and alleged literature. Hoyt was tolerant of the raunchy tone of the poetry and of the tendency of student photographers to get hung up on unfocused shots of breasts and pudenda. They would grow out of that; kids always did.

He was on a downgrade when he wheeled past Little Sem. The sight of the inactive wrecker beside the building froze the smile on his lips. A slight breeze off the lake, magnified by his velocity, stung tears from his eyes. He had been stymied by a handful of old fools. Well, he was going to put an end to that and pronto. He should have acted personally from the beginning. Altering Tumulty's role from adversary to ally had seemed wiser than it was and having a man like Noonan as an enemy was demeaning. Sending Deely to Porta Coeli had been a last lapse. Deely just did not know how to handle these old birds. Hoyt's smile regained its force. His whole career reposed on his ability to handle old birds, beginning with Faiblesse and Tumulty.

They still considered him a mere boy, of course. At forty-four he was among the youngest members of the society still around. The rate of attrition in the society had been high after Vatican II, not that his own eminence could be explained by that. He had no doubt that he would have risen as high and as fast in the most populous of religious orders, if any still deserved that description. Nor did he consider his present post as high as he might go, although there was nowhere higher to go within the society. Father superior? He had made that post subordinate to his own. Misguided friends had wanted to promote him for the position, but he had seen that the center of gravity was where the money was, and Saint Brendan's College was the single moneymaking operation the society had left. The thing to do was to stay with it, free the college from its hitherto umbilical relation to the society and put it on the road to excellence. Meanwhile, an expiring society enjoyed a little reflected glory. His further aspirations were not so much murky as plural. Who knew what opportunities would present themselves to a churchman, the way things were changing? And of course it was Hoyt and others like him who were bringing about those changes. He kept avenues open to the more traditional possibilities, too. His growing friendship with Sean Brophy, the bishop of Fort Elbow, and with Don Oder, his vicar-general, was part of that. Elevation to the episcopate might not be so bad. Of course many a diocese would be a comedown from his present job. He had freedom to speak out, to be noticed, to mold opinion as a college president that he would not have as bishop of a place like Fort Elbow, say. It had been gratifying to observe Brophy's slight condescension fading in recent years. Once the bishop realized he was speaking to a man who handled an annual budget in excess of ten million, his attitude altered. Hoyt had suspected that the thought of walking that sort of financial tightrope scared the hell out of Brophy. Oder was something else. He had a reputation for being

206

a wizard with money and Hoyt could believe it. He was a lot like Fogarty. No doubt Brophy relied on Oder as he himself relied on Fogarty. The true leader learned that there are dozens of second violinists eager to take on the hairy and unrewarding tasks that make leadership possible.

A student couple emerged from the woods on a little-used path. Something like alarm leaped into the girl's eyes when Hoyt slowed and the boy looked as if he were thinking of dashing back and getting lost in the trees again. Hoyt gave the pedals a few pushes and sailed on. What had those two been up to? He did not encourage those who brought him tales of what was going on in the dorms. Drinking, of course; you had to expect that. A few pills and pot, the usual thing. There were coeds who supposedly slept around. In his heart of hearts Hoyt found this difficult to believe. Marriage and related activity remained for him what it had been for Saint Paul, a great mystery. Others were too credulous of these stories. Hoyt had little doubt that it was this sort of rumor, traveling across the lake to Porta Coeli, which explained the absurd opposition to using the site of Little Sem for the new dorm for female students.

Oliver Fleming's phone call had been particularly annoying. He would not have such important benefactors enlisted against him. If Fleming had felt any untutored opposition, it would have surfaced at the board meeting when the plans for campus development were approved. Perhaps Oliver had not fully understood those plans; the wrecking of Little Sem had not loomed large in Hoyt's exposition to the trustees. Preparation of the site. That was the phrase. In any case, they had agreed. Where Hoyt had expected opposition some years ago, when he tore down the old campus church and built the new, there had not been a ripple. It had helped to have the projected new church featured in an article in *Church Architecture*. That article had been reprinted in the Fort Elbow *Tribune*, drawing a stream of approving letters. Had easy success rendered him careless? There would have been a dozen ways of nipping this opposition in the bud. Damn Corcoran for digging up that old document. The man's timing had been diabolical. Found after the rubble of Little Sem had been carted away, it would have been a minor irony of local history. God knows the Founder had not remembered it. He had nodded through Hoyt's description of the projected campus construction without demur. Hoyt had stopped expecting praise or real encouragement. All he asked was a nod of that old head. It was always a great help to be able to refer to the Founder's agreement. Even Faiblesse had been obviously taken aback when told that the Founder had okayed the destruction of Little Sem. And all the while that document had been lying in the archives, ticking like a time bomb. Well, the time for defusing it was long overdue.

Hoyt came to a stop in the parking lot behind Porta Coeli, dismounting with a supple over-the-rear-wheel swing of his right leg. Had Deely realized that he had returned from Porta Coeli with the means of overcoming the opposition among the old priests? Hoyt suspected his assistant had not known, nor had he told him. Let Deely think he had bombed out.

There was a palpable flurry in the house when word spread that he had come. Hoyt asked directions to the Founder's room, needlessly, audibly. Sister Diotima, an anachronistic vision in wimple and robes and clacking beads, sailed to meet him.

"Any change in Father Founder, Sister?"

"No, Father. None. His temperature is normal, respiration clear. He just lies there."

Hoyt nodded gravely. The nun must be as old as the Founder. She had come from the old sod not long after him. A second cousin, she had been one of the associated society of nuns. They, like the brothers, had faded away. Sister Diotima might be the last as she had been the first Brendanite nun. For a brief moment, Hoyt had the sense of being on a sinking ship. He fought the vertiginous sensation and, on the edge of his mind, resolved not to postpone indefinitely the next step, whatever it was to be, of his own career. He did not relish the prospect of ending as the sole surviving member of the society, a not wholly unlikely eventuality.

Once in the sickroom, Hoyt stood at the foot of the bed, hands clasped in prayer. Word spread fast in this house. Old men began to enter the room and cluster around the bed, joining their prayers to his. Did they think his visit would precipitate the death rattle? Hoyt stared at the thin face of the Founder, the pointed nose, hollowed sockets, the enormous closed eyelids. The sunken mouth suggested an absence of teeth and sure enough a denture grinned in a glass beside the bed. Intravenously fed, supported by an oxygen tent, how long would the old man last? He would have a word with the doctor. Sister Diotima, for all her devotedness, was wavering on the edge of tears. In situations like this, one wanted the coldly impersonal report of a professional.

Someone beside the bed smoothed the plane of the tent, as if to get a better look. Phelan. Did the old rascal realize he was wearing his baseball cap while ostensibly at prayer? Hoyt studied this improbable adversary through lowered lashes. A stubborn set of the jaw, fat nose not quite bulbous, rosy-cheeked as a boy. Phelan looked in great shape. Probably relatively young, as age was reckoned here. Phelan had always been a gung ho member of the society. Vocations had come out of any parish he was in as if it were a county in Ireland. The bill of Phelan's cap turned and Hoyt closed his eyes. Having held the attitude for this long, he said a prayer for the Founder. Lord, take his soul and give him rest. He has served you long and well. Hoyt made the sign of the cross and stepped back from the bed.

This broke up the gathering, although those who left the room loitered in the hall outside. Noonan came forward to greet him. Hoyt smiled affably. Phelan came out of the room with them.

"Could we have a word with you, Father?" Phelan looked at him as Faust first looked at Mephistopheles. "We can talk in the office." The last word was emphasized. Ah.

209

"Of course."

As they went down the hallway, Phelan on one side of him, Noonan on the other, a triumphal march with the enemy in custody, Hoyt did nothing to rob them of their moment. He caught Tumulty's eye and indicated that he wanted to see him later. To his escorts he commented on how peaceful and serene the house was. They took him outside and along the cloister walk to show him what a fine view of the campus they had.

"Particularly of Little Sem," Phelan piped, his voice rising lest eavesdroppers have difficulty hearing. "Would you care to take a look through my glasses?"

Phelan unslung his binoculars and handed them to Hoyt. The president focused them, scanned the campus buildings, moving from right to left, arriving finally at Little Sem and the inert crane beside it. He resisted grinding his teeth at the thought of the money this delay was costing. Phelan's binoculars were spectacular, upsettingly so. With these he could easily see student couples emerging from trysts in the woods.

"Very nice," he said, returning the glasses to Phelan. Noonan, to his credit, seemed to find his partner in opposition a bit of a ham.

"No," Noonan said when Phelan suggested a tour of the house. "Father Hoyt has been here before."

"Perhaps we could go to the office?" Hoyt suggested.

Noonan got rid of Phelan somehow; Hoyt walked ahead and let them settle it behind him. His estimate of Noonan rose. Anyone who could get rid of so ebullient a man as Phelan that quickly could not be completely without merit. Would this be more difficult than he had imagined? Once inside the office, he came directly to the point.

"Well, Father Noonan. You still refuse me permission to go ahead with my building plans on campus."

"I'm afraid so."

"The opposition has dwindled to two. Phelan and yourself."

210

"That is right."

"When you agree, he will come along."

"*When* I agree?"

"Father Noonan, I respect your point of view. Frankly I find it more understandable that a senior member of the society would oppose the tearing down of Little Sem than agree to it. In your position I would feel exactly as you do."

"There are many places a new dorm could be built."

"Of course there are. It is also true that the site of Little Sem is the best. Certainly I prefer it. Nonetheless, the dorm could be put elsewhere."

"It will have to be, Father." Noonan's voice seemed to have found the tone he wanted. Firm, but soft. He was not defying Hoyt, simply opposing him.

"In your present position you must make decisions." Hoyt rubbed his palm over the desk that separated them. The office was an attractive one. New but somehow reminiscent of the Founder's old office in Little Sem. The desk and the old crucifix on the wall provided the bridge between past and present. "I mean as acting superior of this house."

"There are not many decisions to make."

"When you make those you must make I will wager that opposition will not stop you."

"If I know I am right, I will act." Noonan's chin lifted and his eyes narrowed with authority.

"Imagine that you are in my spot now. What would you do?"

Noonan smiled. "I would try to get what I wanted."

"How?"

"Let's say that I would try to find a way. But I would be stymied, just as you are. By that document and some old codger like myself."

"Old codger? I don't think so." Hoyt allowed his eyes to drift to the window. "How did you become acting superior, Father?"

"I was asked."

"By your fellow residents. Good. What happens when the Founder dies?"

"There will be an election."

"And Father Noonan will be officially chosen superior of the house?"

Their eyes met and Hoyt saw in the depths of Noonan's what Deely's report had suggested he would. The rest was simple. Ten minutes later, when Father Hoyt left the office, the problem was solved. He had used Noonan's phone to make the call to Deely. Now he faced the more difficult challenge of Michael Tumulty.

"There will be an election," Tumulty said when Hoyt brought the conversation to what would happen at Porta Coeli when the Founder died. They were sitting in Tumulty's room.

"And Noonan will be elected superior?"

Tumulty shrugged. "I'm sure he wants it. Father, I think I can fairly claim to have done what you asked me to do here."

"Everyone has agreed to my taking down Little Sem?"

"Everyone that counts. Garrity has agreed. He was the key."

"But what of Phelan? What of Noonan?"

Tumulty sat forward. "Just go ahead, Father. They cannot stop you. You have overlooked more than they can do in the past."

"Just tear down Little Sem?"

"Yes!"

"Then you have given up on Noonan and Phelan?"

"You know what they're like."

"I've just been talking with them. You are right in thinking that Noonan wishes to succeed the Founder as superior here."

Tumulty clearly found this irrelevant. Hoyt watched him master his impatience. Poor Michael.

"Tell Faiblesse to reassign me. I have to get out of here."

"No."

"But you promised me." Tumulty stopped. His voice had not

212

been under control. Pain and anger shone in his eyes. "I have done all I could."

"I'm sure you did. And I am grateful. Michael, I want you to be the next superior here."

"Superior?" The word seemed to taste bad in Tumulty's mouth.

"Don't be disdainful of it, Michael. Think of it. What other post in the society, in the society as opposed to the college, has the importance of this one? Have you any idea how large the endowment is? This is the largest community we have. To be superior here is no small thing."

"I don't want it. I want to leave."

Hoyt did not find it pleasant to see his former champion reduced to such debility. Tumulty had aged well but he was old. It was unrealistic of him to imagine that he had work to do outside this house. Yet Hoyt respected Tumulty for resisting this truth. He said quietly, "Why would you refuse?"

Tumulty studied the president as if to make sure that he was not being toyed with. When he spoke again it was with the confidential tone among peers that Hoyt himself had used.

"This is not a normal atmosphere, Father Hoyt. We were all boys together, you know. We may look equally old to you but of course that is not so. Old relations reestablish themselves. Men who were senior fifty years ago and have not done a thing in the interval are once more deferred to. I came here with the understanding that it was a temporary assignment. I am not exactly a favorite in the house."

"You think that you would not be elected superior when the Founder dies?"

"I doubt it very much."

"Who then? Father Noonan?"

"Yes."

"That is absurd. You are the obvious choice. I want you to be the superior here."

213

"You do not have a vote."

"I want you to be superior," Hoyt repeated. "And you will be."

Tumulty shook his head. "I will not be elected."

"Who presides when the election is held, Michael? Father Faiblesse does, in his capacity as father superior of the society. And he must certify the vote."

"Of course."

"He can also refuse to accept the verdict of the electors."

"Veto the election?"

"You know he can. Think of the rule."

Hoyt gave Tumulty time to think of the rule, and of other things. He got up and stood at the window. "Father, this is where you will spend your last years. Even if you were given some respite now, quite soon you would be living here. Surely it cannot be a matter of indifference to you who will be the superior of the house. The man who becomes superior when the Founder dies would still be superior when you returned here. I cannot get you reassigned. I do not think it would be wise. Believe me when I say that I understand your reluctance to retire. But as superior you will have more control over your life than you have had in years. You and I and Faiblesse will be a new triumvirate. Nothing outside this house could give you that status. I owe you a great deal, Father. In a sense, I owe you everything. So think about it. I have. What I offer you in return is this final job."

Father Hoyt did not wait for a verbal agreement. He had all he wanted from the expression on Tumulty's face. The president opened the door and left the room.

After he had stopped by Dr. Dowling's office, Hoyt left the building. Wheeling his bicycle toward the lake path, he felt no triumph from his conquests of Noonan and Tumulty. The same lever had worked with both. Faiblesse could veto the election and both men knew that he controlled Faiblesse. He had permitted Noonan to believe that the veto was merely a threat to gain his consent to tearing down Little Sem. But he had made a promise

214

to Michael Tumulty and one he intended to keep. Michael deserved it. Still, it was sad how easily the old fellow had taken it. Father Hoyt inhaled deeply. It was a lovely day. His exhalation became a sigh. Oh, for an opponent worthy of his steel. What would the future be like without conflict and opposition? From now on his path would be like that on which he now wheeled homeward: empty, all his own, full speed ahead.

25

Hoyt had said something about Oliver Fleming making a nuisance of himself but that did not explain why, when the old man telephoned and suggested dinner, Father Faiblesse insisted that he be the host. He would be delighted to entertain Mr. and Mrs. Fleming. As it turned out, Mrs. Fleming was ailing, in the hospital with a broken limb, nothing serious. And Oliver would be glad to come to Father Faiblesse.

If the invitation could not be explained by any desire to relieve the anxieties of Father Hoyt, had it issued from boredom? It surprised Faiblesse to realize that there was something filial in the gesture. His father and Oliver Fleming had both been Fort Elbow businessmen, Oliver the junior, of course, but both men had nursed an essentially small operation into a considerable industry and ended by joining the small economic elite of Fort Elbow. That was not a feat of cosmic importance, perhaps; after all, every community, whatever its size, has its percentage of the wealthy and powerful. It may be that one had to be a citizen of Fort Elbow to consider eminence there to be a matter of privilege. But it was a matter of privilege, of honor earned.

Philip Faiblesse felt that he had always admired those who relied on themselves to build something that otherwise would never have existed. The father superior of the Society of Saint Brendan found that he regarded Oliver Fleming in somewhat the same light as the Founder himself. Formulated, such thoughts surprised, but they pleased even more. Faiblesse felt that he was paying his father a belated tribute.

Philip Faiblesse had been raised before the era when fathers felt a duty to be companions of their sons or sons considered themselves to embody a high moral standard from which their progenitors fell woefully short. Philip Faiblesse had reacted to his father as to a force of nature; that they were not close was merely a fact, neither a failing nor an achievement. When the son had decided to enter the society the father had received the news with compliant incomprehension. Faiblesse senior had been a man in whom the fire of life burned strong. He was burly and boisterous and fond of drink. Had he been unfaithful to his wife? This dizzying possibility was difficult to exclude once the son had become a priest and was acquainted with the frequency and extent of human frailty. His father had been the dominant one at home and his mother, like Philip, would never have dared to question his conduct. There had been business trips, hunting trips, evenings out, hints of great activities elsewhere, so that the portion of himself Faiblesse senior revealed to his family was understood to be a mere fragment of the vast drama of his life.

It had been a relief to Philip to enter a life where he would not be expected to succeed his father, to compete with him and inevitably to fail. As a member of the society he cultivated something akin to passivity, the desire not to assert himself but only to serve. In the end he had been used by others more self-willed. Ah, well, there were worse things. He might have used others. Still, quite often now he assessed his life as his father might have and found that he was not terribly proud of himself. Eventually, of course, his father had aged. Mrs. Faiblesse was carried off in her forties but the father had lived into his seventies, unchanged, it seemed, until the time he sold his business to a national concern and announced that from now on he would travel, golf, sun himself and generally enjoy the leisure an industrious lifetime had denied him. Almost immediately he went into decline. The son was shocked to see his father's body shrink to the dimensions of a lesser purpose. Indecision, reflection, self-questioning set in and Faiblesse senior, become philosophical, turned querulous and talkative. His life, looked back upon, seemed a snap of the fingers in duration, his achievements at once vast and inconsequential. Sometimes, to Philip's embarrassment and with reference to the wisdom of priestly celibacy, he would go on about the absurdity of the role sex plays in life. There seemed to be, however, a disturbingly wistful note in this jeremiad. As a student, Faiblesse had read Cicero's *De Senectute*, a nineteen-year-old boy savoring the stoic withdrawal of the flatulent rhetor. If his father's theme was Ciceronian, it was not sustained by the moral fiber of stoicism. Philip was almost ashamed. And so he had, finally, played the part of the son, the role of assassin. He ended by patronizing his father. Now, when the state of his own health suggested that his end might come halfway between the ages at which his parents had died, he found himself recalling his father more and more. He was in the mood such thoughts induced when he invited Oliver Fleming. A little propitiation, vicarious and too late.

If that had been his hope, it foundered on Oliver's garrulity. From the moment he arrived Fleming talked only of his wife, her absence seemingly giving him an amputee's sense of her ghostly presence. Faiblesse heard that Oliver had moved his wife from the hospital to a nursing home run by the Sisters of Perpetual Help and she loved it, almost against her will. She was in a room with another woman, a Mrs. Hover, and they got along famously. Oliver approved of the spic-and-span look of the home, its chintz curtains and beds that were great nests of white linen. The floor gleamed with wax and above each bed was a crucifix. In short, the place was ideal for mending and reflection. A young priest from a nearby parish brought the patients Communion each day and if Oliver went on to describe him as a bearded dandy in a turtleneck sweater, a medallion bouncing off his chest, he clearly considered such spiritual solace essential to his wife's well-being.

The monologue went on throughout the meal. Mrs. Nickles glided in and out and would have appreciated some sign of approval but she had to be content with Faiblesse's customary praise. When she asked if there was anything else she could bring, Oliver treated the question as an interruption. Father Faiblesse asked him if he had ever seen the chapel in the house.

"No. I'd like to see it."

Upstairs, they stood in the back of the chapel, staring at the altar. Nobis, who had had a tray in his room, insisting that he did not wish to impose himself on the father superior's guest, knelt in a front pew, either asleep or in ecstasy. Faiblesse murmured a prayer and made the first move to go; laymen often displayed an exaggerated devotion on such occasions. When they were outside the chapel, Faiblesse said, "I will offer Mass for your wife in the morning."

"That is kind of you. She is a changed woman since I put her in that nursing home."

"I suppose it helps that she is with people her own age."

"The nuns are her true consolation, Father."

While Oliver extolled the merits of the nursing nuns, his encomium broken by several acid remarks about the state of affairs at Saint Jude's Hospital, Faiblesse poured the brandy. They had withdrawn to his suite, which might have been an error. Oliver settled down like a man who had no intention of leaving soon. Finally, desperate to change the subject, Faiblesse turned to the source of Hoyt's recent displeasure with Oliver.

"I understand that you phoned Father Hoyt about the college's building plans."

"I telephoned him about Little Sem. I told him that I am opposed to its destruction."

219

Faiblesse nodded. "I suppose he reminded you that as trustees we had already approved its destruction."

"I have no memory of it. It doesn't matter."

"Because those at Porta Coeli can veto it?"

"I would be opposed in any case."

"You and I have only a vote. Phelan and the others have a veto."

"So they told me."

"It is true. Father Corcoran found a document in the archives."

Oliver grinned. "Trust the Founder to have provided an obstacle to such a scheme. The man is a genius. Is there any change in his condition?"

"No. That seems to be the best news we can expect."

"Poor man. Old age is a shipwreck. General de Gaulle said that. He lived long enough to prove it in his own case."

"I'm afraid Father Hoyt takes an equally dim view of the old. Your telephone call, on top of the opposition he is receiving from Porta Coeli, upset him. He is used to having his own way."

"Did he ask you to speak to me?"

"Would there be any point in that?"

"Not if the point is to change my mind. Surely you feel as I do, Father. If things go on like this there won't be a brick left on that campus which was laid longer ago than ten years. Father Hoyt has no sense of tradition."

"He is a man of the future."

"No man is that. He is a man of the present, which is a very limiting condition. I know the type. So did your father. Father Hoyt should read history. It gives perspective. He should study the history of the society."

"It has not been written."

"It should be."

A fugitive thought flickered in Faiblesse's mind. He could ask Oliver to underwrite such a project, commission a historian. No.

220

It was a thing only an insider could do. Corcoran? Rejecting the idea, Faiblesse felt suddenly weary. His medicine took its toll, sapping him of what little energy he possessed. Dr. Dowling, after the tests at the hospital, had said little but Faiblesse felt he understood the meaning of that reticence. Oliver took advantage of the lull to return to the topic of his wife.

"Did I tell you that Holy Communion is distributed every morning at the nursing home?"

"Yes, you did."

"Ordinarily Enid and I attended daily Mass together."

"I hadn't known that."

"She is a pious woman, in her way." Oliver puffed approvingly on his cigar, exhaling a wraithlike vision of his churchgoing spouse.

"I regret that I have never come to know her well."

"She belongs to the Third Order of Saint Francis."

"I see."

"It is my great regret that the society has no provisions for a species of lay membership. A third order of sorts."

"That is not permitted to us latecomers in the ranks of religious societies."

"Is it true that members of third orders can be buried in the habit?"

"I think so."

"They can," Oliver said, surprisingly. "I have inquired. I find the thought intriguing. A man who has lived in the world might, late in life, dedicate himself more fully to the church."

Faiblesse thought of his father, thin and brown in the Florida sunshine, rambling on about the absurdity of life. A man married, made money, had a son and then, so quickly, shriveled and died. What did it all mean? His son's reply about good done and service rendered was dismissed with a wave of a tanned arthritic hand. Talk of life as a trial, a test, a journey fared no better.

"A journey to the grave," the old man grumbled.

Faiblesse found it difficult to remind his father of the elements of religious faith. He had asked a local priest to look in on his father, noticing venality dance in the other cleric's eyes. An ailing affluent retiree might conceivably settle some much-needed cash on his stucco church with its rust-stained walls and hideous stained-glass windows featuring the names of their donors. Faiblesse's resentment had been slight. That Sarasota parish was in need of money. Had his father died a good death? The priest, his hopes of a bequest unfulfilled, had said yes, but was stingy with details. Of course Faiblesse remembered his parents every day at Mass.

"There is talk of reviving the diaconate," he told Oliver Fleming.

Oliver frowned. He had heard of this. Married men distributing Communion, even preaching. He did not like it.

He said, "In early ages men entered the monastery after their children were raised."

"Do you have children?"

"Enid could not bear them," Oliver said enigmatically. "Husbands to monasteries, wives to convents."

"The traffic is in the opposite direction nowadays."

That was a mistake. In the manner of the shocked laity, Oliver began a tirade on the modern clergy. As courteously as he could, Faiblesse cut him off. He feared that he would fall asleep in his chair while Oliver reviewed the sad state of the Church. He went downstairs with his guest and, at the front door, they said good-bye. Faiblesse found the night air slightly reviving but he longed to crawl into bed.

Oliver said, "I would be most appreciative if you would visit Enid."

"Of course."

"This Sunday? I will come for you."

Faiblesse agreed. It was a way to end the evening.

26

Sunday, High Mass in the chapel of Porta Coeli, the rite the madly altered one put into effect since Vatican II but orchestrated by Goudge in such a way that it bore at least some resemblance to the Latin liturgy whose demise they lamented to a man. More penitential than the liturgy was the sermon. They took turns. They had been trained in an era of the fulsome sermon, twenty minutes long at least, a discourse blending instruction and exhortation, history and dogma, and salted with examples of pith and point. The Founder himself had taught them homiletics and forbidden them to have recourse to the canned sermons available in handbooks for the unimaginative preacher. No doubt each of them had cheated from time to time, but with the saving awareness that that was what he was doing. A genuine sermon was worked up by oneself. Needless to say, it could be used again and again when the proper Sunday rolled around, but it was delivered with embellishments, it grew and altered and improved with use.

Thus thought Father Tumulty, leaden with boredom in his place in chapel. The special trouble in this house was that a man too often brought to the pulpit matters discussed during the week in the recreation room and at table, matters of opinion now taken up in a role that assured one the last word, or personal hobby-horses ridden with a vengeance for twenty minutes while the house sat captive before the preacher. Henley, for instance, loved to expatiate on the vanity of talk of space exploration, adorning his scornful treatment with a bouquet of texts from the Apocalypse that somehow suggested that the desire to escape the earth and alight on other planets was a clear sign that the end was near. "Inner space," he would urge them sibilantly, the words whistling through his dentures. "Inner space, dear brothers in Christ. *That* is our concern." Noonan, hands shoved up the sleeves of the alb, head thrown back, eyes on the ceiling, would go on and on about the humility each of them must feel when he looked back on the ineffectual years in the vineyard of the Lord. The opportunities missed, the failure of zeal, the mediocrity of times past must not induce despondency now. Our God is a merciful God. Each man arrives before His throne empty-handed, in need of pardon and pity, deserving little praise. Garrity in his turn would try to put things back in proper perspective by urging his fellow priests to pray that the great works they had begun during their active ministry would be continued by worthy successors now that they had withdrawn to this anteroom of eternity, soon to give an accounting of the use they had made of their talents. False modesty about past accomplishments was not the sacrifice God asked of them now. He wanted their hearts, whole and entire, still beating with the enthusiasm that had animated their deeds throughout their careers as priests. His peroration was often spoiled by the sound of Noonan's audible snore.

This morning old Father Ucello was putting on a strange performance in the pulpit. His text was the fallen sparrow verse, which was good enough, but he had gone on in a choked voice

224

to describe Saint Francis's love for our feathered friends. Not that birds are made in the image of God, but they do bear His likeness, the imprint of His fullness of being. Let us not forget that the Holy Spirit appeared in the form of a bird. What then was to be said of a man who would deliberately bring death to these little ones? What manner of human being would put 10–10–10 fertilizer in a bag of bird seed? There is a word in the language which, like so many words in use today, is a euphemism to cloak in inoffensive verbiage a dastardly deed. Father Ucello was thinking of the word "pesticide." He found it a loathsome word. The only thing to commend it was its obvious affinity with "homicide." Phelan rolled with discomfort in his seat. "What in hell is he talking about?" he whispered to Trask, who, without opening his eyes, arms folded, shrugged his shoulders eloquently. Tumulty was trying to tune out the mad analogy Ucello was drawing, something about chemical fertilizer—a lovely word, that, redolent of man's efforts to aid nature in its noble task, and yet a chemical manufactured for the laudable purpose of fructifying the vegetable kingdom could so easily be perverted and bring death to the animal. Mineral, vegetable, animal, Ucello keened, the natural friendship of the levels of being turned to enmity by sinful man. Tumulty groaned. What did this have to do with anything?

It had been only two days since his conversation with Father Hoyt, more than time enough for him to see himself as a permanent resident of Porta Coeli. These sermons had once been half listened to with an eye for future anecdotes when he returned to the real world. Now Ucello seemed the spokesman for his own condition. He opened his eyes and imagined himself seated where Noonan was. Pride of place. *Superbia vitae*. He wanted to sit there. If he must stay in this house he wanted something to do. He would make something of the job. Hoyt had been right in that: the superior of Porta Coeli could be, if he had the imagination to see it, one of the three top men in the society. Or one of the two. It was difficult to think of Hoyt as a member after that conversation about the election. Everything was grist for Hoyt's mill: the society, its rules, its home for retired priests. Well, God can bring good out of evil. However Michael Tumulty became superior of this house, once he was in, it was a lifetime post. He would comport himself in it as the Founder might have if he had come to Porta Coeli as a younger man. Of course there would have to be a time for healing. Noonan and Phelan could not be expected to take their betrayal without protest.

Phelan was thinking of the letter in his desk. "I, Leo Phelan, having celebrated three years ago my golden jubilee as a member of the Society of Saint Brendan, do, under the provisions of the document found in the archives by Father Corcoran, give my consent to the use of the site of Little Sem for the new dormitory." How easily the dread words had come from his pen. He had read them over, waiting for revulsion to overcome him. The sense of treachery he thirsted for did not put in an appearance. The concession had been extorted from him and he wondered if he should not put into his letter the quid pro quo that explained his writing it. He had not yet signed and delivered the letter, despite Noonan's impatience. As much as anything else, Phelan dreaded the reaction of others in the house when Little Sem came down. That would make it clear as day that Leo Phelan had given in. Noonan was furious when he suggested that they explain to the others why they did what they did. The man who could veto an election could also remove the superior of Porta Coeli from that post. Hoyt's cleverness approached the diabolical. What Phelan wanted to hold out for was some assurance, preferably written, that Hoyt would keep his side of the bargain.

That afternoon Phelan was heading outside with a nine iron when he encountered Corcoran, dressed in street clothes. The day was warm and, when they were outside, Phelan mentioned that Corcoran would not be comfortable in that attire on such a day. He was not a champion of informal clerical clothing, he added needlessly, but around the house a suit and Roman collar seemed an affectation.

"I am off to town," Corcoran said.

Watching Corcoran go off without, Phelan was sure, so much as a by-your-leave from Noonan, he thought grimly that things would be different soon. Perhaps very soon. There had been a scare two days before when the Founder's temperature had begun unaccountably to rise. Sister Diotima and Miss Bishop had packed the old man in ice to bring his temperature down to normal. They had succeeded but now the doctor feared that pneumonia might have been brought on by the method used. Considering this, hacking listlessly away at three old scrubs with smiles in them, Phelan decided that he had best not delay further his consent to Hoyt. He went to his room, got out the letter, read it almost without emotion and signed it. *Quod scripsi, scripsi*. He decided to deliver the letter himself.

Hoyt had a suite of rooms on the top floor of the administration building, an aerie from which, Phelan had been told, he had an unrivaled view of the campus. There was no answer to Phelan's knock on the door. He should have telephoned before coming. What to do now? To slip the letter under the door might suggest an unseemly urgency, if he could indeed get the letter into the room that way, which seemed doubtful. To find out, he dropped to his knees. He ran the edge of the envelope along the narrow aperture; it just fit.

"Phelan! My God, is that you?"

Still on his knees, Phelan looked over his shoulder to see Huff advancing, a horrified expression on his face.

"Did you fall? Are you hurt?" Huff, beside him now, got his hand under Phelan's arm and began to tug.

Phelan shook himself free. "Let go. What are you doing? I'm all right." But he did not find it easy to get to his feet again and had to accept Huff's help.

"What are you doing prostrate at Hoyt's door?"

"I was not prostrate," Phelan snapped. "I was pushing a letter under the door."

Huff stepped back while a comprehending smile stole over his face. "Aha. A threatening note? You are a true adversary, Leo. But come, face your enemy." Huff advanced on the door and began to pound vigorously upon it.

"He is not in," Phelan said.

"And how do you know that?" There was definitely a malevolent twinkle in Huff's eye. "Did you phone first to make sure the coast was clear?"

"You are being ridiculous, Huff. What are you doing here?"

"Not delivering letters. I do not compete with the postal service."

Huff stuck to his side when Phelan went downstairs. Phelan seethed with indignation and embarrassment. What ignominy to be discovered on his hands and knees at Hoyt's door, and by Huff of all people. He would never hear the end of it.

"I'll walk back to the house with you," Huff said.

"I am not going back."

"Where then?"

Phelan glared at him. Huff would get his when the Noonan regime began. This brazen taunting was too much. Phelan's eyes narrowed. The toad. Could that have been Huff? He turned on his heel and marched away. It was almost worth giving in to Hoyt in order to gain ascendancy at Porta Coeli.

Tumulty, seeing Noonan on a bench across the lawn, turned to go in another direction, then stopped. He crossed the grass and sat down beside Noonan.

"I have just come from Little Sem, Noonan."

"There isn't much to see."

"At our age the eye needs little stimulus to see much. I was able to understand your intransigence on the matter. I admire you for it."

"Sooner or later it will be torn down, Michael."

"It could have been restored. It is in basically good condition."

"Are you an architect, Michael?"

They sat in silence for a time. Tumulty was tired from the walk around the lake. He had thought he was providing Noonan with an opportunity to say that he had given in to Hoyt but he seemed only to have tempted him to circumlocution. How odd to realize that they would both be staying here. And would Noonan resent the reversal of their past relation? He looked at Noonan and found that he had fallen asleep. Tumulty left him there, dozing in the shade. Was Noonan weary at the prospect of reassuming the authority that had been his so long ago? Poor fellow.

Noonan was not asleep. He listened to Tumulty get up, hesitate, then go away. A moment later, Noonan opened his eyes. It took another moment for his vision to clear. The lake shimmered in sunlight and it was a pleasant spectacle, seen from the shaded bench. He had swum in that lake as a boy. Whatever the case with rivers, one can step twice into the same lake. Students no longer went swimming in the spring. It was a time of caution and prudence, and of insurance. The college could no longer accept the risk. Nowadays brother sued brother, children their parents; quite impersonal. The vice of gambling and the virtue of insurance. Unquote. Who had said that? Noonan could not remember. He did not care. The mind is a tireless plagiarist. How many of his thoughts were really his own? Augustine regarded truth as a common good, everyone's, no one's, but truth is the object of thought. Its expression bears the mark of individuality. Noonan felt his mind to be an echoing hall, littered with odds and ends picked up just anywhere. Imagine Tumulty, rambling along the hallways of Little Sem. He tried to imagine himself as a young man of nineteen or twenty, the school prefect, a figure of respect and authority to the high school boys. Little Michael Tumulty. *Ecce aqua benedicta.* The sweet wine of nostalgia was filched from him by Tumulty young and old. Did he in his heart really feel affection for that old building, the scene of his youthful triumph? It had been more bother than honor to be head prefect of the school, always at the beck and call of the Founder, the middleman between faculty and students, neither fish nor fowl, no time unequivocally his own. He had learned then an odd truth. Those at the top envy those who are not, who bear no responsibilities, who are free. No wonder he had formed the resolution never again to be at the top of anything.

If that had been his hope, it had been fulfilled, pressed down and running over. And now he ran the risk of being elected superior of Porta Coeli when the Founder died. Did it really matter? Bottom and top were indistinguishable here. He did enjoy presiding at table and in chapel, and what else was there to the job after all? The Founder had lent it the vast prestige of his long life of service so that the post of superior of Porta Coeli seemed a good deal more important than it was. It was the Founder who was important. And the Founder lay dying. Noonan stopped the whirl of his mind to see if he might surprise in himself a pang of sorrow at the thought. How does one grieve over the death of a man in his nineties who has been in a coma for weeks? In chapel each night they prayed that the old man would receive the grace of a happy death. The prayer seemed to have been answered already. If the Founder's death lay at the end of a coma, how could it terrify? Perhaps it would only be a kind of awakening. But then, when he suffered his seizure, the Founder may have experienced the bottomless dread death evokes. It was a terrible thought to think of the old man's brain frozen in the moment of terror beneath the external calm of the coma, these days a prolonged agony with death the only release.

Noonan shivered and shifted on the bench, moving into the

sun. It was morbid to dwell on death. Better to live like Tumulty, as if life still stretched before them, years and years of it left. Noonan got up. He was thirsty. He would find Trask and open the liquor cabinet. They would have a gin and tonic together.

27

WHILE SAYING MASS that Sunday morning Father Faiblesse was swept by nausea and dizziness. He managed to get to the front pew of the little chapel and he sat there for fifteen minutes before he could continue. Thank God he was saying a private Mass. Of course Nobis was there and afterward pestered Faiblesse about what had happened. The father superior dismissed the suggestion that he was ill, praying that Nobis would not float a rumor. He did not want inquiries, curiosity, sympathy. The same stubbornness decided him to keep his promise to Oliver Fleming and pay a visit to the nursing home where Mrs. Fleming was staying. As they drove across Fort Elbow, Faiblesse felt surrounded by the possibility of debilitating pain; at any moment it might return. This did not help his mood. He told Oliver he must return to the house in an hour.

"What a scene they make." Oliver had halted Faiblesse and pointed into the parlor. Enid Fleming in a wheelchair, a nun beside her, awaited them. Bright curtains at the windows behind the pair were alive with sun; Enid wore a quilted housecoat, the nun a white habit. Oliver led Father Faiblesse almost reverently toward this tableau.

"You look like twins," he announced. The nun, Sister Margarita, still in her fifties, did not look flattered. When Oliver had completed the introductions, the nun, saying something in a fluting voice, sailed from the room. Faiblesse had the sense of being abandoned.

"Have you read the novels of M. Raymond?" Oliver asked when they were settled in chairs. "He is a Trappist."

"A Trappist novelist?" Faiblesse said. The nursing home affected him in much the same way Saint Jude's had when he went in for his tests. The chance of illness rendered a certainty by the surroundings.

"I have been reading him. *The Man Who Got Even with God. The Family That Overtook Christ.*"

"Got even with God? What a curious idea."

"Beautiful stories." Oliver tipped back his head.

"I have never liked the Trappists," Faiblesse said. "It is a prejudice, I admit. Of course I have grounds. Saint Bernard of Clairvaux was an impossible man." He remembered Nobis fussing over him in chapel that morning. Nobis should have been a Trappist.

"You can't mean that," Oliver protested. "Saint Bernard figures in these novels."

"He was a fascist," Faiblesse told Mrs. Fleming, who seemed delighted by his contrariness. "His treatment of Peter Abelard was cruel, atrocious, uncharitable. He set his ecclesiastical dogs on the man." An Abelard who looked much like Faiblesse was hounded across his imagination by a pack led by Hoyt and Phelan. Tumulty, too.

"Who is Peter Abelard?" Enid wanted to know.

"A renegade monk who seduced his logic student," Oliver snapped.

"He was not a monk at the time," Faiblesse corrected. "Perhaps he was in minor orders."

"I thought he was a monk."

"Minor orders?" Enid said.

"He became a monk after he had been emasculated by the uncle of Heloise."

"Emasculated?" Enid said.

"Castrated," Faiblesse explained, surprising himself.

"I don't understand."

"It doesn't matter." Oliver glared at his wife but Faiblesse sensed he was the real object of that ire. Had they come here to visit with Mrs. Fleming or to discuss Oliver's reading? Faiblesse wished that he were home, alone, where the onset of pain could be met with dignity.

Faiblesse said, "Abelard became a monk. Poor devil. He was still hounded by righteous asses like Bernard." He had the silly notion his father would have approved the line he was taking.

"You praise the lecher and condemn the saint?"

"Abelard was certainly not a saint. He was given to self-pity. And of course to become a monk when one has been made impotent is scarcely a sacrifice."

Oliver took a cigar from his pocket and was asked by Enid not to smoke it there.

"I will smoke if I want to. Father, would you care for a cigar?"

Faiblesse put it in his pocket. Oliver left his unlit.

He said, "What interested me in those novels was the frequency with which family men betook themselves to the cloister. Husbands to the monastery, wives to the convent, children distributed among their parents' religious houses."

"A barbaric custom," Faiblesse said, shaking his head. "The Middle Ages, whatever is sometimes said, were not a high point in Church history."

"Surely the practice I mention was exemplary."

"Breaking up a family?"

"For a higher purpose," Oliver said. "Surely it is permitted in canon law?"

"What canon law permits is hardly a moral guide."

"But is it legal?"

"I wouldn't be surprised. Canon law always bored me. I never understood why I was asked to study it. The Founder just told me to."

"How is your Founder, Father? Oliver tells me he is ill."

"He is dying. It is only a matter of time."

"I'm so sorry."

"I consider him a second father," Oliver said unctuously.

Faiblesse looked at him. "You do?"

"That is how he treated us. In Little Sem."

"You were there?"

"Of course I was there. Before your time, of course."

Faiblesse felt that he should have known this. It explained so many things. To Mrs. Fleming he said, "Your husband has been very generous to the society. We are grateful to him. The retirement home he built for us is not unlike this place, I suppose."

"Enid loves the nuns here. They are all holy women."

"They are kind," Enid said.

"Have you met our Sister Diotima, Mrs. Fleming? She is as old as the Founder. I think they are cousins."

"She is still active, Enid," Oliver said. "Nuns live to an incredibly advanced age, vigorous to the end."

"Working?"

"They do not consider it work."

"Here they are run off their feet, poor things. It must be a depressing life, caring for the old."

"It is well to remain active," Faiblesse said. "The residents of our retirement home complain of boredom."

"It is the same here."

"I envy the men at Porta Coeli," Oliver insisted.

"Most of them would change places with you."

"I don't believe that. They are close to God. It is I who would change places with them."

"You can't mean that."

"Oh, but he does," Enid said. "Can't you tell? Oliver still wants to be a priest."

Enid Fleming threw back her head and laughed. Father Faiblesse joined in. Oliver Fleming stared at them, enraged.

"He wants to get even with God," Enid trilled.

Faiblesse's laughter took new impetus from her remark. Oliver rose, glared at the two of them and left the room. Enid Fleming wiped her eyes and grew serious.

"He would like to leave me here and join the monastery."

"I doubt that."

"No. I mean it." She clutched his arm. "Could he really do that?"

Sun still shone at the windows but joy had fled the parlor. Enid Fleming was a worried old woman. Father Faiblesse felt that he himself was only waiting for the onset of pain.

"I'll go get your husband."

"I won't stay here," she called after him. "I won't."

Faiblesse found Oliver in another parlor down the hall. He told him to come back to his wife but Oliver shook his head.

"You must not laugh at me, Father. What she said is true. I want to become a priest."

Faiblesse stared at the spare personage sitting rigid in a chair. Oliver's eyes searched his face for some reaction. Faiblesse said, "You can't be serious."

"I am perfectly serious. Have you understood me? I should like to enter the society. It would be the crowning joy of my life to be ordained a priest, to offer the Holy Sacrifice of the Mass . . ."

"And to live at Porta Coeli?"

"Yes."

Had this absurd ambition been behind Oliver's generosity in building Porta Coeli, a minor pharaoh ordering his pyramid? "How old are you, Oliver?"

"I am younger than many of the men living there."

"You are a married man."

"Father, at my age, to be a husband or to be a monk comes to much the same thing."

"Nonetheless, you have a wife."

"She will want for nothing."

"Except for you."

"She will learn to accept it."

"Do you propose to abandon her here?"

"Your phrasing is tendentious."

"I mean it to be. Forget this foolishness, Oliver. You are an old man. You have lived a long life. You have taken on obligations. You are what you are. You must accept that."

"I want to enter the society."

"No."

"You refuse me?"

"I refuse to let you dream of demanding such a sacrifice from your wife. You do not regard this idea as demanding any sacrifice from you, do you?"

"It would be a pleasure to live my remaining years for God."

"Nothing prevents your doing that."

"You know what I mean."

"The answer is no."

Oliver began to speak obliquely of his wealth. He seemed to regard it as a dowry. Faiblesse was glad when Sister Margarita looked in.

"Where is your wife?" she asked.

"In the parlor."

"She is not there."

"Perhaps she went to her room."

"She is not there either."

Father Faiblesse did nothing to aid in the search for Enid; he found himself rooting for her. But Sister Margarita was alerted by a filling station attendant across the street. An old woman in a wheelchair was out on the sidewalk waving at passing cars.

Wheeled into the parlor, Enid tilted her chin defiantly. "I am going home, Oliver."

"Nonsense. You are not well. What kind of spectacle were you making of yourself? Do you want to be put away in another kind of place?"

"I want to go home."

"There, there," soothed Sister Margarita.

Enid rejected the consolations of religion. "I mean it, Oliver. You must take me home now."

Oliver avoided looking at Faiblesse. "You can't be moved."

"You moved me here from the hospital."

"So that you could receive adequate care. When you are well I will take you home."

"No, you won't. You mean to leave me here. You want to go live with those old priests."

"Hush, Enid."

She turned to Faiblesse. "Now do you believe me? This foolish old man wants to become a priest at his age."

"You mustn't worry yourself, Mrs. Fleming."

"Take her to her room, Sister," Oliver said.

"No." Enid gripped the wheels of her chair. "I will scream."

"It's time for your back rub, Mrs. Fleming."

"If you touch this chair, I will scream. I will cause pandemonium. My husband is going to take me home."

"Dr. Bloomer would not permit it," Oliver said.

"Dr. Bloomer is an ass, as you have told me. He permits what he is told to permit. I am ready to go, Oliver. Where is the car?"

It was a day of defeats for Oliver. Sister Margarita, downcast, embarrassed, took Enid to her room for her things. Oliver looked at Faiblesse as if from the depths.

"I'll get the car," he said hollowly.

"This is best, Oliver. Take her home. I will call a cab."

Faiblesse stood in the service door when Oliver drove up. On the tinted windshield the sun glowed, blurring the driver's face. Inside, the air conditioner would be purring. Faiblesse felt an involuntary pity for the old man. He wanted to make some quixotic gesture to redeem his life. His wife arrived, a suitcase in her lap. Sister Margarita pushed his huge, broken Heloise toward Oliver's car and he, unlucky Abelard, got out to open the door. Faiblesse went inside the nursing home in search of a telephone. Poor Oliver. Poor Enid. A stab of pain brought his pity swiftly home. He decided to call Mr. Nickles.

28

*F*ATHER FOGARTY'S NOTE informing the father superior that he was eloping with Miss Liczenski was typewritten and Father Faiblesse wondered if the prospective bride had done it. A picture formed in his mind: Fogarty pacing the room, dictating. But surely the note had not been typed on the electric machine Miss Liczenski used in her office here. Where then had it been typed and under what conditions? His mental picture began to assume lascivious contours; Faiblesse erased it from his mind. He folded the note, slipped it under the blotter on his desk and wondered what he should do.

It was heedless of Fogarty simply to run away like this. God knew that the process of laicization had been speeded up to such a tempo that the delay would have been inconsiderable. He found it difficult to believe that either Fogarty or Miss Liczenski had been so overcome by carnal impetuosity that the brief interval a legal leavetaking would have dictated could have loomed impossibly large. Assuming that they had not already consummated their union, prior to obtaining a civil license. The

240

mental picture returned and Faiblesse grew mildly wrathful. What kind of shenanigans might not have been going on under this very roof? And for how long? The two of them were at an age where curiosity rather than passion would have motivated their liaison, or was that a churlish, self-protective thought? Faiblesse had been immune to attacks of concupiscence for years. The only personal analogy he could find for Fogarty's flight would be his own absconding with Mrs. Nickles. Good God. He had best call Hoyt.

The president of Saint Brendan's College was both angry and amused.

"I am flabbergasted," Faiblesse said.

"You had no inkling?"

"None whatever."

"Well, these things happen. With damnable frequency, too. He might have chosen a better time, though I can't imagine when that would have been. Who knows of this?"

"So far as I know, only myself."

"What of her family?"

"I wanted to talk with you before I contacted them. There is no immediate family but she has, I gather, many cousins and uncles and aunts."

"I'm coming over there. I'll decide how to handle this when I arrive."

Having hung up, Faiblesse realized that he did not deserve to be resentful at Hoyt's usurpation of his function. After all, by telephoning him, he had in effect delivered the problem into his hands. He lit his pipe, feeling silly and inadequate. Would anyone else have noticed some sign of what had been going on between Fogarty and Miss Liczenski? He wanted to think they had been so discreet it would have been hidden from any eye, even the most suspicious. He rose from his desk and went downstairs to the kitchen. As luck would have it, both Mr. and Mrs. Nickles were there, sitting at the table, cups of coffee before

241

them. The little domestic scene surprised Faiblesse, he did not know why. The Nickleses pushed back their chairs when he came in but he urged them to remain seated. He pulled up a chair and sat with them. Mrs. Nickles brought him a cup of coffee.

"I have some rather shocking news." He looked at Mr. Nickles. He felt that it would have been easier to say if Mrs. Nickles were not there. She had expressed more than passing interest in the Church. Perhaps Mr. Nickles would follow her in, if she ever made the move, but he would not take the initiative on something like that. It would have been possible to speak to Mr. Nickles as a man of the world.

"What is it, Father?" Mrs. Nickles asked.

"It is about Father Fogarty." Faiblesse sipped his coffee. "And Miss Liczenski."

Mr. Nickles grinned and nodded his head. "Gone off, have they?"

"How did you know?"

"He didn't know," Mrs. Nickles snapped. "Surely it isn't true."

"I'm afraid it is. I'm as surprised as you are."

"I'm not surprised," Mr. Nickles said.

"Why do you say that?"

"Woodie, will you please be quiet."

"No, Mrs. Nickles, I want to know. I feel I should have had some intimation of this."

Nickles tipped his chair back slightly and adopted a knowing expression. "It was plain as the nose on my face. I've said for weeks there was something up, but Mrs. Nickles told me I was wrong."

"You observed things?"

Mrs. Nickles said, "He wasn't prying, Father. Nothing like that."

"Of course I wasn't. There wasn't any need to."

242

What Mr. Nickles had to say did not strike Father Faiblesse as particularly significant. The two had often been alone in the office together. Of course they had been. They had driven away in Fogarty's car on several occasions. Had things reached a point where Fogarty could not drop Miss Liczenski off at the end of the day without arousing suspicion? Nickles ticked off his items with the annoying suggestiveness of a prosecuting attorney. It seemed to Father Faiblesse that Mr. Nickles was enjoying this scandal. He was glad to leave the kitchen and return to his room. Hoyt came right upstairs when he arrived.

"You have to give it to Fogarty," he said. "He certainly made a shrewd choice."

"Shrewd? You've seen Miss Liczenski, Father. She would be safe in the navy."

"Money, Father. Money. The woman is loaded. Fogarty told me so himself. She inherited a suitcase full of shares in the original issue of Flamingo stock. It stunned Fogarty that she had no real idea what they were worth. I should have suspected something then."

Money. Faiblesse remembered hearing of Miss Liczenski's stock. Well, at least that provided an intelligible motive for Fogarty. Miss Liczenski, being a woman, would have needed no rational reason for doing this.

Hoyt said, "Have you talked to the others in the house?"

"The housekeeper was as surprised as I am; her husband claims to have suspected it all along. I think he is flattering himself."

"And Father Nobis?"

"I have not yet spoken to him."

"Let's call him in."

When he arrived, summoned from a holy hour in the chapel, Father Nobis listened impassively to the news.

"Did you know anything of this?" Hoyt asked him.

"Father," Nobis said to Faiblesse, "I cannot discuss this case."

243

"Why not?" Hoyt demanded.

Still speaking to Faiblesse, Nobis said, "I sometimes acted as Father Fogarty's confessor."

"Ah. Very well, Father. You may leave us."

Hoyt frowned after Nobis had left. "Surely not everything he knew would have come under the seal of the confessional. He must have seen things, heard things."

"Oh, he was quite right, Father. I would not have wanted to put him in the position of trying to distinguish between what was and what was not confidential. Father Nobis is very conscientious, almost scrupulous. It would have been too unsettling for him."

"It's pretty damned unsettling for me, too." He looked at his watch. "We haven't much time. I made an appointment at the chancery office."

"You did?"

"Don't tell me you're not free."

"Did you tell them what the problem is?"

"I didn't even tell them that there is a problem. For all they know, it's just a friendly visit."

"They?"

"I wanted Bishop Brophy in on this, too. He will see the need to smooth things over fast to make certain no discussion begins. Fort Elbow has had enough trouble of this kind. He won't want us dropping more of it on his doorstep. I could wring Fogarty's neck when I think of having to tell Oder and Brophy about this."

And so, feeling like an appendage, Faiblesse was driven away to the chancery office and an appointment with Donald Oder, the vicar-general of the Fort Elbow diocese, and Sean Brophy, its bishop. Hoyt put a hand under Faiblesse's elbow when they climbed the steps of the chancery and Faiblesse actually felt in need of help. More and more it was dawning on him that it was his right-hand man who had defected and that he would inevitably be on the defensive in the interview ahead.

Oder came out to greet them as soon as the receptionist let him know they had arrived. The smile on the vicar-general's face was one of oily sympathy and it was directed primarily to Hoyt. Oder nodded vaguely to Faiblesse as if he were not absolutely sure who he was. The vicar-general, some not wholly unreliable sources claimed, had once described the body Faiblesse headed as "our Mickey Mouse society." Faiblesse followed the two younger men down the hall to Oder's office. They walked in pregnant silence. Who were Oder's informants that he should have heard already, as he obviously had? Hoyt was managing to remain unsurprised, at least in manner, in the face of Oder's knowledge. The newspaper on Oder's desk dissolved the mystery. Hoyt took it from the vicar-general, glanced at it, uttered a vulgar word and passed it on to Faiblesse. When he saw the story, the photographs, Faiblesse sat down as if he had been pushed into the chair.

"Fogarty-Liczenski Marriage Announced." Beneath that heading, side by side, were photographs of the happy couple. He scarcely recognized Miss Liczenski; her photograph could not be a recent one. Fogarty's was obviously his ordination picture and that was the shock: in it he wore a Roman collar. Fogarty, who had long forsworn clerical clothing, smiled at the readers of the Fort Elbow *Tribune,* unmistakably a priest. Faiblesse could not bring himself to read the story. His arm went limp and the newspaper dragged on the floor. Oder, who had been commiserating with Hoyt, though not without a chuckle or two, asked for the paper back.

"Bishop Brophy hasn't seen that yet."

"Does he have to?"

"He'll see it eventually, Father. Better to have all the grisly facts before us from the start,"

Hoyt took the paper and handed it to Oder. "That must have been her idea."

"Perhaps. The notice was sent to the Fort Elbow *Catholic,* too. They certainly don't mean to be secretive."

"The Fort Elbow *Catholic*?" Faiblesse was aghast. "Did they seriously expect it to be printed there?"

"It might have been, Father. Fortunately Miss Muscatelli, the editor, consulted me first."

"How long have you known?" Hoyt asked testily.

"Just since this morning. Of course I assumed you people have known for some time."

"Father Faiblesse hadn't a clue. Fogarty left him a note."

Oder and Hoyt looked at Faiblesse as if trying to comprehend his density. Faiblesse said, "Why would I suspect him? I trusted him." He added, more feebly, "We all trusted him."

If he had expected Hoyt to inform Oder that Fogarty was his protégé, Faiblesse was disappointed. The president sat forward, establishing some distance from the grieving father superior. "The point is what do we do now?"

Oder tipped back in his chair as if to escape the range of Hoyt's pronoun. "You could be in worse shape, you know. The reader might think the whole thing is kosher, that Fogarty had been dispensed from his vows. It's a pretty careful statement." He glanced at the paper. "Is that a bad photograph of her, or what?"

"She has money."

"Ah."

"What is particularly thoughtless about it," Faiblesse said, "is that our Founder is now on his deathbed. He could die at any minute. Imagine if he had died today. The news would have been eclipsed by that." He gestured at the newspaper.

A buzzer sounded on Oder's desk. He rose. "The bishop will see us now."

Sean Brophy wore his hair somewhat longer than he had as auxiliary bishop to George Caldron, but that was the least of the transformations in the man. What had formerly been a presumptive authority, one founded on the promise of competence and innovation, was now an authority ex officio. The bishop waited beside his desk for the three priests to approach him. Oder got them seated, putting Faiblesse off to one side. He so placed his own chair that he and the bishop were facing the visitors.

"How is your Founder?" Brophy asked. Belatedly he directed the question to Faiblesse, too.

Faiblesse said, "His condition remains serious."

"Would there be any point in my going to see him?"

"He is in a coma, Your Excellency."

Brophy was momentarily pleased by the archaic form of address, but he frowned away his pleasure and asked Hoyt what he could do for him. Oder had brought in the newspaper and he now handed it to Father Hoyt. Brophy followed this exchange with interest. He settled back in his chair, receptive, distant, a spiritual father.

"We've had a bit of shock, Bishop. Father Faiblesse's assistant has just announced his marriage to the father superior's secretary." He passed the newspaper to the bishop. Brophy read it with obvious interest. When he had finished, he glanced at Faiblesse with raised eyebrows. He waited for Hoyt to continue.

"This comes, needless to say, at an inopportune time. I am thankful he wasn't directly connected with the college. In the past he was, as that story points out. Without being Neanderthal about it, I want to disassociate the college from all this. You will notice that the story leaves his canonical status conveniently vague. How quickly can an ex post facto laicization be put through?"

"Fogarty himself must petition for it, of course."

"Of course."

"Do we know where he can be reached?"

"Father Faiblesse can take care of that."

"Well, then." Brophy, his hands flat on the desk, outlined the procedure. Listening, Faiblesse wondered why Hoyt had insisted on bringing him along for this interview. He felt completely superfluous. Fogarty's misadventure had significance for

Hoyt only insofar as it might affect the fortunes of Saint Brendan's College. After the inquiry about the Founder's health, the society dropped out of the conversation. Did it loom any larger in Hoyt's mind than in Oder's and Brophy's? It was the president who had turned the conversation to his building plans and was now speaking with diffident enthusiasm of the new dorm for coeds.

"It is a self-liquidating government loan," he said. "As good as a gift. There is no donor demanding the building be named for him."

"Construction has started?" Oder asked.

"It will, shortly."

The bishop was interested in the nature of the loan and Hoyt satisfied the episcopal curiosity with a detailed account. Oder, too, listened with rapt attention. Perhaps Hoyt was right to divert them like this, balancing the embarrassment of Fogarty's marriage with a reminder of the efficiency with which the society ran its college. Except that it was no longer the society's college. The conversation drifted on to the diocesan building fund.

Faiblesse was relieved when the interview came to an end. In recognition of the father superior's presence, Brophy reminded Faiblesse to contact Fogarty and have him make a formal request for dispensation from his vows. Faiblesse knelt and asked the bishop for his blessing. After a moment's hesitation, Hoyt, too, dropped to his knee. Brophy murmured over them, sketching with his ringed hand the sign of the cross.

In the car Hoyt turned angrily to Faiblesse. "Why did you ask for his blessing? That was neither the time nor the place. When you do business with a bishop you've got to be in an upright position. And there we were groveling on the carpet like mendicants. Did you see the look on Oder's face?"

"I didn't notice."

"Lucky you. Please don't ever do that again."

"We always asked the Founder for a blessing at the end of an interview."

"I never did. It's not as if we had been going to confession, Father. I hope you noticed that Brophy himself was surprised."

They drove on in silence. Faiblesse had lamented the waning of the practice within the society and hoped to bring it back. Few members asked for his blessing after a visit with him. He felt that they should. It was not a personal thing. Spiritual son, spiritual father. All the better if it stung the pride to kneel before a fellow man who was, after all, God's representative. Whatever one felt toward Brophy personally, the man was a bishop, his blessing desirable.

Hoyt swung into the driveway of the house on Cavil Boulevard. He waited with the motor running for Faiblesse to get out.

"Got any ideas on how to reach Fogarty?"

"None at all."

"There must be some clue. I'll look into it."

"When you were telling Bishop Brophy of the new dormitory, you spoke as if all obstacles had been removed."

Hoyt looked at Faiblesse, then reached for the key and turned off the motor. "I have been meaning to speak to you about that. Yes, the obstacles have been removed. Noonan gave his consent and the other fellow, Phelan, followed suit."

"Incredible."

"I suspected all along that they were after something else. Their devotion to that decrepit old building never rang true."

"And what were they after?"

"Noonan wants to be superior of Porta Coeli after the Founder dies."

"Yes, of course. He is acting in that capacity now. He would have to be elected."

"Anyway, that's what it was all about."

"But what good was knowing this to you? You could scarcely promise him that he would be elected. I imagine he will be in any case."

"The fact is that I don't want him to be superior there. My choice is Michael Tumulty."

"Tumulty!"

"Yes. He was as helpful as he could be during this delay. I had told him I would do what I could to get him reassigned if he got rid of the opposition to the building program. Now I see that was a foolish promise. Still, I owe him something."

"Did you promise him he will be the next superior of Porta Coeli?"

"I did."

"How can you keep such a promise?"

"You."

Father Faiblesse stared at Hoyt. The man was incredible.

"When the election is held," Hoyt said patiently, "you will preside. You do not have to accept the results of the election. If Tumulty is not voted in, you void the election and appoint him superior of Porta Coeli. That is perfectly within your rights. You know the rules of the society."

"I see."

Hoyt smiled. "There is a solution for everything, Father. Just wait. Even this Fogarty business may turn out to be a blessing in disguise."

"What did you tell Noonan?"

"I don't understand."

"Noonan. Why did he give in?"

"I reminded him of your prerogative in the matter of elections."

"You threatened him with that?"

"No. I reminded him of the rule which permits you to refuse the outcome of any election. Well." Hoyt reached for the ignition key.

Faiblesse got out of the car and closed its door carefully. He stood watching the car go down the driveway. When it was gone, he turned toward the house. Mr. Nickles waited for him in the open door.

"The Mrs. wondered if you would be in for dinner, Father."

250

"Yes. I'll be in."

Did the Nickleses now fear that one day they would wake up and find the house empty of priests? Father Faiblesse tried to smile, but neither the thought nor the pain in his stomach would permit it.

29

*I*T WAS HENLEY who noticed that the razing of Little Sem had begun. Accustomed to view with incredulity whatever he saw on the television screen, he had come to mistrust the unphotographed world as well. He had just got up from a nap and come outdoors for a breath of unconditioned air. The temperature within the house was cool, which was welcome enough, but the chilled air seemed to affect his joints. Sometimes, after a night in front of the television, he had difficulty stretching his legs straight. The body could no longer be trusted—limbs, muscles, organs. Henley was often brought embarrassingly awake at night because he had wet his bed. That loss of control was a grim omen. At the moment of death, the sphincter muscle relaxes and a lifetime of self-control deserts the body along with the soul. Did others have his problem? He was too ashamed to ask. After a nocturnal accident he made his bed quickly, concealing the evidence. He should change the sheets or at least air the bedding, but either course was risky, exposing him to suspicion. His room was redolent of urine, the odor of old age. On bad nights the damp bed was scant protection from the air conditioning, and, though he might awake relatively dry, his limbs were stiff and sore. No, he could not trust his body now. Thus, when he saw the wrecking ball swing into the side of Little Sem, he was prepared, at least for a moment, to doubt his vision. The effect was not immediate. The ball swung back, described an arc and again crashed into the side of Little Sem. Peering across the lake, Henley could see the destructive effect of the ball now. He turned and went back to the house, moving with prudent swiftness.

Noonan and Trask were in the recreation room. The liquor cabinet was open and both men had glasses in their hands.

"They are tearing down Little Sem," Henley said excitedly.

Noonan's gaze was blurred. "You don't say."

"They are. I saw it."

"You must be mistaken." But Noonan would not meet Henley's eyes.

"Come see for yourself."

"I believe you," Trask said.

"You're drunk," Henley scolded him. "Noonan, come look."

"I believe you, too, Henley. We both believe you."

Henley stared at him, shocked. "You're drunk, too."

Noonan did not deny it. Henley slapped his thighs. "I'm going to tell Tumulty. Do you hear me? I'm going to tell Tumulty about this."

Trask lifted his glass insouciantly, as if toasting the suggestion. Henley huffed from the room. He was both furious and confused. What tribunal could he bring Noonan before? Noonan was acting superior of the house. This was shocking. Tumulty would know what to do.

But he could not find Tumulty. He was not in his room. Henley knocked on other doors, thrusting his head in whether or not there was an answer. "Little Sem is being torn down!"

"You agreed to it," Corcoran reminded him. "Why all the excitement?"

"I never thought they'd really do it. Did you?"

"I thought they would do it no matter what we said. What is Noonan's reaction?"

"Noonan is drunk in the rec room."

Corcoran looked at his watch. "At two in the afternoon? I didn't think he would take it this hard."

"Trask is with him. They are both drunk. It's a scandal."

"The wrecking of Little Sem is a blow to Noonan."

"He didn't even know about it. Not till I told him. It is a scandal. The Founder ill, Little Sem being torn down, everyone napping. Trask and Noonan drunk." Henley threw up his hands.

Corcoran sat up in his bed. "Can you see from here?"

Henley did not understand.

"Little Sem. Can we watch from this side of the lake?"

"Yes, yes. Come, I'll show you."

"Go tell the others. I'll be out in a minute."

Ten minutes later six old priests stood looking across the lake. The wrecking ball had eaten a great cavity in the wall of Little Sem and a haze of dust hovered over the building. The watchers wore solemn expressions. It was really happening. Until now it had been only a logical possibility, like one's own death. If they felt sadness, there was fascination, too. They knew again the delight the child feels when the tide comes in and washes away the sand castle laboriously constructed during the afternoon. Was there anything that could not be destroyed in an hour, in minutes? Suddenly it seemed miraculous that anything man had made survived: cathedrals, statues, pyramids. Such relics could be reduced to dust in an afternoon. Little Sem was being knocked down like a house of cards. What would Leo Phelan's reaction be?

Eventually Henley went back to his room. He wanted to be alone. Noonan's behavior had upset him almost as much as the destruction going on across the lake. The man was obviously not a fit candidate to succeed the Founder as superior here. Henley resolved to convince others of that truth. Little Sem, the Founder

—with so much already crumbling, they could not run the risk that Porta Coeli would become a chaotic community. They needed someone strong as their head. Someone like Tumulty.

Huff came in with yesterday's paper opened to the society page. "Look at this, Henley. Do you know Fogarty?"

Henley looked at the pictures, at the headline, and shook his head. "Why should I? I don't know many ministers."

"Minister? This man is a priest."

"Don't be ridiculous. He has married. Can't you read?"

"That's the point of it. Man bites dog. Henley, Fogarty is a member of the society. It says he was once stationed at the college."

"Don't be a fool. Give me the paper. Look at his face. The man is obviously an Episcopalian."

"But his name is Fogarty."

"He is not a priest. He cannot be."

"Henley, it happens all the time nowadays. It is the sixteenth century all over again."

"Nonsense. Huff, Noonan must not be our next superior."

"I thought you were for him."

"Not any longer. Tumulty is the man. I shall cast my vote for Michael Tumulty."

"Is the Founder worse?"

"I don't know."

"Perhaps we should go see."

Phelan had noticed what was happening to Little Sem when he stepped outside after lunch. He was stricken with such an acute sense of remorse that almost against his will he had gone down the steps to the lake path and started toward campus. He had not gone one hundred yards when he stopped. What was the point of getting a closer look at the effect of his perfidy? He did not even have the heart to lift his binoculars to his eyes. He shuffled slowly back toward Porta Coeli but did not climb the steps to the lawn and visibility. He dreaded encountering the others now. Since writing the letter to Hoyt, he had managed to keep silent about what he had done. Noonan refused to commiserate with him on how they had been blackmailed by Hoyt. Now their secret was out. Everyone would know that they had capitulated. Phelan could not face their surprise, their questions, perhaps their jeers. He would deserve them. Nothing could be said against him that was not true. He had betrayed his own best instincts. He had betrayed the Founder. And why? For Noonan.

When he was sure the others would be in their rooms taking afternoon naps, Phelan crept up the steps and crossed the lawn to the building. As he came along the cloister walk and neared the recreation room, he heard voices. He peeked inside and saw Trask and Noonan at the liquor cabinet. Alcohol was insufficient solace for Leo Phelan. He waited a moment, then scooted unseen past the window. Once inside the building, he decided against going to his room. Someone might already be waiting for him there, someone who would demand to know why he had permitted Hoyt to override his veto. Phelan went into the parlor off the lobby and sat down. He felt very tired. What he had done seemed worse than sin. The pottage he had traded for was not even his own; it would be served to Noonan.

Phelan lit a cigarette and left it in his mouth. Hands plunged into the pockets of his jacket, he slumped down in the chair, letting his feet slide out. His shoes were dusty from the lake path. Hoyt would not veto Noonan's election as superior. Thirty pieces of silver. Phelan drew back his feet, placed them solidly on the floor. At least they would get the price of their agreement. He got to his feet and began to pace back and forth in the parlor. The tile floor was a checkerboard. He crossed to the far side of the room. King. Now he could move in any direction he chose. Well, kingmaker anyway. He took the cigarette from his mouth and spilled its ash upon the floor. He ground it beneath his shoe. A mothlike smudge. This house would know a little discipline soon. Dear God, what if the Founder recovered? What would

256

his reaction be to learn that the senior men of the society had agreed to the destruction of the first building he had put up? And learned that, after a noisy show of defiance, Leo Phelan, too, had acquiesced? Why, Leo? Why? Phelan stood stock still in the center of the room. It would be impossible to lie to the old man. The whole business had taken on the aspects of a medieval intrigue: the Neapolitan succession, Callistus III waiting for King Alfonso to die, Callistus the first Borgia pope.

Phelan stubbed out his cigarette, tugged at the bill of his baseball cap and left the room. When he was standing by the Founder's bed, cap in hands, the sight of that wasted old figure lying inert, suspended between time and eternity, brought tears to his eyes. He started to kneel beside the bed, stopped, then did ease himself onto his knees. Gripping the railing at the foot of the bed, he lowered his forehead onto the backs of his hands. Forgive me, Father, for I have sinned. I could have stopped them. My opposition alone would have sufficed, forget about Noonan, but I weakened. I sold my birthright. Finally he stopped mumbling and just knelt there, numb with self-disgust and some genuine grief. It did not help to let his mind fill with anecdotes from Church history, continuing the line of thought begun in the parlor. The government of the Church had always been in the hands of mortal men, often of weak, immoral men. Lecherous popes guilty of nepotism and worse. But there was no consolation for Leo Phelan in thoughts of corrupt cardinals and bishops. He had been trained in the school of the Founder, he was a member of the Society of Saint Brendan. He should have acted better. He was not worthy.

Voices in the hallway. Phelan started to get to his feet but decided to remain on his knees. Perhaps he would be left alone if come upon in an attitude of prayer. He recognized Henley's voice and took heart but then he heard Tumulty. The voices grew louder and, at the doorway, stopped. Phelan listened to them come into the room. A hand was laid on his shoulder.

"Leo?"

He nodded.

"It is not your fault," Henley said. "It is ours. We should have listened to you."

Phelan got one foot on the floor. Henley helped him up. Huff and Ucello looked sheepish and Tumulty looked only kind.

"You tried to stop them," Henley said.

"How could he go ahead?" Ucello wondered. "He was supposed to have permission from us all."

"What does Hoyt care?" Henley said indignantly. "Leo, could you sue? Could you take him to court?"

"I am not a lawyer."

"Corcoran is a canon lawyer."

"It is too late," Phelan said, looking at Tumulty. Why did he think that only Tumulty knew that Hoyt had not gone ahead without Leo Phelan's permission? Henley was saying that he would never vote for Noonan as superior of the house.

"But he was head prefect of the school," Phelan cried.

"That was a long time ago. He is in the rec room now, drinking with Trask."

"I know. He is crushed." Could they understand the self-disgust one felt in betraying his conscience?

"He joked when I told him about Little Sem."

"He is not himself."

Huff said, "Tumulty, do you know Father Fogarty?"

"Of course. He is assistant to Faiblesse."

"The assistant of Faiblesse!" Huff and Henley spoke together.

"What's wrong?" Phelan asked.

Henley said, "Did you bring the paper?"

Huff shook his head. "He has married. It was in the paper. A picture, too, him in a Roman collar, bold as brass. Thank God the Founder will never know."

"Amen," Tumulty said.

"We must not be overcome by what has happened to Little Sem," Phelan said, avoiding Tumulty's eyes. "The Founder

258

would not want that. We must not give Hoyt a double victory, our spirit as well as that building."

"The man will try to take over here next," Henley said. "He may have plans for this building. Another dorm for girls."

"Nonsense," Tumulty said.

"We are safe here," Phelan agreed. "As safe as men can be on this earth. Oliver Fleming saw to that."

Alma Bishop appeared at the door, surprised to find this reunion taking place in the Founder's room.

She came to the bed and they made way for her. She fussed with the oxygen tap and checked the amount of fluid in the bottle from which the Founder was fed.

"He seems unchanged," Henley said.

Miss Bishop glanced at the Founder's face.

"Is there any chance, any chance at all, that he will recover?" Phelan asked.

"Oh, I don't think so, Father."

She slipped her hand beneath the plastic tent and took hold of the Founder's wrist. Her eyes dropped to her watch. Her fingers moved about on the old man's wrist. Suddenly she threw back the plastic and leaned over the body. A moment later she raced from the room.

"What is the matter?" Phelan cried. "What is it?"

Tumulty leaned over the bed for a moment, then turned to the other priests.

"The Founder is dead."

30

THE BODY of the Founder had been taken away, to be returned to Porta Coeli after it had been prepared for burial. Faiblesse, the father superior of the Society of Saint Brendan, had been summoned in order that the residents might gather to elect a successor to the Founder as superior of the house.

> The leaving leaves have left
> The stark trees bereft
> Of green and awkwardly in wind
> They lurch, cavort and bend.

Ambrose Huff did not like it but at least it was done, a quatrain perhaps, the resolution of a chord, a complete thought. He would have liked to write some lines to mark the death of the Founder but his mind quickly settled into the grooves provided by a lifetime of reading the psalms. *De profundis clamavi ad te, domine.* Perhaps his small gift could be turned to translation. Hopkins's version of the *Justus quidem tu es, Domine.* The metaphysical poets. Ronald Knox. It had all been done too many times before, and too beautifully. How tragic that the English liturgy had not been developed at a time when there were men who were both Latinists and possessed of an ear for their native tongue. The versions of the Gospels now read at Mass suggested corporation prose. Huff smiled and pushed the bitterness away. The Founder had survived into this mad age without a murmur of complaint. Nothing had shocked him. The house was abuzz with gossip about some young priest who had run away with Father Faiblesse's secretary. Surprise. Disbelief. How would the Founder have reacted? Perhaps the wonder is that there are still a few shreds of fidelity left. It became a temptation to regard tenacity as a virtue. All of them at Porta Coeli had given a long life to God, but who could claim that his living of it had matched the standard set by the Founder? *Requiescat in pace.*

A tap on the door. "Come in," Huff called. The somber face of Henley appeared. O'Leary was with him. "Come in, come in."

"What are you writing?"

"Memoires d'outre-tombe."

"Ah," O'Leary sighed. "Other times, other times."

"Faiblesse should be here soon," Henley said. He sat on the bed. "Would you object to talking about the election?"

"O'Leary has a candidate?"

"Do you mean Noonan?"

"He could make a good superior," Huff said.

"I don't think so. We don't think so. We are going to vote for Tumulty."

"Why on earth would you do that?"

"It is a matter of principle. He is a leader. Noonan is not."

"We have no need of a leader. Tumulty would have us in a constant turmoil. Whatever your misgivings about Noonan, I would think twice before voting Tumulty in."

"We have thought about it more than twice."

They left after ten minutes. Huff would not vote for Tumulty. Tumulty with his remembered insolence of office was a menace to the peace of the place. His insistence on living in the present was in its way more oppressive than nostalgia. Perhaps. Huff had read the poems of his youth, brought to him Xeroxed by Corcoran. Ambrose Huff had no desire to be further reminded of those days.

Stokes returned from town to learn that the Founder was dead. Corcoran, meeting him on the cloister walk, gave him the news. Stokes stopped as if he were required to make some decision and was reluctant to do so.

"God rest his soul," he said finally.

"Amen. Have you noticed that Little Sem is being torn down?"

Stokes dragged his eyes toward the lake. He seemed surprised by what he saw on the campus side.

Corcoran said, "Did you give your consent?"

"I was asked only if I would make a fuss."

"And you said no. Ah, well. Father Hoyt must have received permission from us all."

"From Phelan, too?"

Corcoran indicated the activity across the lake.

"I thought Phelan would never agree," Stokes said.

"Perhaps he didn't. But what of Noonan?"

Stokes shrugged.

"And now, Father," Corcoran said heartily, "we must elect a new superior of the house."

Panic shone in Stokes's eyes. "When?"

"Very shortly. The father superior will preside. Do you have a favorite?"

"I haven't thought about it. Do you?"

"Anyone but Noonan. But what of yourself, Stokes? Would you like to be superior?"

Stokes was assailed by memories of an awful year when he had been pastor of a parish. He had been carried from the rectory to half a year of recuperation in a rest home. But if he knew fear, he retained his sense of humor.

"Passionately," he said, and Corcoran punched him on the arm.

Michael Tumulty decided to wait in his room until he was summoned to the meeting. His hour had arrived and he was ready for it. He refused to belittle the post he aspired to. Much could be done this side of the Rubicon, too. It was a new era. How often over the years they had discussed what would happen when the Founder died. But the problems this had seemed to promise grew progressively less vexatious; dozens of discussants had preceded the object of their concern into eternity. In more recent years the tendency had been to lament the fact that the Founder had lived to see the dissolution of his society. Faiblesse as father superior was a disaster and Hoyt was thought to be worse. Porta Coeli had come to seem the last bastion. Here the original spirit of the society could be preserved, but first it must be revived and that required a strong superior. Tumulty looked at his watch. Soon Faiblesse would arrive and the election take place.

Dear God, if only it were over. Until it was, the worm of doubt could munch at his confidence. He wanted to trust Hoyt, he had to trust him. Yet the man had already reneged once on a promise. Tumulty told himself that Hoyt had nothing to lose by keeping this one. He truly wanted the job now. It was as if this were what he had wanted all along. And Porta Coeli *was* the society now. Cause for sorrow there, perhaps, but the Founder had always worked with what he had. Who but an optimist could have got through the first years of the society? Porta Coeli would be the yeast that raised the loaf again. Long ago the college had performed that function but those days were gone forever. Thanks to Oliver Fleming, Porta Coeli was economically secure, independent of the vagaries of Hoyt's ambitions. Fleming. Had he been informed of the Founder's death? Tumulty picked up the telephone and dialed. He was surprised when a woman answered.

"Mrs. Fleming? I had thought you were still in the hospital."

"Oliver brought me home."

"Are you able to get around?"

"In a chair, yes. But you want to speak to Oliver."

"Please. It's important."

After a delay, Fleming came on the line. Without preliminary, Tumulty said, "Oliver, Father Cullen is dead."

"Good God. When?"

"Just an hour ago."

"It is the end of an era."

"We have all been thinking the same thing. But we must go on. Shortly we will be electing a new superior of the house. That is the rule."

"Who will it be?"

"One never knows until after the election."

"When is the funeral?"

"The arrangements are incomplete. I shall of course keep you informed. The house will need your continuing support. I hope I can count on that."

"Certainly."

"Good. It must be pleasant to have Mrs. Fleming home again."

"Yes."

Mrs. Nickles was not speaking to Mr. Nickles. This was a state of affairs he always longed for until it was upon him. It was damnably annoying to have one's questions go unanswered, one's remarks ignored. His insistence that Fogarty's defection had come as no surprise to him had called forth a withering contemptuous blast, followed by this silence. But it did seem to Mr. Nickles that he had seen it coming. It was not natural for a young man, in the full vigor of his age, to be living a life of self-denial. A man needed a woman. Mr. Nickles thought this thought with a little inward swagger. It seemed to have nothing to do with Mrs. Nickles. He had not known Fogarty well, but those few occasions on which the priest had gone beyond a mere greeting seemed, remembered now, fraught with significance. A good-looking young fellow, seemed to know his job, whatever exactly it was. But Miss Liczenski! She presented a puzzle to Mr. Nickles. He had not shared his wife's envious antagonism toward the secretary: Mrs. Nickles had considered it beneath her dignity to serve another employee's meals. Miss Liczenski was dumb. There was no other word for it. Mr. Nickles had never heard her utter a word that suggested intelligence, wit or humor. As for looks, well, her face was homely and she was straight as a stick. Fogarty must have seen her as a starving man regards bread and water. Mr. Nickles was prepared to believe that the union would not last. In fact he was sure that it would not. He said so to Mrs. Nickles, thinking it might melt the frost, but it only worsened things. What a loyalist she was. She wanted to believe both that a priest would never run away with a woman and that, if he did, he would always remain faithful to her, even if she was Miss Liczenski. There were times when Mr. Nickles preened himself on his own long marriage. In an uneventful life, it seemed some claim to distinction. A life sentence.

Mrs. Nickles found him in the pantry, coming in so quickly he did not have time to conceal the glass of beer he had been drinking.

"Father Faiblesse wants you," she said coldly. "With the car. He is going out."

Mr. Nickles did not get to his feet as quickly as his elation dictated. She must not think him servile. On the other hand, what a break to get the hell out of the house.

The meeting was called to order in the refectory since the table there could easily accommodate them all. Father Faiblesse took his seat at the head of the table and did not insist that the old priests fall immediately silent. Trask had not come and

Phelan went to fetch him. Noonan drifted, not saying much, just showing the flag. Michael Tumulty was already seated but the others seemed reluctant to get started. What they were about to do was the first official recognition that the Founder was indeed dead. Father Faiblesse looked at these aged priests with affection and with wistful envy. As usual he had felt, upon entering Porta Coeli, peace descend; he was free of the outside world's petty annoyances. He could almost forget what the doctor had finally told him. Today it had been a particular relief to get inside the house after the long, chatty drive with Mr. Nickles. Mr. Nickles had asked, quite seriously, if the son of a priest was automatically an altar boy. Had he read that the sons of popes had been made cardinals? Trask, puffy-eyed, obviously just wakened from a nap, came in. Father Faiblesse tapped his water glass with a pencil and, slowly, the residents of Porta Coeli took their places at table.

"You all know why we are gathered here this afternoon. Father Cullen passed away several hours ago. We will begin the meeting with a prayer for the repose of his soul. I think we can remain seated during the prayer."

The old heads bent over the table, already set for the next meal. "Would you say the prayer, Father Noonan?" Faiblesse asked.

Noonan, at his accustomed place at the side of the table, rubbed a hand over the expanse of his pate. "Heavenly Father," he began. "As we look back over the disappointments of our lives . . ."

Garrity cleared his throat with unnecessary vigor.

". . . it is consolation to realize that such bright spots as we see are due in large part to the labors of the servant whom you have called to yourself today. May his soul and the souls of all the faithful departed, through the mercy of God, rest in peace."

"Amen."

"Thank you, Father. We will now proceed to the election of a new superior of this house. You are all eligible to vote. I will not call for nominations. If you will each take a piece of paper from this tablet and write on it the name of the man you want to succeed Father Founder as superior of Porta Coeli, we will see where we stand."

It took some minutes for the tablet to make its way around the table. Not everyone had brought a pencil with him, a contingency Leo Phelan had foreseen. He had filled his pockets with the short pencils that accumulated in his desk during the golf season. These were now distributed.

"Please fold your ballots after you have made your choice. Father Corcoran, would you collect and count them, please?"

Corcoran went round the table with a soup bowl, collecting the folded slips of paper. He took them to a serving table against the wall, where he began to unfold them. The old men murmured among themselves; few seemed to have any deep curiosity about the result of the voting.

"Would you like me to announce the result?" Corcoran asked.

"Please, Father."

The first ballot was inconclusive. Stokes, to much merriment, received one vote and was accused of voting for himself. A demand that the handwriting be examined was smilingly denied by Father Faiblesse. Noonan received four votes, Tumulty five, Garrity two.

"Tumulty has it," Henley said with satisfaction.

"The winner must receive a majority of the votes cast, Father. That means seven votes. We will have another ballot."

On the second ballot, Garrity retained his two and Noonan and Tumulty were tied at five apiece. Father Faiblesse asked if a recess would be desirable before the third ballot. The suggestion was turned down. Leo Phelan said they wanted to get this over with.

Once more the tablet went around the table and the old heads bent over the ballots. There was tension now when Corcoran took the bowl of votes to the serving table. The solemnity of the occasion had impressed itself upon the electors. Noonan and Phelan were fidgety; Garrity frowned at his companions, as if he were seeking his two enemies among them. Michael Tumulty, head tipped back, stared at the ceiling. Father Corcoran was ready to announce the results of the third ballot. Faiblesse asked him to come back to the main table to do so. Standing beside the father superior, Corcoran counted out the bundles he had made.

"Tumulty," he said. "One, two, three, four." He paused. "Noonan." The old men hunched attentively over the table. "One. Two. Three. Four. Five. Six. Seven—"

Cheering broke out and Phelan's plea for a standing ovation was heeded. Tumulty remained seated but nodded at Noonan, smiling the good loser's smile. His eyes flicked in the direction of Faiblesse.

"Congratulations," Phelan cried, pumping Noonan's hand. *"Non placet."*

Phelan's delight elicited new applause and Father Faiblesse had not been heard.

"Non placet," he said again.

Goudge was shaking Noonan's hand now and Trask got into position to be next. Noonan was unable to retain the serious expression he had worn throughout the voting. His face broke into a boyish grin.

Father Faiblesse said more loudly, *"Mihi non placet."*

Faces turned to him with expressions of curiosity and surprise. Only Corcoran seemed to understand what Faiblesse was doing.

He announced, "Father Superior has nullified the voting."

"Mihi non placet haec electio," Father Faiblesse said formally, using the phrase dictated by the rule of the Society of Saint Brendan.

Noonan now grasped the significance of the statement and so did Leo Phelan. Phelan shook his head at Faiblesse, as if to say there was no reason for what he was doing.

"No, Father. It's all right. We agreed."

Corcoran said, "In nullifying the election, the father superior assumes the responsibility of appointing our new superior."

Faiblesse was on his feet. "I appoint Father Garrity the new superior of Porta Coeli. Thank you, gentlemen. The meeting is adjourned."

There was a tinkle of tableware when Garrity fell back into his chair. Water was called for. Phelan was trying to get the floor. Michael Tumulty, having sat with noticeable composure through the surprise of the veto, was stunned. Faiblesse gave him a wide berth and got out of the refectory without being accosted by Phelan. He hurried to his car. Mr. Nickles was dozing behind the wheel. The sound of the door opening wakened him.

"Through already?"

"That's right. Let us be on our way, Mr. Nickles."

As they drove off, Faiblesse felt that he was leaving Porta Coeli forever. Quite soon it might have been his own home. Well, he was leaving it in good hands. As they rounded the lake, the pain started up again and, moving into a corner of the seat, out of range of Mr. Nickles's curious eyes in the rear-view mirror, Father Faiblesse took one of the pills the doctor had prescribed.

31

AFTER PHELAN managed to escape from the refectory, his passage slowed by his defiant persistence in meeting the eyes that tried to avoid his, he hurried through the kitchen and outside in time to see Faiblesse's car leaving the parking lot. Phelan quickened his step, moving after the car, whose distance from him, despite his own pursuit, increased according to some obscure ratio reminiscent of grade school math problems. The hand he lifted in the hope that Faiblesse might look back held his binoculars. He put them to his eyes, coming to a halt as he did so. The car leaped large to his retina and he took a step backward.

Traitor. He realized that he had been forming the word like an incantation since he came outside. He said it aloud. He would have liked to bellow it to the skies. The numbers on the car's license plate seemed to spell the word in some simple code. Phelan's grip on his glasses was crushing. He half believed that he could crush them, as frantic mothers filled with miraculous adrenaline lifted automobiles to free their struck-down children.

Betrayed. Oh, God. He let his binoculars drop and they bounced painfully off his belly. His whole body quivered with postponed rage and his eyes blurred with tears. Anger. Humiliation. They had deceitfully gained his consent to the destruction of Little Sem and then had cast Noonan aside despite the fact that he had been the choice of the house. Phelan's eyes lifted to the sky as if justice hovered there as visible as cloud cover.

Deely was in the outer office joshing with the secretary. He turned with a smile. Tumulty searched the young man's face but found no telltale clue to what had happened. Perhaps Deely, too, was a mere instrument and had not known the ultimate plan. Tumulty had left the refectory and, without forethought, without question, had set out on foot for the campus. Now he moved directly to the president's door.

"Is Father Hoyt expecting you?" the secretary trilled.

"I doubt it."

He opened the door without knocking. Hoyt sat at his desk, a plastic bug in his ear, an appraising but generally pleased smile on his face.

"Hello, Father," he said, showing no surprise at this unannounced visit. Not too many years ago it had been a frequent thing, popping into one another's offices.

"We have just held our election."

Hoyt looked at him steadily as if trying to comprehend this remark. He took the bug away from his ear. The muted sound of Hoyt's voice issued from the plastic earpiece when he laid it on the desk. He punched a key on a machine to turn it off.

"What election?"

Still standing, Father Tumulty felt the cold superiority of one unjustly treated.

"The election of the new superior of Porta Coeli. You may remember our conversation on the matter."

"But how could there be an election . . ."

271

Silence. Tumulty realized that Hoyt had not known of the Founder's death. He sank into a chair opposite the president. "The Founder is dead."

"I see." Hoyt put his hands flat on the desk and stared for a moment at the far wall. "And his successor has already been elected. Congratulations, Father."

"Oh, no. It is I who must congratulate you."

"Was the veto necessary?"

"It was invoked."

"How did the others react?"

"Father Garrity almost fainted when he was named the new superior."

"Garrity!"

"Father Faiblesse pronounced his *Non placet* and then appointed Garrity. Are you surprised?"

But there could be no doubt that Hoyt was surprised. He had risen from his chair as if propelled. A repertoire of seldom required emotions flickered across his face like stage lightning. In a moment his expression was calm.

"Who won the election, Father?"

"Noonan."

"And Faiblesse overturned it?"

"He did. And appointed Garrity."

"So naturally you think that I betrayed you. I did not. I gave you a promise I intended to keep. I still intend to keep it. Is Faiblesse still at Porta Coeli?"

"He left immediately after the election."

"Okay." Hoyt glanced at his watch. "I will clear this up before the day is over. That is another promise."

Hoyt came around the desk and put his hand on Tumulty's shoulder.

"I owe you a great deal, Father. My promise was given in payment for that debt. I am going to keep that promise. I have no idea what Faiblesse is up to. He cannot possibly have misunder-

272

stood me. Let Deely take you back to Porta Coeli. I am going to pay a visit on our father superior."

Tumulty allowed himself to be led from the office. Deely and the secretary turned when the priests came into the waiting room. Tumulty refused the offer of a ride back to Porta Coeli. As he left, Hoyt called after him.

"I shall keep my promise, Father. Depend upon it."

Tumulty took that thought with him on his slow return along the lake path. Depend upon it. Depend upon the word of Father Hoyt. To such disfavor he had come. Hoyt and Deely. Faiblesse no longer. The father superior was playing some game of his own. Tumulty stopped and looked for Little Sem but it was no longer there. Gone. That quickly half a century of tradition had been erased, a landmark obliterated, a horizon redeemed. He had not expected to be affected so. Erosion and change are constant, in the physical world, in the human world, too. The society. He had sold his soul in order to have some continuing influence in the society. He had not flinched at the thought of betraying Noonan. He had gone along with Hoyt's willingness to use the rule of the society for private advantage. His grief was not explained by the disappearance of Little Sem.

But he was still alive. He had not died. He was still a member of the society. The sun had not yet set on this eventful day. But his efforts to stir up hope in what Hoyt could do now were unsuccessful. They had lost. He had lost.

"I'm sorry, Michael."

It was Noonan, his naked head pushed around the door of Tumulty's room, a sad expression on his face. Tumulty shrugged.

"The joke is I gave my consent to Hoyt on Little Sem. I guess Faiblesse wasn't told."

"Perhaps not."

"He would have vetoed your election, too, Michael."

"We'll never know. You were the choice of the house."

"Well, Garrity has it now. He's welcome to it."

"He is a good man." It felt good to mean that, even as his mind was on what Hoyt might be doing now on his behalf.

"Come to the rec room. We are toasting our new superior."

"In a minute."

The door closed. Tumulty had no intention of going to the rec room. Let Garrity enjoy his moment. He deserved it. He had not wanted to be superior. Wouldn't he resign if asked to do so by Faiblesse? Of course he would. Hope began to rise again. He had to trust Hoyt. There was no one else to trust. With all his faults, the man had undeniably accomplished things. He had twisted Faiblesse around his finger so often in the past that it scarcely strained credulity that he would do it again. Tumulty decided to go to the recreation room. He wanted Garrity to remember that he had rejoiced in his good fortune, however brief it turned out to be.

32

FAIBLESSE HAD EXPECTED a telephone call from Father Hoyt but the president came in person, sounding his horn impatiently at the gate until Mr. Nickles let him in, then speeding up the driveway and braking noisily in front of the house. Faiblesse, drawn to his window by the sound of the horn, decided to receive his guest in his room. He sat at his desk, intending to look busy. Since returning from Porta Coeli he had changed from street clothes to a cassock. Only his desk light was on. The atmosphere was not unlike that of the Founder's study when one had been summoned for an interview.

His phone rang. It was Mrs. Nickles downstairs, telling him he had a visitor. He told her to send Father Hoyt upstairs. Hardly had he hung up than he heard Hoyt on the stairs, taking them two at a time. He puffed as he came down the hallway, stopped briefly outside the door, then entered the room without knocking. Father Faiblesse did not look up, though he was unable to focus on the type of the book that lay open before him.

"What in the world have you done?" Hoyt demanded.

When Faiblesse looked up he had difficulty seeing beyond

the puddle of light created by the desk lamp. "Is that you, Father Hoyt?"

Hoyt came closer, entering the light. "What in hell happened at Porta Coeli?"

"Ah. Then you've heard of the Founder's death."

"I'm talking of the election."

"Won't you sit down, Father?"

"No, I won't sit down. Where is the light switch?" Hoyt stamped away, found the switch beside the door and flicked it on. He was clearly in a rage.

"Sit down, Father," Faiblesse said.

Hoyt looked at the father superior through narrowed eyes. When he spoke again, his voice was calmer. "Father Tumulty called on me as soon as the election was over. Of course he was furious with the stunt you apparently pulled."

Faiblesse got to his feet, slowly, his fingertips remaining pressed to the desk. "Father Noonan received a majority of the votes cast on the third ballot."

"And you nullified it?"

"Yes."

"Then what?"

"So you approve of what I did to that point?"

"Did you name Garrity as superior of the house?"

"Father, I won't continue this conversation with you pacing up and down the room. Please sit down."

A short contest ensued. Hoyt glared at Faiblesse. The father superior's expression communicated nothing. Hoyt strode to a chair and flung himself into it. Faiblesse resumed his seat.

"Why didn't you appoint Michael Tumulty?"

"I hope you're not contesting the legality of what I did. It was you who reminded me of my prerogative."

"I can't believe this. I thought we had talked it over, that you understood—"

"I remember you talking to me, Father. I do not remember talking it over. I said not a word."

Hoyt put his hand on the desk and leaned forward. "What is it, Father? What's eating you?"

A cloud passed over Faiblesse's face. "You know my position."

"Tell me. What is your position?"

"I mean in the society. I am the father superior, am I not?"

"Of course you are. How could *I* not know that?"

"You created me, is that it?"

"I supported your election, yes. I doubt that you would have been elected otherwise. In fact, I am sure you would not have been. What does that have to do with Tumulty and Porta Coeli?"

"I was doing my job as father superior."

"We promised that job to Michael Tumulty."

"*You* promised it to Father Tumulty."

"Very well, I promised him. You knew I had. You said nothing to suggest you felt differently. Naturally I assumed that you agreed."

"Naturally."

"So what happened to change things?"

"I decided to act as the superior of the society. I am not answerable to you, Father. That comes as a surprise to you, I know. The realization came as a surprise to me. I saw what a mockery of the society my mode of acting had been."

"And you wanted to assert yourself."

"That is right."

"For the sake of the society." The word sounded unflattering in Hoyt's mouth. "You know as well as I do that the society is on its last legs. Why did we sever relations between the college and the society? So the society could not pull down the college with it. The society is little more than a handful of old men at Porta Coeli, men in their seventies and older. Dying men."

"You and I also belong to the society, Father."

"And after us?"

"I don't know. But while there is a society and I am father superior, it is my duty to serve it. I have failed in that duty. I may have been wrong to agree to the secularization of the college. If the college must sustain us, well, for decades we sustained the college. I mean to work for close relations between us again. No doubt things cannot go back to what they were, but they can be made a good deal more favorable to the society than they are now. Above all, members of the society must have a more decisive say in what the college becomes. They built the college, Father. It is not right that the college should not recognize its responsibility to the group that founded it."

Hoyt was shaking his head incredulously. "You have only one vote on the board of trustees, Father Faiblesse. Moreover, I can have you removed from the board just like that."

"I know you could."

"Just so you understand that."

"Oh, I do. But I also have some power, Father. The time is long overdue that I exercised it. I am relieving you of the presidency of Saint Brendan's College."

"You're what!"

"I am going to reassign you."

"You haven't the power to fire me from the presidency. I thought you just acknowledged that. You have only one vote. And you will lose that at the next meeting of the board. You're through as a trustee. If you think I'm going to let you interfere with the running of the college, you're wrong. I am angry about Tumulty because you have made me look like a liar. All right. I can't do anything about that. But I do run the college."

"I am not speaking as a trustee of the college, Father. I am speaking as your religious superior. You have taken the vow of obedience. It pains me that I must remind you of that. I am going to reassign you and you are obliged to do what I say."

"The trustees won't stand for it."

"You may be overestimating their gloom, Father. I do not know. In any case, this does not concern them. This is between you and me."

278

"And who do you have in mind as president?"

"That decision is not wholly mine. I have only one vote as a trustee."

"You're not serious, Father. You can't be."

"I am quite serious."

Hoyt sat back in his chair and studied Father Faiblesse. For the first time the father superior detected some semblance of respect in the younger man's expression. He felt a new self-respect. It had been during the ride back from Porta Coeli that he had decided on this course of action. He had not imagined that he would be having this conversation so soon. He had expected a phone call, during which he would have asked Hoyt to come see him tomorrow. Thank God there had been no delay during which he might have wavered. He was convinced now that Hoyt's successes had been won at the expense of the society of which he was a member. Garrity had been right all along. Matters could only be rectified by removing Hoyt from the presidency of Saint Brendan's. It would be unrealistic to expect Hoyt to dismantle what he must regard—and not without reason—as signal achievements. How strangely easy it had been to act, egged on as he was by the dull pain inside him. Hoyt had been caught completely off guard.

"You can't expect me to take this without a fight."

"With whom would you fight, Father? Surely not with me."

"Because you are my religious superior?"

"Yes."

"Things have been changing, Father Faiblesse. Or haven't you noticed? The day that a religious superior can get away with arbitrary decisions is over."

"My decision is not arbitrary. I am acting for the welfare of the society."

"You want to sacrifice the college to the society."

"I intend to sacrifice neither the one nor the other. But my greater concern is that the society not be sacrificed."

279

"It is doomed, Father."

"I refuse to accept that."

"Look at the evidence. How many active members do we have?"

"Every religious community is having a difficult time just now. Things will change, vocations will increase. I am determined that the society shall survive to see a better day."

"It's Fogarty, isn't it?"

"What do you mean?"

"Fogarty. You blame me for Fogarty. I wished him on you."

"This has absolutely nothing to do with Father Fogarty."

Hoyt got to his feet. "The only benefit of this conversation is that I can turn Tumulty over to you. The man is understandably angry. Now he will know who did him in and why."

"He would not have made a good superior. Nor would Noonan. Those old men deserve something better after their years of service."

Those old men. He would have liked to mean himself as well. When Hoyt had gone—having made it clear that he considered no questions closed by this interview—Faiblesse sat down, not at his desk but in the easy chair near the window. He had turned off the overhead light when he closed the door after Hoyt. He felt weary. He felt old. The medication left him dull. The sense of righteousness began to ebb. What he had done at Porta Coeli, in nullifying the election, had been made possible by what the doctor had told him. An exploratory operation. Faiblesse had no illusions about the result. His strength had been the strength of a dying man. He knew that he would not have wanted to live out his last days under either Noonan or Tumulty. Nullifying the election had led to the decision concerning Hoyt. Was his motive the good of the society or only an imagined self-interest? Both, he decided. Inextricably both. The demand for absolute purity of motive was too much, at least when it is human beings who act. In any case, he had acted and his action could not

280

be undone. The satisfaction of knowing that seemed an acceptable substitute for his waning sense of rectitude.

It was quite dark outside now. Soon it would be time for dinner. The Founder was dead. *Requiescat in pace.* The thought no longer surprised. After all those weeks of coma, the old man's death seemed oddly posthumous. Still, it was the end of an era if not of the society. The day after tomorrow they would bury the Founder in the community cemetery not far from Porta Coeli.

33

FATHER TUMULTY was not contacted by Father Hoyt before dinner. From the refectory the old priests went to chapel, where they recited the rosary, offering the prayer for the repose of Father Cullen's soul. His body had not yet come back from the mortician's to be waked in this same chapel. Father Tumulty was anxious to have the rosary over. He was certain that Hoyt must be trying to reach him, yet when he hurried to his room he sat for an hour and his telephone did not ring. He put it to his ear to make certain that it was in working order and then, since he held the instrument in his hand, he dialed the number of the president's office. No answer. But of course he would not be in his office now. His rooms then. The phone there rang many times but finally it was answered.

"Father Tumulty here. Did you speak with Faiblesse?"

There was silence on the other end of the line.

"Father Hoyt? Are you there?"

"He wouldn't listen to me. He won't change his mind."

"But why?"

"It doesn't matter why. He appointed a superior and that's the end of it."

"It matters to me. It matters a good deal. I thought that it mattered to you."

"No, Father. It does not matter to me."

"But you promised. We had an agreement."

"Don't blame me, Father."

"I do blame you."

"Father Tumulty, do you really think I give a damn who is superior of Porta Coeli? Do you think anyone besides yourself gives a damn?"

"Apparently Father Faiblesse does."

"He has lost his mind."

"What do you mean?"

There was a thin laugh on the wire. "Father Faiblesse told me he intends to replace me as president of the college."

"What!" Tumulty felt delight bubble up within him. Faiblesse get rid of Hoyt? It was too good to be true.

"That's right. He fired me." The president spoke as if he were learning a new language. "Any quarrel you have is with him."

Hoyt hung up. When Tumulty had returned his own phone to its cradle, he felt like laughing aloud. Quarrel with Faiblesse? What about? The father superior was finally standing up to Hoyt. That made him and Tumulty allies, not enemies, no matter the contretemps of that *Non placet*. The father superior's action had been aimed at the president, not at Michael Tumulty. Once that was clear to Faiblesse, well, who knew what might lie ahead? Tumulty decided to visit Faiblesse first thing the following day.

He greeted Mrs. Nickles with a lilt in his voice, offered to go upstairs to the father superior's room, but the housekeeper insisted that she announce him. The airless, dusty parlor reminded Tumulty of *Great Expectations*. He feared that inhaling deeply would bring on a fit of coughing. To protect his lungs, he lit a cigarette. He was puffing contentedly when Faiblesse came downstairs and peered warily in at his visitor. Faiblesse looked like a man who had spent a restless night.

"You're here about the election, Father?"

Tumulty waved his cigarette, relegating that matter to a lesser plane. "I spoke with Hoyt last night."

"I see." Faiblesse sat on the edge of a chair and gathered his cassock about his legs. "Father Tumulty, any bargain you may have made with Father Hoyt—"

"I thought he was acting in your name."

"He was not."

"Is it true that you are going to reassign him?"

"Did he tell you that?"

"Yes."

"You seem delighted by the prospect."

"Of course I am." Tumulty slid forward on his chair. "Father Faiblesse, we see eye to eye, you and I. On the society, on the college, what they have been, what they can be."

"On Porta Coeli, too?"

"That was a misunderstanding."

Faiblesse stared at him. "I wish Father Hoyt had not reported to you the substance of our conversation. Have you told others?"

"Father, don't hesitate now. Go through with it. I'm behind you on this. Do you think I ever sided with Hoyt?"

"He has done notable work."

"But at the expense of the society. All he really cares about is the college. That and his own career."

"You are harsh on him, Father."

"He has been a Trojan Horse, a fifth column. He should have been stopped long ago. But it is not too late even now. You have to do it."

"Father, why have you come here?"

"To offer you my support."

"In exchange for what?"

Faiblesse had never been so direct and Tumulty was startled. "That isn't fair. Don't wait, Father. Act immediately."

"You are a storehouse of advice this morning, Father Tumulty."

"I know how lonely and agonizing decisions can be."

"You amaze me, Father."

"In what way?"

Faiblesse put his head back and rubbed his eyes. "How can you still trouble yourself with the petty politics of the society?" He opened his eyes and looked in a blurred fashion at Tumulty. "I envy all of you at Porta Coeli. You have earned the right to put ambition and pettiness behind you. Haven't you had enough yet? God knows I am sick of it, sick and tired. If I remove Father Hoyt it is not to win a triumph over him. We must move beyond the notions of triumph and defeat. Think of the Founder, rest his soul. Did you ever once hear him complain of Father Hoyt?"

"We have to fight for what the Founder stood for."

"We? No, Father. I, perhaps, but not you. Father Tumulty, I acted as I did at the election to stifle your ambition once and for all."

"Ambition!"

"Father, you must stop trying to stir things up. Let the men at Porta Coeli spend their last days in peace."

"We are not dead men, Father."

"No. Thank God for that. You must pray for the rest of us. That is what we expect of you."

"Every member of the society prays."

"Perhaps at your ages you are closer to God. Thank you for coming, Father. I would be grateful if you said nothing of what Father Hoyt told you. How will you get back to Porta Coeli?"

"Father, we must talk. You have accused me of ambition."

Faiblesse had risen and reluctantly Tumulty did, too. He could not leave, not now, not like this. Faiblesse did not understand why he had come. He did not see that they were natural allies.

"Father Faiblesse, I am old but I am not feeble. There are many things I could yet do. I am at your disposal."

Faiblesse took his elbow and they walked together to the front door.

"I want you to return to Porta Coeli, Father. Mr. Nickles will drive you. Free your mind of these small vexations. You have earned some years of peace."

"I don't want peace!"

"I know, Father. I know. But you must try."

Enid's motorized wheelchair and the staircase elevator enabled her to be as mobile as she had been before she broke her leg. Her plastic bathtub chair made sitz baths possible. Oliver lifted a staying palm when Enid threatened to go into detail on this activity. The ash on his cigar, gray, inches long, a parable like geological layers, fell to his vest. He left it there.

"How the skin itches beneath a cast."

"Offer it up," Oliver advised.

"I do. Are you still angry with me?"

"Certainly not. Your antics at the nursing home were a source of amusement to me. I enjoyed your announcement to the world that my deepest desire is to abandon you to the care of strangers."

"Mrs. Hover was nice."

"We must visit her."

"The poor woman is a widow. Needless to say, her children consider they have met their obligations by paying her bills at the nursing home."

"I thought it a pleasant place."

"You would not have thought so if you were an inmate there."

"No one smoked cigars there."

"I do not mind. I offer that up, too."

"Where is that woman?"

"Miss Quirk? She is in her room, reading. She has a taste for nasty novels."

"What do you mean?"

"They are paper-covered and have lurid covers. Much nudity."

"I will not have them in the house."

"It doesn't matter. She is not a Catholic."

"How do you know?"

"I asked her."

"She must be fallen away. Catholic or not, she should not fill her mind with trash. I will speak to her."

"I doubt that it will do much good. In any case, she is a nurse. Her view of life would not be ordinary. It may not seem trash to her."

"Perhaps."

Enid took a knitting needle and inserted it between the cast and her leg. "Ah. That feels lovely."

"I thought you were going to offer it up."

"Isn't our pleasure as acceptable to God as our pain?"

Oliver frowned at this dangerous doctrine.

Enid said, "It was a lovely write-up in the paper. About Father Cullen."

"Yes."

"Did you have a nice visit with Father Faiblesse?"

"He seemed to find it useful."

"I am happy you are not angry with him. It was very nice of him to visit me at the nursing home."

Oliver puffed at his cigar, sending great billows of smoke into the room. His own eyes watered but he welcomed the discomfort. Life is tragedy. When Faiblesse had invited him to the house on Cavil Boulevard that afternoon, Oliver had gone in the mad hope that Faiblesse had reconsidered the feasibility of Oliver's delayed vocation to the priesthood.

"Put such thoughts out of your head, Mr. Fleming. They are a temptation. You must not wrap your selfishness in the mantle of sacrifice."

"You dare to call me selfish?"

287

"I dare many things these days. Please sit down again, Mr. Fleming. There is something I want to tell you, something I should like your counsel on."

"My advice would be worthless. I am a selfish old man. You have just told me so. No doubt my generosity to the society is more disguised selfishness."

"I am sorry to have offended you."

"I had expected a change of heart, a sympathetic ear. I am sorry that I came."

"Sit down, Mr. Fleming. Please. I am glad you are here. I have decided to remove Father Hoyt from the presidency of Saint Brendan's College."

Oliver sat down. "Can you do that?"

Father Faiblesse smiled. "My past actions justify your asking that question. I have been a very poor superior of the society, Mr. Fleming. I have done little more than obey the orders of Father Hoyt, a man whose religious superior I am supposed to be. The society has suffered because of this. The college, too, has suffered, I think. Now I am putting my house in order. It is my hope to reverse recent trends."

"Have you told Father Hoyt of this?"

"I have."

"And?"

"I do not know. He did not like it, of course. He thinks me arbitrary. No doubt he would like to contest my decision. But there is very little he can do but obey."

"He can leave the society."

Faiblesse's eyes widened. Obviously this possibility had not occurred to him. "Yes. He could do that."

"And remain as president of Saint Brendan's. Unless, of course, the trustees asked him to resign."

"Do you think they would do that?"

"No."

"Nor do I." Faiblesse stared blankly before him as if for the

288

first time contemplating the vista his decision had opened up for him and for the society.

"The society is more than the college."

Faiblesse looked at Oliver. "Not very much more."

"There is Porta Coeli."

"Yes."

"Why did you ask me here, Father?"

"I want your help. As a trustee. Can I interest you in a lost cause?"

"I am beginning to wonder if there is any other kind. Yes, of course. We shall fight the battle together."

When Oliver rose to go, Father Faiblesse came outside to the car with him. "Forgive me if I seem unkind, Mr. Fleming. You have been very generous to the society and we all appreciate it. Where would we be without Porta Coeli? It is a lovely place."

Oliver nodded wistfully. "Yes, it is."

"Will you attend the Founder's funeral tomorrow?"

"That is my intention."

"Good."

It seemed a repetition, after almost sixty years, of his expulsion from Little Sem. The sadness was perhaps deeper because it was no longer replaceable by hope. His destiny, too, was the same. The girl in the orange canoe. Enid.

"Will we attend Father Cullen's funeral, Oliver?" Enid asked him now.

"Would you go with your leg in a cast, riding in a wheelchair?"

"I would like to go with you, Oliver."

He put out his cigar and waved the smoke away.

"Then we shall go, Enid. Together."

34

Aᴛᴇʀ ᴛʜᴇ ʀᴇǫᴜɪᴇᴍ Mᴀss in the chapel of Porta
Coeli, the cortege formed in the parking lot behind the building
and on foot they followed the hearse carrying the Founder's body
to the community cemetery on a small hill overlooking Saint
Brendan's Lake. Bishop Brophy, who had preached at the Mass,
his sermon receiving low marks from the old priests in the pews,
brought up the rear, resplendent in episcopal regalia. In front
of him, Oder and Hoyt walked together, their conversation
animated. Then came the old priests, two by two, in cassock and
surplice, their birettas set at various angles on their heads. Leo
Phelan walked with Oliver Fleming, who was pushing his wife
before him in her wheelchair. The day was clear and warm.

"Would you like me to push the chair for a while, Flamingo?"

"Thank you, Father. It is no trouble."

"She's not heavy, she's my wife?"

"Eh?"

"What kind of bird is that, Oliver?" Enid asked, pointing to
a feathered blur.

"Do you know, Father Phelan?"

"That is your finch, Mrs. Fleming," Phelan said, after a moment's hesitation.

"Such a brilliant red."

"Yes."

Oliver said, "Father Faiblesse tells me he is reassigning Father Hoyt."

"Our father superior has become an autocrat."

"I had not realized he had a will of steel."

"A whim of iron."

"There is another finch," Enid Fleming cried.

Phelan nodded. He had no idea what species of bird it was that so caught her fancy. Faiblesse had called him a bird watcher when he came upon him looking through his binoculars. Was that his destiny? He could learn the names of birds, their migratory habits, which species were endangered and which were not. He imagined himself lecturing to poor housebound souls on the bounties of nature. Bah. He could never compete with Ucello. He exchanged places with Noonan, who walked behind them with Tumulty.

"What is the name of that red bird?" he asked Tumulty.

"Brophy."

"Ho ho."

Noonan became aware that Fleming was speaking to him. "I didn't hear you."

"I said Father Faiblesse is a good religious superior. He speaks truths hard to accept, but they are truths."

"He vetoed my election as superior of Porta Coeli."

"When did this happen?"

"Immediately after the Founder's death we held an election. That is what our rule requires. I was elected on the third ballot. Faiblesse overturned the result and installed Garrity."

"What were his reasons?"

"He is under no obligation to give reasons."

"You are disappointed?"

"The will of the house was thwarted by Faiblesse."

"Mine, too."

"Thank you, Oliver."

"You misunderstand me."

Noonan changed places with Tumulty.

"How much farther, Father?" Enid asked. She could not see around the hearse.

"We are nearly there."

The road had risen. To their left was the lake and, beyond, the campus. Where Little Sem had stood there was only empty space. Tumulty pointed this out to Oliver Fleming.

"Mortar and stone, Father. Mortar and stone. All things pass."

"You have become a philosopher."

"Nothing so silly as that, I hope."

"It cannot be undone now," Tumulty said sadly. He might have meant many things.

"At least the old man was spared the sight."

"Yes."

The hearse had entered the gates of the cemetery. There were rows and rows of identical small headstones, beneath which the departed members of the society lay. An endangered species. The Founder's headstone would be indistinguishable from the rest. The casket was carried to the freshly dug grave and they gathered around it. Faiblesse read, in English, the final prayers.

Eyes downcast, Tumulty reflected that Oliver's remark was only superficially true. The Founder had not been spared the sight of his lifework crumbling to dust. Whatever the outcome of the struggle between Faiblesse and Hoyt, the society was doomed. Tumulty felt that the Founder had known that. The Society of Saint Brendan would not figure prominently in any historical account of the time in which it had briefly flourished. Tumulty let his eyes roam over the grim geometry of the gravestones. The dead members of the society seemed summoned to take part in these final rites for the Founder. Had they given their lives to a failed hope?

And what would success have been? We have here no lasting

city. Even if the society, the nation, mankind were not endangered, each individual must die, and if death is failure no one can succeed. Let go, the Founder had urged Leo Phelan. Let go. Who can guarantee the results and consequences of our efforts? The living write a story unreadable by them, entering and exiting without knowledge of the ultimate script. It does not matter. Let go, let go. For a moment, listening to the burial liturgy, looking over the rows of the society's dead, Michael Tumulty had an intimation of what matters and what does not and he knew a fugitive peace.

"May his soul and the souls of all the faithful departed, through the mercy of God, rest in peace," Faiblesse prayed.

And, answering, the bishop and his retinue, Faiblesse and Hoyt, Phelan and Noonan, Garrity, Oliver and Enid Fleming, Michael Tumulty and all the old man's followers, aged, distracted, a dwindling band, let go for a moment of all that divided them.

"Amen."